WAGER FOR LOVE

"Show me how you'll win this wager and financially rescue us both," Garreth said. "You'll have to be very convincing to catch Sebastian."

"Mr. Armstrong—"

"Garreth, please. If we're going to be lovers"—Lacey gasped and he quickly held up his hand—"even for pretend, we should be on a first-name basis. Don't you agree?"

Lacey rose, inadvertently lessening the distance between them. Her skirts swished around Garreth's boots and he felt a stirring in his veins. He could be playing a very dangerous game himself if he let this farce go on much longer. His own body reminded him what a desirable woman he was dealing with.

"You know I'm a betting man, Lacey. And you've stirred my competitive spirit despite my better judgment. So I'll make a little wager with you. If you can convince me that we stand a chance of pulling this off, I'll do everything I can to see that you become Mrs. Sebastian Avery. That is, if you still want my help."

Lacey barely had time to nod before Garreth took her in his arms, drawing her small, slender body against his.

He saw the flash of surprise in her eyes as she realized his intent. Gently he lowered his mouth to hers.

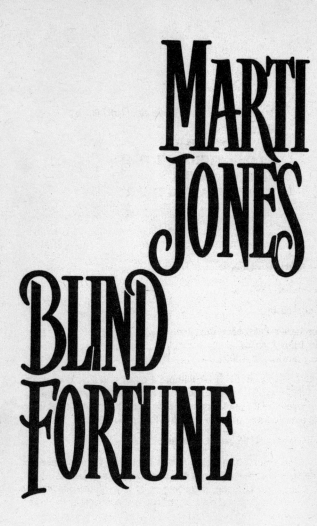

MARTI JONES

BLIND FORTUNE

LEISURE BOOKS **NEW YORK CITY**

A LEISURE BOOK®

November 1995

Published by

Dorchester Publishing Co., Inc.
276 Fifth Avenue
New York, NY 10001

Printed in the United States of America.

This book is dedicated to the kind and generous people of Mobile, Alabama, who gave of their time and knowledge to help me make this story as true to life as possible.

Among them: Rusty Henderson and the ladies of Oakleigh; Sally Blair and Jonni Burke of the Conde-Charlotte Museum House; Ethel Hase and the ladies of the Richards-DAR House; Mary Brittin of the Bragg-Mitchell Mansion.

Special thanks to a guy named Walker III at the Holiday Inn, who can get you anything at a moment's notice. And a very friendly carriage driver who tolerated many strange questions without losing her smile.

"That even our love should with our fortunes change."
—*Hamlet*, William Shakespeare

BLIND FORTUNE

Prologue

Mobile, Alabama
August, 1891

"Mr. Stone, are you telling me we're penniless?" Lacey Webster asked, her knees going rubbery. She sank into the huge leather chair, which still bore the shape of her father's form. She imagined she could feel his warmth through the folds of her black silk mourning gown.

"Not penniless. Not yet. But definitely in difficult circumstances." He tugged the waist of his vest over his paunch, his fleshy face alive with eager triumph.

She had always been aware of her father's aversion to Thaddeus Stone. Now, as she stood before him watching the delighted gleam in his eye as he told her of their desperate situation, she was beginning to comprehend the depths of his evil.

"H-how difficult?" she asked, tucking a strand of chestnut hair behind her ear. Her blue eyes watched his unsettled fidgeting closely, trying to ascertain its meaning, and yet she was already certain she wasn't going to like what she found.

Once more he shifted in the brocade chair facing the massive desk and cleared his throat. "Your father signed over the mortgage on Emerald Oaks to me three months before his death. He had already sold off most of the land. All that's left is a small portion of land west of the house, and the residence itself. That is the parcel I now hold the deed to."

"Dear God," she whispered, clasping a trembling hand to her white lips. "He sold over a hundred acres?"

Again he cleared his throat, opening the leather satchel on his lap. "Here are copies of the bills of sale, and the mortgage agreement."

She took the proffered pages and scanned them, her heart missing a beat.

"As you can see, there are approximately eight months until the balance comes due."

Lacey felt the bottom drop out of her safe little world. Icy fear gripped her heart. "So much money. Why would he do this? I don't mean to offend, Mr. Stone, but my father never considered you a friend while he was alive."

He stared down at his carefully manicured nails for a full minute, then glanced up at her, his eyes unsympathetic. "He had no choice. He'd lost a good bit to bad investments and he needed to recoup his losses in a hurry. Unfortunately, his reputation as a good businessman dwindled with his funds. In the end, I was the only one willing to loan him the money to try to start again."

"Why? You were Mother's beau before she chose Father. It's been no secret there were bad feelings between you two. Why would he go to you?"

"As I said, he had no other choice."

She didn't accept that, but she nodded. "And why did you agree?" she asked, knowing that was the more important question at this point.

He grinned. "Let's just say I had my own reasons."

A chill rippled along Lacey's spine. She saw something in his eyes then that caused a shiver of foreboding to sweep away the last of her confidence.

"What are we going to do?" she breathed, unaware she spoke the words out loud.

"I'm afraid you, too, have little choice. The house will have to be sold to pay off the loan, and whatever furnishings you still have will barely cover the other debts your father left behind."

"Sell the house! Mr. Stone, you've seen my mother. You know about Georgie. How can you even suggest I sell their home? They'd never be able to handle a move like that now. Besides, where would we go? Any employment I could get, if indeed I could find work at all, wouldn't support their needs."

He grinned, and again his eyes shifted to his

clasped hands on his lap. "There is another option."

Lacey felt a thrill of relief and she sat forward eagerly. Then his grin widened, showing a row of short, sharp teeth.

She drew back sharply. "Another option?"

"Yes. I'm sure we could work out some sort of arrangement."

"That—that's kind of you," she whispered, somehow certain kindness had no place within this man.

He met her gaze and the false cheer had disappeared. "Not at all. You see, I knew your father would never be able to come up with the money he owed me in time. This was going to be my revenge for the way the two of them cuckolded me all those years ago. I was going to take Emerald Oaks away from them. However, I didn't count on your father dying before my plans were complete. Now I'll just have to take my revenge some other way."

The coppery taste of fear stung Lacey's tongue. The evil permeating the room was almost a living force now. Stone had harbored hate and resentment for all these years, and he was here to get vengeance. Nothing in Lacey's sheltered life had prepared her to deal with such a fiend. Her cheeks grew cold and she could tell by his smile that the color had drained from her face.

"Katrina may have rejected me in favor of your father when we were young, but she will never rebuff me when she learns I hold the title to her precious Emerald Oaks."

"Rebuff you? I'm afraid I don't understand."

"I mean to have Katrina, once and for all. If it means threatening to take Emerald Oaks away to get her compliance, then that's what I'll do. But make no mistake, she will be my wife before too long."

Lacey jumped to her feet, her shock stealing her breath as she stared down at the evil visage before her. "Your wife? You can't be serious! You've visited with Mother since Father's death. You know how she's been since then. She can't marry anyone. And even if she were able, she would never agree to such a scheme. She loved my father dearly."

His answering smile stretched his lips over his teeth until he appeared to grimace at her.

"I'll wager she loves Emerald Oaks as much. Besides, I can be charming when needs be. I wooed her once; I'm sure it will pose no challenge to do it again in her present state. When I give her the choice between being thrown into the streets or becoming my wife, I'm certain she'll see the wisdom of my plan. But if she doesn't agree, you will just have to convince her."

"No, never! You can't believe I would help you force my mother into such a detestable union."

"Oh, you will help me," he told her confidently, the gleam in his eyes devilish. "You will do whatever I tell you to do. Because once I have Emerald Oaks, your dear mother will be totally at my mercy. As will your little brother, Georgie."

"Georgie? What has he got to do with this?"

"I need Emerald Oaks and your mother to

make my revenge complete. What I don't need is a moronic simpleton hanging around. No, I'm sure everyone will agree once they get a good look at him that the kindest thing I could do would be to find a nice, secure place to send him."

He slowly rose, his dark, narrowed eyes never leaving hers. "Just how nice and secure a place it is will depend on you."

"Me?" she choked. God, how had her mother ever been attracted to this man? Why had her father ever turned to him, even in desperation?

"Yes, you." He reached across the desk and laid his finger against her cheek. "You remind me so of your mother when we were courting. She's nothing but a shell of her former self, but you—you are a fresh young thing."

Lacey jerked away, slapping at his damp, fleshy hand. "You're mad if you think I'll allow you anywhere near my mother or Georgie. Get out of this house, Mr. Stone."

Laughing, he reached out and cupped her chin hard in his hand. "I'll go, for now. But you have eight months, Miss Webster. And while you are a pretty thing, and no doubt smart as well, I don't believe you will be able to come up with the money to stop me in that length of time. So rest assured, I will be back."

A ruddy stain colored his cheeks as though he could barely contain his delight. "I warned your father about his business deals. They were risky, and he grew more reckless the deeper he got into trouble." He closed the satchel and cleared his throat. "You have no one to blame for your predicament but him, Miss Webster. Remember that."

Lacey's head spun dizzily. She felt as though she were drowning in a wave of terror. Her heart pounded against her ribs until she thought he must see it trying to burst from her chest. Distantly she heard him mutter something about showing himself out, but she couldn't force a response. She wilted into the chair, gasping for air.

She heard the sound of the front door slamming as though from a great distance. The pounding of her heart filled her ears until she clasped her hands over them in desperation. She sat that way for a long time, feeling more lost than at any other time in her life.

"Miss? Miss?"

As the sound of Tess's voice finally penetrated the fog of her despair, Lacey looked up. The woman stood in the door of the study, a worried frown creasing her aged face. Her strawberry-colored hair, streaked with gray, was held back from her face in a severe bun, making her appear stern. But Lacey knew her appearance to be an outward illusion. Tess had always taken care of them. More than a housekeeper, more than a nursemaid to Georgie and now Katrina. She'd been their rock since the swift, unexpected death of her father.

Stumbling to her feet, she crossed the room in an unsteady rush and threw herself into Tess's sturdy arms.

"Oh, Tess, what am I going to do? I've never

had to handle anything worse than one of Georgie's spells. Everything is happening too fast. I can't deal with this alone."

"You're not alone, dearie," the older servant soothed, her callused hands smoothing Lacey's chestnut hair. "Tess is here."

Noticing her eyes were oddly dry, despite her reeling emotions, Lacey stepped back. Her legs trembled and she had to clasp her hands together to keep from biting her fingernails.

"I'm afraid even you won't be able to fix things this time, Tess. That man will destroy our family if I can't stop him."

Tess went to the portable bar in the corner of the study and poured a snifter of brandy. She pressed it into Lacey's hands. "Drink."

"Strong spirits? Tess, how will that help anything?"

"Well, it might not help, but at this point it surely can't hurt. You're near hysterical. Drink."

Lacey sipped the liquor, its warmth spreading through her veins. Her legs felt stronger and her hands steadied. She sipped again.

"Tell me," the woman said, after giving Lacey a moment to compose herself.

Gripping the crystal glass until the carved edges cut into her palm, she pulled her scattered thoughts into focus.

"Father sold everything except the house and a bit of land. And that is mortgaged heavily. Mr. Stone—oh, Tess, Thaddeus Stone is an evil man." She shuddered and took another drink of the liquor. Then she relayed the conversation with Stone to Tess.

Lacey could see Tess was as shocked by the revelation as she'd been but was trying to hide her astonishment. After a moment the older woman stated matter-of-factly, "Well, as I see it, we'll just have to find a way to get the money before the loan comes due."

"You didn't see the amount, Tess. There is no way I can get my hands on that kind of money. Besides, I have a feeling Mr. Stone isn't going to give up that easily. He looked...insane with hatred."

"No doubt. He'd have to be to devise such a scheme. I never did like that man. Oily, he always seemed to me. But he hasn't won yet. Now for starters, you can keep my salary," she offered generously. "I don't need it anyhow. I've got all I need right here."

Lacey smiled weakly. "Thank you, Tess. That's very sweet of you. But I'm afraid it will take a lot more than that to pay off Mr. Stone."

"Then we'll just have to think of something else. How much time have you got?"

"Eight months," she said, shaking her head in despair. "Only eight months."

The woman patted Lacey's shoulder sympathetically. "I'd better go see about your mama and little Georgie. Try not to worry so. Eight months is long enough to come up with a solution."

"I can't sell the house," Lacey told her, her tone

emphatic despite the fact that her voice was little more than a whisper.

"No, miss. Not as long as your mama and Georgie are alive, you surely can't do that."

"I've got to think, Tess. There has to be another way."

Soon after, Tess left the study, leaving Lacey alone with her thoughts. She returned to her father's chair, but this time she found no comfort in the supple leather. How could her father have done this to them? How could he mortgage Emerald Oaks to Thaddeus Stone? She felt anger at him such as she'd never known while he was alive.

Immediately she shook off the animosity. She couldn't start placing blame or she'd be playing right into Thaddeus Stone's hands. Her father couldn't have known he would die before having a chance to pay off the loan. She felt certain he must have had a plan to get them out of this financial mess.

Her hands played over the stacks of papers and files littering the polished heart-of-pine desk. Maybe he had already found a way to solve his financial troubles. Perhaps time had run out before he could implement it. She had to know.

Feeling somewhat like an intruder in her own home, she began to shuffle through the papers. She would have to go through all his things until she found a solution. It was the only way.

Since Katrina's breakdown, her mother refused even to believe Lacey's father was really dead. There would be no help from that quarter. And Georgie...

She loved her brother dearly, but his infirmity only added to her predicament now. She would have to do this by herself, she thought, truly alone for the first time in her life. Even Tess, though kindhearted and a source of emotional strength, couldn't help her this time.

She picked up the first stack of papers she came to and began to read.

Lacey stared down at the paper in her hand, her father's handwriting achingly familiar. After nearly three hours she'd found her answer. But how could she follow through with her father's plans?

Horrified, she wondered how her father would have gotten her to go along with the scheme. It was true none of them had ever been able to withstand his charm for long. But this seemed so calculating, so coldly mercenary.

Lacey watched from the doorway of the master bedroom her parents had shared since before her birth. Her mother slept restlessly.

Katrina Webster groaned and shifted, haunted even in repose. Her mother's small frame looked lost in the huge bed with the mounds of covers. Even the summer heat could not warm her. The breakdown that followed her husband's death showed no signs of releasing Katrina's tormented soul.

Closing the door silently behind her, Lacey left her mother to the escape of her afternoon nap.

She slept so little these days that Lacey dared not disturb her.

Down the hall she pushed open the door of her brother's room, the nursery he should have long since outgrown. His dark head was bent over a wooden puzzle. The tiny pieces fell from his fingers, finding the right spot every time as if by magic. In seconds the complex puzzle was complete and he immediately tipped it up, letting the small, odd-shaped pieces fly in every direction.

At ten, his intelligence was easily comparable to an adult's. His mental abilities astounded her, even after all these years. If only they could reach him emotionally. But Georgie lived in a world of his own making, a place no one else could reach.

It was up to Lacey alone to keep her family together. She had no choice but to do whatever was necessary for the well-being of her mother and Georgie. Thaddeus Stone had not been bluffing. He would destroy her mother. And he would send Georgie away if she didn't stop him.

But could she do this? Could she put aside her own fears and doubts and shoulder such a huge responsibility alone?

Again she studied the page in her hand, knowing without a doubt that it was the only way. Despite her aversion to the plot, no matter how distasteful and frightening the idea seemed to her, she admitted with a shudder that it was the only hope for all of them now.

Chapter One

Mobile, Alabama
September, 1891

Her eyes were an everyday shade of blue, not special in any way. But the way those eyes gazed down at him was anything but ordinary.

It was the first thing Garreth Armstrong noticed as he looked up from the ledger on his desk. Indeed, little about the woman standing before him could be termed average.

"Thank you, Gramb," he said, rising to his feet and dismissing the thin, balding man still standing in the doorway. His secretary stepped out, closing the door behind him, and Garreth motioned his visitor to the sturdy wooden chair facing his desk. He took the opportunity to study her more closely as she carefully positioned the voluminous skirts of her gray poplin day dress beneath her.

Circling his desk, he propped his hip against the corner of the rich oak and took in her carefully coiffed auburn hair and porcelain-perfect skin. The woman reminded him of a portrait come to life, and her regal bearing unnerved him. He cleared his throat.

"What can I do for you, Miss—" He tried to remember what Gramb had said the woman's name was, but realized he'd been too absorbed in trying to balance the ledger still open on his desk.

"Webster," she provided, meeting his gaze briefly. She eyed his lackadaisical position on the desk corner and her mouth pinched into a frown.

Garreth resisted the spark of conscience that told him to return to his seat. His position on the desk could only be taken as rude. But her priggish attitude disconcerted him and he found a perverse pleasure in her disapproval, which was at least a human reaction.

"Well, Miss Webster, what brings a fine lady like you to the docks of Mobile Bay?" His voice held a touch of the acerbity he felt, and he saw her dark, mahogany-colored brows rise a fraction.

"I'm here on business, Mr. Armstrong," she said. Opening her small, jet-colored reticule she withdrew a folded sheet of linen stationery and a pair of tiny, round, gold-rimmed spectacles.

Perching the spectacles on her nose, she unfolded the paper. Garreth felt a wide grin slide

24

over his face. Such a small thing, her need for glasses, but enough to ease his discomfort. Now she looked merely beautiful, something he knew how to deal with.

"According to the information I have here it seems your business, Armstrong Shipping, has fallen on hard times," she stated matter-of-factly.

She glanced at him over the top of her spectacles and Garreth's smile vanished. His arms crossed defensively over his chest.

"May I ask where you got your information?"

She waved away his question, which sent his ire boiling over, and looked once more at the paper in her hand. "That's really irrelevant at this point." She removed her glasses and her suddenly cool blue eyes met his steadily. "What is important is how we can rectify the matter."

Garreth sprang off the desk and strode back to his chair. Once seated, he pierced her with an angry glare and leaned forward.

"Just who the hell are you, lady?"

Tucking the spectacles calmly back into her bag, she edged forward in her chair.

"I told you, my name is Lacey Webster."

Suddenly her artless naivete seemed deceptive to Garreth. Despite her guileless appearance, her presence in his office and her knowledge of his finances proved she possessed a measure of intelligence and a great deal of courage.

"Look, Miss Webster, I don't know what someone like you—"

"Someone like me, Mr. Armstrong?" A white line of irritation appeared around her lips. Her annoyance pleased Garreth, rivaling his own.

"You're obviously a well-bred young lady. Why are you interested in the state of my company?" He couldn't help the sarcasm that tinged his words as he added, "Shouldn't you be having tea about this time, or embroidering doilies or something?"

Her gloved fingers tightened on the page she held and he felt some of his good humor return. Miss Lacey Webster would think twice before she poked her button nose into his business again.

"Actually, Mr. Armstrong, I prefer coffee. And my embroidery has always left a great deal to be desired."

Garreth felt a slap of surprise hit him, followed by grudging admiration. His smile returned fully. The lady certainly had spirit. Surprisingly, he found he couldn't fault her for that. With an answering nod he conceded the first point to his picture-perfect guest.

"Please continue."

Lacey hadn't known what to expect from Garreth Armstrong, so she'd never practiced this part of the meeting. She hadn't known he would be so attractive either, with his sun-streaked blond hair and tanned complexion. She almost wished he were the one her father had chosen for her to marry, instead of his best friend.

How would he react to her proposition? She took a long, slow breath and counted slowly to ten. Her eyebrow twitched nervously. Hadn't she known this meeting would be difficult? She'd prepared herself for two weeks so nothing could go wrong, and she'd not let her temper flare now and spoil everything.

Reining in her heated emotions, she offered a conciliatory smile, deciding to proceed with complete honesty.

"As I was saying, I know you're in need of funds." She held up her hand quickly. "Please don't ask me again how I know that: I have no intention of telling you and you'd only be wasting both your time and mine."

"I see. And are you here to offer me the money you seem to believe I'm in need of?" He carefully avoided acknowledging the fact that she was correct. His financial situation was quickly deteriorating.

"Of course not. My situation is as desperate as yours."

"Then I'm afraid I don't understand the point of this meeting. If it's money you want you certainly must know you've come to the wrong place."

"We both need money, Mr. Armstrong. I've come here to discuss with you a way in which I think we can both get what we want."

Garreth nodded, leaning back in his chair. He steepled his fingers and lifted them to his pursed lips as he studied Lacey. Her ready admittance of her own financial difficulties surprised him. But then, she'd managed to do that more than once since her arrival.

"You have my undivided attention," he said

flippantly, closing the ledger on his desk with a casual wave of his hand.

Lacey shifted in her seat, unnerved by the intensity of Garreth's gaze. His green-gold eyes pinned her to the chair as he slowly closed the fingertips of his large hands together.

"Some time ago, in your last year at Barton Academy I believe, you made a wager with a school chum, Sebastian Avery."

Once more Garreth straightened in irritation. His smile died and he fought a wave of indignant anger at the woman's intrusion into his affairs.

"You've certainly gone to a lot of trouble to find out some very personal details of my life, which are none of your business. Let's cut to the heart of the matter, shall we? What do you want?"

Lacey had expected his reaction this time and she felt prepared. With a deceptively confident air she rested her hands on the man's desk and smiled.

"I want to be the woman who helps you win that bet, Mr. Armstrong."

She watched his eyes widen slightly, then narrow once more. She'd surprised him, even shocked him. But he quickly hid his reaction, and if she hadn't been expecting his response she would have missed it.

"Is that so?" he finally asked, a false air of calm disinterest about him now.

"It is indeed."

Garreth pressed his fingers to his mouth and eyed Lacey as though he intended to purchase her at auction. After a long minute he shook his head.

"It would never work."

Of course she hadn't expected him to jump at her proposal, she reminded herself. And even if he did, he could only help get the idea off the ground. After that, it would be completely up to her. But she'd convinced herself she could do it. She didn't want Garreth Armstrong deflating her hopes before she even began.

"What do you mean?" she asked, her tone defensive. "I've thought this through completely, I assure you. The wager clearly stated—"

"I know full well the terms of the wager," Garreth interrupted.

"Then let me explain my plan."

"That isn't necessary. I can guess what it is and I still say it won't work."

Lacey felt unaccountably insulted that he'd dismissed her so readily. "But why? I'm not ugly, Mr. Armstrong." She was pleased her voice sounded strong, since the bravado was forced.

"Certainly not." His eyes boldly raked her figure. A smoldering flame lit in his gaze. "In fact," he drawled, "you're possibly the loveliest woman I've encountered in all of Mobile County."

A blush rose swiftly to Lacey's cheeks and she looked away. Garreth's words caused a tightening in her chest, and a rush of pleasure coursed through her.

"I've been taught all the social graces," she said, adding quickly, "and I *can* embroider, a little."

Garreth saw the embarrassment and decided she needed another dose of humbling before he sent her on her way.

"I'm sorry, Miss Webster, I'm afraid you've wasted your time and," he added, raising an eyebrow at the page in her hand, "your resources."

"You mean you won't help me?"

"I mean I can't help either of us. There is nothing you or I can do to assure that I win that bet. Besides, it was the foolish act of a couple of spoiled schoolboys, nothing more."

"I see." Lacey gazed at the man before her with a sharp glint in her eyes. "You mean if you'd lost Mr. Avery would never have claimed the money each of you put into the Bank of Alabama?"

Clenching his jaw, Garreth wondered how the woman had learned so damned much about the wager. "You have done your research, haven't you?"

Lacey remained silent, aware that his statement had not been intended as a compliment. Still, she would endure almost anything to get him to comply with her wishes.

"Tell me, why is my winning this bet so important to you? You must have other options."

She debated how much she should reveal to this man, then decided to tell him as much as she felt able to reveal. No matter how painful it would be for her to dredge up her own personal troubles, she'd aired his and couldn't help feeling he would react more favorably to an honest explanation than a whitewashing of the facts.

"I, too, need money, Mr. Armstrong. My father

passed away recently, failing to mention the enormous debts he'd incurred in the past few years. Soon after his death I was informed that a large amount of money was owed on my home. The loan comes due in eight months. I've sold everything we owned of value but it simply isn't enough."

"Sell the property."

"My father also sold all of the surrounding acreage before his death. All that's left is the house and about five acres of land. Nothing like the one hundred and twenty we originally had. My father built that house for my mother thirty years ago when he brought her to Mobile as a bride. When my father died my mother suffered an emotional breakdown, so great was her love for him."

She leaned forward, fighting the tears that always seemed so near the surface lately. Under the strain of the recent turbulent events, beginning with her father's death, she'd felt unequal to the burden she bore.

"I can't tell my mother she has to leave her home now, Mr. Armstrong. I simply cannot."

"What you're asking—"

"What I'm asking is nothing more than an introduction."

He quirked a brow, his eyes slanted in distrust. "An introduction?"

She squirmed, her gaze falling to her lap. "Yes."

Her hesitation told him it would be slightly

more than that. He could guess the direction her mind was taking.

Garreth turned his chair away, avoiding Lacey Webster's sad face. God, the girl was lovely, even distressed as she was now. He wished he *could* help save her home.

But what she wanted would be a betrayal of Sebastian. Not that he didn't deserve it, the reprobate. Garreth smiled, thinking it had been too long since he'd spent time with his incorrigible friend.

Sebastian had the wealth necessary to be a gentleman of leisure, and he divided his time between the ladies and the driving club at Bayside Park.

Garreth, on the other hand, had had to work hard every day since taking over Armstrong Shipping three years ago.

The late Wilson Armstrong and Sebastian's father, Lawrence Avery, had both come to Mobile Bay from England in the years before the war. They'd been drawn into a lifelong friendship by their mutual positions as younger sons of nobility. Without the probability of an inheritance from their families they'd left for America to build their own fortunes.

Garreth sighed. If only his father hadn't been such a bad gambler. Betting on anything from a horse race to which raindrop would reach the bottom of a windowpane first, his father gambled incessantly. As did Lawrence Avery. However, Sebastian's father always seemed to have

Lady Luck on his side and Wilson Armstrong did not.

Now Garreth wished he had never made that absurd bet with Sebastian. They'd been as obsessed with gambling in their school days as their fathers were. Right now the trust his mother had set aside for him would more than pull Armstrong Shipping out of the slump it was in if he hadn't put it up to cover his side of the wager.

But it was no use. They'd made the wager and if he married first, thereby losing, the trust money would automatically go to Sebastian and vice versa. They'd made sure of it when they retained a lawyer to draw up the appropriate papers to make the disbursement of the funds legal and binding.

And his earnest pride and honor, not to mention the skinflint lawyer, kept him from reneging on the bet now.

"Mr. Armstrong?"

Garreth spun his chair about and frowned at Lacey. He had no idea what she'd said. She peered at him as though expecting a reply and he was struck once again by her natural beauty. Lacey Webster would be a good match for Sebastian, he thought, then straightened. Why not? It was common knowledge his friend didn't choose women with the best of discretion. Why, he might be doing Sebastian a favor, setting this lovely woman in his path.

With a dry chuckle he shook his head. No, he couldn't do it. Even if Sebastian did deserve it for all the rotten tricks he'd played on Garreth over the years.

"I'm sorry, Miss Webster, but what you're asking me to do would be underhanded and dishonest."

"Stories of your exploits are common knowledge around Mobile. Most of the better-known pranks you two have played on one another over the years have been more deceitful than what I'm asking you to do," she said, once more using her carefully collected information. "Besides, I come from a very good family, I'm not unattractive, and I was raised to run a household expertly. Mr. Avery could do a lot worse. From what I've heard recently he almost did just that."

Garreth clenched his jaw. "Again, I must insist you tell me the name of your source."

Lacey smiled. "Again, I must refuse." Her look gave no quarter and he backed off once more.

"You certainly come well informed." He leaned back in a leisurely stretch and threaded his fingers behind his head, making the fabric of his shirt pull tight across his broad chest. He saw her swallow hard.

"Yes, Sebastian's sudden trip to Springhill didn't come as a great surprise to anyone. His father would never have approved of a Cajun daughter-in-law; Sebastian should have realized that. But I don't see how that can help you: he isn't even in Mobile at present."

"No," she said, her expressive eyes alight with renewed spirit. "But his father is planning a boating party for next weekend to try to cheer up his son. I'm going to be at that party."

"I'll be sorry to miss it," he told her, his crooked grin stealing the fire from her eyes.

"You're not going? But you're his best friend."

He shrugged. "I'm up to my eyes in work here. Not all of us can live a life of endless parties and socials."

Lacey heard the slight touch of bitterness beneath his light tone. She licked her dry lips and hurried on. "I need you there," she admitted, her unsteady voice hinting at the desperation she felt.

Garreth suspected as much, but he was now ready to hear her state her plan aloud. "Why?"

He watched her flush and sat forward, anticipating her answer. When she remained silently fiddling with her gloves, his interest was piqued. "You're very pretty. Sebastian will notice you, make no mistake about that."

"Perhaps. But alone I'll be just one young woman among many. With you..."

"Me?"

"I've heard about the rivalry between you and Sebastian Avery. Everyone has. If he thought you and I—that is, that we were..."

"Ah." His interest soared. She *had* done her research. Garreth suppressed a grin at the woman's scarlet cheeks. Damned if she wasn't right, too. If Sebastian thought Garreth was interested in Lacey Webster he'd go after the girl with all the ammunition in his arsenal. The challenge stirred Garreth's gaming blood.

But that reckless streak had always led to trouble for him, so he tamped it down, remembering his business and Lacey Webster's predicament. He settled back in his chair.

Friendly rivalry was one thing, but these were people's lives they were discussing. He would have to refuse Lacey's offer, no matter how tempting it might seem.

Still, he couldn't resist letting Lacey Webster stew in the juices of her foolishness just a bit longer. Obviously her father had left her in a desperate situation: he could see the fear and uncertainty in her eyes she'd kept hidden in the beginning. But didn't the beauty realize the danger of what she was suggesting? Another man might take advantage of her naivete—and her beauty—the way he longed to do. Honor forbade him to accept her offer, but he couldn't resist showing her the folly of her plan before he sent her on her way, hopefully wiser.

"Let me see if I have this straight," he said. "You're proposing I pretend to be in love with you for the weekend so Sebastian will try to steal you away from me."

"Love! Well, no, not exactly—"

"Lacey," he cut in, liking the way her name sounded on his lips but using it mostly to unsettle her. "You don't mind if I call you Lacey?"

He could see she did, but she shook her head.

"Sebastian is known as something of a rogue when it comes to the ladies. And I don't doubt for a minute he'd try to steal someone as lovely and desirable as yourself, despite our friendship. But the bet stated that the first one of us to succumb to the velvet bonds of *matrimony* would forfeit the stakes of the wager. How can you assure me Sebastian will want to give up his freedom *and* his money to wed you?"

"I don't know what you mean."

"Don't you?" Garreth stood slowly, walking around the desk without taking his eyes off Lacey's face. He stopped directly in front of her, the narrow space between her chair and his desk forcing an intimate closeness. He could see her swallow hard, her blue eyes going wide.

For a moment his conscience smote him, but he pushed it aside, telling himself he was doing the right thing for both of them. Lacey Webster needed to see the folly of asking a man to participate in a plan laden with such pitfalls. Just in case she thought to go elsewhere after his refusal.

"Show me how you'll win this wager and financially rescue us both. You'll have to be very convincing to catch Sebastian, though, I warn you."

"Mr. Armstrong—"

"Garreth, please. If we're going to be lovers"— she gasped and he quickly held up his hand— "even for pretend, we should be on a first-name basis. Don't you agree?"

Lacey rose, inadvertently lessening the distance between them. Her skirts swished around Garreth's boots and he felt a stirring in his veins. He could be playing a very dangerous game himself if he let this farce go on much longer. His own body reminded him what a desirable woman he was dealing with.

"You know I'm a betting man, Lacey. And you've stirred my competitive spirit despite my better judgment. So I'll make a little wager with you. If you can convince me that we stand a chance of pulling this off, I'll do everything I can to see that you become Mrs. Sebastian Avery. That is, if you still want my help."

Lacey barely had time to nod before Garreth took her in his arms, drawing her small, slender body against his.

He saw the flash of surprise in her eyes as she realized his intent. Gently he lowered his mouth to hers.

Chapter Two

Garreth's mouth descended. Lacey knew she should protest. But she needed his help, and if she had to go along with his little test to gain his assistance, so be it. It wasn't as if she were actually kissing him because she wanted to, she rationalized.

Claiming her lips, he crushed them beneath his own with an intimacy Lacey had never dreamed existed. Shivers of unaccustomed desire raced through her body and she felt her resistance melt beneath his skilled ministrations.

All thoughts of protest scattered, leaving her without even the smallest defense. Her lips parted and she caught a sharp gasp as he deepened his ravishment.

Then, just as Lacey feared she would faint from lack of oxygen, Garreth grasped her upper arms and shoved her body away from his.

Damned if the little minx hadn't put him in his place, he thought, slowly releasing her arms. Whether she'd felt the all-consuming heat he had, or she'd faked the response to win the wager, he didn't know. By all rights, he should certainly concede defeat, though.

His head cleared as he watched her vivid blue eyes gaze up at him. Why had he ever thought them ordinary? They pierced him as though she could see into his very soul. Knowing he was about to lie to her, he hoped that wasn't the case.

"Well, that wasn't bad," he managed to say in a steady voice. His loins screamed in unfulfilled desire and his arms ached as he forced himself to release her.

"Not—um, not bad?" she whispered.

"Yes. You obviously have some natural ability," he told her coolly. Turning away from her dazed expression, he settled in his chair behind his desk to cover the truth of the passion he couldn't hide. What a fool he'd been to think he could frighten her with his advances. She'd responded with the enthusiasm of a seductress, and he'd been the one left dazed and breathless.

"But you're lacking in experience," he said, thanking his lucky stars that statement was true. If her kiss had been any better he'd have found *himself* asking for her hand in marriage.

Lacey's eyes flew wide. "Of course I have little experience. Just what sort of woman do you take me for, Mr. Armstrong?"

Her anger should have cooled his reaction, but

instead he found himself aroused further by her show of spirit. A hot streak in that one, he thought.

"Yes, well, I meant no offense, of course," he muttered, shuffling some papers on his desk. "However, I'm afraid Sebastian is accustomed to women with a bit more—seasoning. I can appreciate your situation, and I sympathize as I said. But I'm afraid I can't help you."

Still apparently bewildered by what had transpired between them, Lacey blinked rapidly. The desperation that she'd fought to hide flashed briefly across her face, and Garreth had to fight his urge to reassure her. He steeled himself against the weakness and faced her with a look of mild boredom.

"I see," she said softly, her eyes unable to hide her disappointment and embarrassment that he'd not only kissed her, but found her lacking. The soft, low voice shot daggers of hunger straight through him. "Well, I'm sorry I bothered you."

Garreth realized her haughty aplomb had melted like misty fog under the hot Alabama sun. No longer did she possess the calm self-assurance she'd worn like a mantle since entering his office. Her hopelessness hung about her now like a black pall.

Clearing his throat, he continued to stare down at his desk. He wished there were some way he could help her, he truly did. But dammit, he could barely help himself right now. And he simply could not deceive Sebastian by going along with her plan.

"Good day, Miss Webster," he said, not even looking up as he dismissed her.

He heard her gather her skirts in a rustle of starched fabric and step around her chair. The door to his office opened and closed and he let his head fall back against the top of his chair.

Releasing a heavy sigh, he burrowed his fingers into his thick mane of hair and tugged. The pain cleared his head, made rational thought possible. And kept him from jumping to his feet and racing after her.

He couldn't help her, he repeated to himself like a litany. There had been nothing he could do. Sebastian might be a rakehell and a boor sometimes, but for better or worse he was still Garreth's best friend.

He smoothed his tawny hair back into place and tried to force Lacey Webster and her proposal from his mind. He had work to do if he planned to keep Armstrong Shipping in business for the remainder of the year. Opening the ledger to the last page, he stared blankly at the rows of figures. Even with the money he'd get for the shipment due in next month on the *Mirabella*, he couldn't hope for more than three or four more months of stability.

Damn, he almost wished he could go along with Lacey Webster's plan. And after her display of passion, he strongly suspected she could pull it off. He certainly needed that trust money....

He straightened abruptly, his fist clenching the

edge of the ledger until the heavy stock of the cover dug a groove in his palm. That was the answer. Why had he thought it impossible? Honor and legalities be damned, it was the only logical thing to do. His whole future was at stake.

Slamming the book shut, he jumped to his feet and grabbed his coat as he rushed out, leaving Gramb standing in the doorway, staring dumbly.

His pride was about to take the beating of its life, but Garreth knew he couldn't live on pride. He needed money. And the only funds he had left were the ones he'd put up as his share of the wager with Sebastian. It had cost him half a day to ride out to Springhill, but if Sebastian went along with his plan it would be worth it.

He rode up to the horse-head post in front of the massive fluted columns of the house and dismounted, tying his reins securely. He passed the Jenny Crane fountain surrounded by late-blooming azaleas and stepped onto the front gallery. The door opened as he approached and a smile creased his face.

"Mrs. Avery, how have you been?"

Sebastian's mother tidied her henna-enhanced hair and fluffed her skirts. "Garreth, what a marvelous surprise. Sebastian will be so happy to see you. I hope you've come to stay a while."

"No, ma'am, I'm afraid I can't stay. But I needed to speak with Sebastian."

She waved him into the main hall and closed the door. "I do wish you would talk some sense into him," she said. "He's been impossible since...well, since we came to Springhill."

Garreth nodded and allowed her to take his hat and gloves. She set them on the hall tree. "He's in the back parlor," she said. "If you'll excuse me, I have to speak with the cook."

There was no reason to show him the way. Garreth had spent as much time while growing up at Sebastian's house as he had his own home. Anna Avery briskly headed for the kitchen, obviously certain her son's mood would improve with the arrival of his friend.

Garreth found Sebastian standing by the oak sidebar in the parlor, nursing a whiskey. Apparently not his first one of the day. His eyes were bright, his voice already unsteady.

"Damn good to see you, man," he greeted Garreth overloudly with a resounding clap on the back. "Come in, have a drink." Without waiting for a reply he poured another glass of whiskey.

Taking the drink, Garreth noted the level of liquor in the bottle. It was nearly half empty.

"How have you been, Sebastian?" Garreth asked, studying the pallor of Sebastian's skin and noticing he'd lost a few pounds since the last time he'd seen him. "How was the trip upriver?"

"Grand," Sebastian said roughly, slamming his glass down hard on the table. He poured another healthy slug of the amber liquor and lifted it to his lips. After a great gulp, he grinned. "Why don't we take the horses out for a run and I'll tell you all about it."

Obviously Sebastian was not going to make this easy for Garreth. He was temperamental at the best of times, used to getting his way and liking things thus.

This apparently was not the best of times for Sebastian, and his usually innocuous selfishness seemed to have an edge of bitterness to it. Garreth strongly suspected this might not be the ideal time to discuss business affairs. However, he'd come this far and he realized he had little choice.

"I need to talk with you about business." Garreth leapt in with both feet. He had to talk with Sebastian and get back to the office. He'd be burning the midnight oil tonight to make up for the hours lost today.

"Screw it," Sebastian bellowed, emptying his glass. "I never cared a whit for honest work, you know that."

"*My* business, Sebastian. This is important."

"I feel like taking a ride. Coming?" Sebastian made to walk past Garreth and out of the parlor, but Garreth placed his hand on his arm and stopped him.

"I don't have time for that. I need to talk to you now."

"Then you'll make time for a ride. And after that, you'll stay the night and we can deal a few hands of cards."

"Dammit, Sebastian. I have to get back to the office right away."

Releasing his arm from Garreth's grip, Sebastian looked up at his friend and grinned. Throwing his hands out to his sides, he rolled his shoulders. "So, talk. And then we'll ride."

Garreth blew an exasperated breath and set his own glass aside, the whiskey practically untouched.

"I need money, Sebastian. The company—"

Sebastian waved his hand. "Why the hell didn't you just say so? How much do you want to borrow?" Already he was reaching for the wallet he carried beneath the tailored lapel of his coat.

"No, this is more than an advance on my allowance, Sebastian," he said tightly, annoyed that he'd had to take over the reins of a failing business to survive and Sebastian still considered the biggest problem of his life to be running short before his monthly allotment was due from his father.

Garreth took another deep breath and tempered his resentment. If his father had been a better gambler, or hadn't gambled at all, he knew he'd still be thinking the same way Sebastian did.

It wasn't Sebastian's fault he'd been allowed to go on with his frivolity while Garreth had had to learn the true hardships life could deal. Besides, no matter what Sebastian did, he would always be Garreth's best friend. The alliance went back too far to be severed easily.

"So, what's up?"

"The company has had a few minor setbacks," Garreth said, even in his desperation refusing to admit the depths of trouble the business was in. His pride might not sustain him, but he had more than enough to stop him from revealing the whole truth of his situation.

"The company?"

Seeing the sneer Sebastian didn't bother to hide, Garreth realized his mistake too late. "I know how you feel...."

Sebastian's hand dropped from his front pocket and his jacket fell closed. "The company," he repeated. "Why do you bother with that piddling enterprise? It's a damn waste of time. And money," he added, pushing the button of his coat through its matching hole, as though closing the subject as easily.

"I've explained it all to you before, Sebastian. My father started Armstrong Shipping when he first came to Mobile. It's important to me to keep it going." Not for all the money in the Avery accounts would Garreth admit, even to his closest friend, that the company and the town house were all he had left. The last shreds of his pride wouldn't allow him to bare his soul to that extent, and Sebastian could never understand anyway.

"And I've told you before that company has made you into a complete bore. You never have time for anyone or anything since you took this fool notion to make something out of it. Let it go. You damn well would be better off without the headaches it causes."

"I can't let it go, Sebastian," he confessed. "I—I need the income."

His friend made a rude noise in his throat and turned to pour another drink. Garreth watched the whiskey in the bottle drop another fraction and he shook his head. It had been a mistake to try to talk to Sebastian when he was clearly in his cups. Especially about Armstrong Shipping,

47

a subject the other man loathed on a good day.

"I've told you before, the venture is worthless. It's pouring money down a hole to try to keep it going. Your father let it go to ruin after he made his money. Forget it. Besides," he added, grinning, "it's been damned dull in town without you."

"I'm sorry about that, but I won't give up on Armstrong Shipping. I have to make a go of it."

"Well, not with help from me," Sebastian said snidely, a cold smile adding to the chill of his words.

Garreth's temper rose. "I didn't come here to ask for a loan. I came to talk to you about my trust. You remember the money—"

"I don't want to hear any more of this," Sebastian cut in. Downing the remaining liquor in his glass, he turned away. "I'm sick to death of listening to speeches about responsibility and maturity. And quite frankly, I'm tired of being compared unfavorably to you. Maybe it'll do us all a world of good if people find out you're not such a brilliant success."

So that was it. Sebastian's own pride had obviously taken a beating recently. His father had been making unflattering comparisons between the two friends again. A habit which had nearly cost Sebastian and Garreth their friendship more than once in the past. He tried to smooth things over.

"Well, we've all got to grow up sometime," he whispered, feeling the hope he'd carried in his breast all the way from Mobile die within him.

Slowly he picked up his glass and sipped the smooth whiskey. He felt certain he was going to need its succor.

"Like hell," Sebastian cursed, a hint of his good-natured joviality returning. "You grow up, you just grow old. I like things the way they are. Besides," he added, the forced gaiety quickly vanishing, "damned if they'd let me grow up anyway, even if I wanted to." He waved an unsteady hand toward the stairs, but Garreth knew he was speaking about his parents and their recent mandate concerning his latest paramour. They wanted him to show initiative, as long as it didn't conflict with their plans for his future.

"I heard about the Cajun," Garreth said cautiously, thinking they'd finally hit on what was really bothering Sebastian. "She was special to you?"

Another curse was followed by a dry laugh. "You know better than that," he told Garreth. "Just another woman, the same as a hundred others."

"Serious enough to throw your father into a fit and get you banished to the country out of season. I'd say that's a tad more than the usual, even for you."

"I said it was nothing," Sebastian snapped. "A pretty face, that's all. Drop it."

"It's dropped." Garreth could see he'd hit a sore spot and he suspected it was the reason Sebastian had been drinking so much today. It would also account for him being more tempestuous than usual.

"You're staying the night?"

"Sorry, I can't. I have to get back. Listen, I can see you're not in any mood to discuss business; maybe we can finish our talk later."

He started for the door, but Sebastian called his name. When he turned back there was a light of fury in Sebastian's eyes.

"When it comes to your father's worthless company, my answer will always be the same," Sebastian warned, his slight show of good humor gone.

It was a felling blow to Garreth's hopes. He knew the timing would not matter now. He'd made a fatal error in telling Sebastian why he needed the trust money. Now he'd never convince him to dissolve the wager.

Sebastian met Garreth's stormy glare and his lips turned up slightly. "Anything else I can do for you," he said jovially, "just let me know."

But Garreth knew it would be useless. Sebastian would never give in to his request if it meant a chance to save Armstrong Shipping. He resented the time Garreth spent working, used to his friend's constant attention and company. And he resented the way his father threw Garreth's conscientiousness up in his face whenever Lawrence Avery felt Sebastian didn't measure up. In any other matter, Sebastian would go to the mat for Garreth. But Garreth knew without a doubt he'd never get Sebastian's cooperation in saving the business.

"I'd better get back," he said, putting his glass aside once more. There wasn't enough whiskey in the world to curb the disappointment and dread he felt. Dissolution of the wager was his last hope. Like Lacey Webster, he'd played his final card.

"You'll be here for the weekend?"

Garreth paused, meeting Sebastian's eager look. "The weekend?"

"The party. I've invited a group to come up for some boating before the weather gets too bad. I'd like you to come."

The weekend party Lacey had asked him to attend as her new beau. Garreth took a moment to absorb the irony of the invitation. If only Sebastian knew...

"I'll see what I can do," Garreth said.

Sebastian walked him out and Garreth couldn't help the burning resentment he felt at his friend's easy dismissal of Garreth's troubles. To Sebastian, life was one big party or social. No worries, no cares.

Ah, well, he should be so lucky, he thought, mounting his horse. Once, in another lifetime, he had been as carefree and apathetic toward the trials of indigence as Sebastian. If only his father hadn't been such a bad gambler, he thought for perhaps the hundredth time.

All the way back to town Garreth's ire grew, fertilized by the offhanded way Sebastian had dismissed him. Damn the fool. Couldn't he see how desperate Garreth had been? Didn't he care? But Garreth had not known Sebastian for twenty-odd years without realizing what a pampered snob he could be at times.

The Averys had coddled and indulged their only son to the point that very few people could stand the younger man's manner. If it hadn't been for their lifelong friendship, Garreth would have considered severing their ties long ago. Each time Sebastian got his way, he became more and more demanding. And now, to have finally been reprimanded for what his parents considered bad judgment on his part, well, it seemed Sebastian did not take censure very well. He probably couldn't care less about the Cajun girl. Most likely she was just a passing fancy. Sebastian's interest was no doubt fueled by his parents' objections.

Again Garreth fumed. Why did his friend have to act so childish and unreasonable when it came to Armstrong Shipping? And would it have made a difference if he'd poured out his soul and confessed the whole truth of his penury to Sebastian? Undoubtedly not.

The streets of Mobile were dark save for the occasional glow of a gaslight when Garreth made it back to the docks. He stabled his horse and climbed the two flights of stairs to his office, surprised to find a light still lit within. Had Gramb forgotten to extinguish the lamp? That hardly seemed in character for the man.

His office door was ajar and Garreth slowed his steps as he passed the secretary's deserted desk.

Slowly gripping the edge of the wooden door, he eased it open and peered inside. On the couch in his office, Gramb snored raucously.

Garreth grinned. He'd known the man was dedicated, but he certainly hadn't expected him to wait for Garreth's return.

He went to the couch and shook the man's bony shoulder. Slowly, the secretary peeled open his eyes, startled by Garreth's face looming over him. He jumped and Garreth stepped back.

Sitting up quickly, he rubbed his hand over the back of his neck. "Oh, Mr. Armstrong, I'm so glad you're finally back."

"Gramb, why didn't you close up and go home? I certainly didn't expect you to wait for me. In fact, I'm so tired I might just forget the paperwork and go on upstairs to my rooms."

"Mr. Armstrong, I had to wait for you. This came right after you left." He handed Garreth a well-worn envelope.

The scrawl across the front read *Garreth Armstrong, Armstrong Shipping*, with the address of their waterfront offices. Nothing else gave a clue as to the sender's identity.

"What is it?"

"Well, I opened it, just like I always do," Gramb informed him. Garreth nodded and he continued. "You read it, Mr. Armstrong. I can't bear to tell you. It's just dreadful news."

A heavy wave of foreboding crashed around Garreth, dampening his anger at Sebastian and chasing his other worries from his mind. He didn't need dreadful news now. He didn't need anything else unpleasant to go wrong in his life. He'd had more than his share the last year.

Slowly he removed the heavy sheet of parchment from the envelope and peeled it open. His eyes scanned the writing, and a vulgar expletive erupted into the silence of the office. Gramb jerked reflexively and twisted his hands together nervously.

"This can't be," Garreth said, pacing the small area in front of his desk. "This cannot be true."

"I'm sorry, Mr. Armstrong. I know how you must feel."

"How I feel? How the hell could you know how I feel? I don't even know how I feel." He paced again and slammed the paper on top of the stack already littering his desk. "Buried. That's how I feel," he said, his voice a harsh whisper. "Buried alive."

"The man doesn't know for certain. He could be wrong."

"Could be. Could be," Garreth repeated, cupping his hand over his mouth as he tried to think rationally. This would mean the end for Armstrong Shipping.

He snatched up the letter and read it again. The man didn't sound mistaken. He swore he'd seen the *Mirabella* capsize in a hurricane off the coast of Hispaniola. After the storm no trace of the ship had been found. She was presumed lost, all hands and cargo included.

Chapter Three

"Garreth Armstrong, you villain," Francine Thomas cried with delight as she hurried down the walk to meet the carriage. "What are you doing here? I haven't seen you in an age."

Garreth paused, momentarily stunned by her unfortunate choice of address. He felt like the villain in this piece. For a brief second he considered turning around and getting back into the carriage.

Instead he brushed aside his misgivings and stepped down onto the shelled drive. Francie raised on tiptoe and pressed a kiss to his cheek.

"Francie, how are you?" He accepted the rather bold welcome with casual interest.

"I'm wonderful," she cooed. "And I can certainly see you're as devilishly handsome as ever. What brings you over?"

"I came to speak with your houseguest. She's still here, isn't she?" he asked, though the question was rhetorical. He knew from the knowledge he'd been able to glean that Lacey Webster had not left Mobile. He had his own sources of information in town and, though apparently not as well versed as Lacey Webster's, they had managed to find out where she was staying.

"Lacey? Of course. But what...?"

"I believe we have a bit of unfinished business together. I thought perhaps we could go for a walk and discuss it."

A twinkle lit Francie's wide green eyes. "A stroll? Well, I don't suppose that could hurt anything. Come along, I'll get her."

She stepped lightly along the flagstone walk toward the modest white two-story house. The four heavy columns along the front went from ground to roof, and the upper story boasted a veranda that reached from one end of the house to the other.

The building was formerly a jail, but the previous owners had restored the structure, making it into a private residence. Looking at the pristine white railings and double-shuttered windows no one would guess its original purpose.

Garreth followed Francie into the main hall past the open door of the front parlor. He could smell the scent of lavender potpourri coming from the decorative jars in the open front windows. She paused at the bottom of the stairs, placing her hand delicately on the newel post as she glanced up.

"Lacey," she called. "You have a visitor."

She looked back and smiled at Garreth, her left foot going to the first step. The position tilted her figure slightly, jutting her curvaceous backside out.

Garreth's eyebrow tipped upward as he studied the enticing pose. No doubt Francine Thomas knew exactly what the position did to her figure. He looked away. Somehow her harmless flirtations seemed blatant compared to Lacey Webster's cautious innocence.

"Did you call me?" Lacey was saying, her feet just coming into view on the twisting staircase. She looked past Francie and stopped. Gripping the banister, she felt her rosy cheeks pale.

"Garreth has come to take you for a stroll."

Lacey's eyes went from her friend to the man who had so completely humiliated her two days before. Color rushed back to her face, staining her skin a glowing crimson all the way to her hairline. Her hand tightened on the polished banister.

"You two know each other?"

"Oh, of course," Francie said, stepping back and clutching Garreth's arm with her other hand. She tugged, drawing him nearer to the bottom of the stairs. "Mobile isn't nearly as big as folks would like to make out. Is it, Garreth?"

"Small, indeed," he agreed, smiling at Francie and wondering how someone as serious-natured as Lacey Webster had ever become close friends with such a silly society chit like Francine Thomas.

Of course, he now understood where some of Lacey's information had come from. Francine was one of the town's biggest busybodies. That still didn't explain her knowledge of the wager, though, since he felt certain Francie knew nothing of that.

"I believe we have some unfinished business, Miss Webster," he said, noticing her grip on the railing and the way she stood, steady as a statue. He forced a smile and was disturbed to see her draw back.

"Do we? I was under the impression we had said all there was to say."

He cleared his throat and stepped closer, his neck arched to stare up at her. Damn, but he wished she'd come the rest of the way down. He felt ridiculous looking up at her this way.

"I may have been a bit hasty in dismissing your proposition," he said, glancing over at Francine and wondering just how much the girl knew about Lacey's proposal. She blinked at him, feigned confusion in her heavily lashed eyes, and he knew he'd been right to think some of Lacey's facts had come from her.

"I see." Finally, Lacey took the remaining stairs to bring her down on a level with him. "I'll get my things and be with you in a moment."

As she stepped around Garreth's large frame, his eyes followed her. She went to the petticoat table by the front door and picked up the small straw bonnet she'd worn in his office. Tugging on her gray gloves, she glanced up once into the hatpin mirror and straightened her hat before meeting his gaze.

"I'm ready." She turned to Francie. "I'll be back shortly. This shouldn't take long," she added, shooting Garreth a questioning glance.

"I promise I won't keep you. Thank you for agreeing to accompany me."

"You be on your best behavior," Francie called after Garreth. "Mama will have my head for letting Lacey go alone if anything should happen."

Garreth saw the bright flush cover Lacey's magnolia-white skin as she pretended not to hear her friend's teasing admonition. Garreth grinned and assisted Lacey along the uneven walk.

As they strolled toward the old Spanish park on the corner, they discussed the weather and every recent happening they could remember.

Long, uneasy silences punctuated their excursion. Garreth noticed how the sun brought out the red highlights in her auburn hair. He thought once again how beautiful she was and what a shame she'd been forced to seek an advantageous marriage rather than wait for love to find her.

Her courage struck him once more. How brave she must be to have come to his office that day, alone and exposed. She'd put her own ego and self-respect aside to help her family. He wouldn't have thought such soft, smooth shoulders could bear the weight. Valor and strength of character were rare, and he couldn't help but be attracted to them. Especially in such a pleasing package.

She had a low, silvery voice that seemed to whisper through the small hairs at his nape, and settle heavily in his loins. He had to fight to keep his mind on the conversation.

Lacey meandered at a relaxed pace, but her insides continued to flutter like a thousand butterfly wings. She rambled on with no thought to her words, just to ease the tension tightening in her breasts. She'd daydreamed of outings such as this in her youth. A strong, handsome man, a beautiful day, and feelings she'd never felt before. It took every ounce of resolve she could muster to keep from forgetting the real reason they were together.

The park was crowded with mothers and nannies and their charges. Garreth searched for a secluded spot where they might talk, but nothing presented itself.

"I wanted to speak to you privately," he said, eyeing the area. "But this isn't what I had in mind."

Scanning the picturesque scene, she nodded. "It is rather full, isn't it?"

"We could go to my office, I suppose." He hoped she'd decline. He was afraid to be completely alone with her when his feelings had grown so muddled. It had been easier before that first kiss. But since then he'd had trouble keeping his mind off the pleasure of that moment, and his desire to repeat it.

Her eyes widened and a flush colored her cheeks. So she remembered it, too. Somehow the thought stirred him even more.

"That's so far away," she stammered, her gaze darting around the crowded park and congested streets. "Perhaps we could just find a carriage; a ride might be more solitary."

Relieved, Garreth hailed a closed carriage so they could converse in private. Unfortunately, the only available cab happened to be driven by Crazy Larry.

Lacey climbed in and took the seat facing the driver. Garreth warned the man to keep his antics down to a minimum, but Larry only grinned his toothless grin. He hadn't gotten his reputation as a crazy driver for nothing.

As Garreth sat down across from Lacey, he could see her nervously twisting her fingers together, and once more he marveled at the courage she'd shown in coming to his office in the first place. That, more than anything, spoke volumes about her desperation, even if he hadn't been able to see the despondency when he'd rejected her offer.

They started off slowly, but at the first corner Garreth muffled a curse as Crazy Larry took the bend without slowing. He tried to think of some way to begin the conversation, but nothing immediately came to mind. He cleared his throat and saw Lacey start.

"Have you changed your mind?" she finally asked, again surprising him with her candor and bravado.

Garreth met her gaze, cringing at the fragile spark of hope he saw there. Her voice, though bold, held a forlorn note.

"You might say it has been changed for me. If you still plan to attend the boating party this weekend, I will join you."

"Why?"

He saw a brief flash of expectation cross her face. It gave him the courage to continue.

"I went to Sebastian to try to dissolve the wager. He refused to listen to me. Sebastian is my closest friend, but he has a personal dislike for Armstrong Shipping, and his frame of mind is not the best right now. I don't know, maybe I'm rationalizing, but I've begun to think you might be good for him. He could use someone like you, levelheaded and earnest, to keep him in line."

"And this sudden change of heart has nothing to do with the fact that your ship, the *Mirabella*, has been lost at sea?"

A choked sound escaped Garreth's throat, and he stared hard at her set features. Her beauty had lulled him; he'd almost forgotten how dogged she could be in her determination. "You've heard about that?"

"Mr. Thomas mentioned something about it at dinner last night. As Francie said, Mobile isn't nearly as big as you might think. You have my sympathy."

He nodded tightly. "Thank you. It was quite a blow, personally as well as professionally. I spent the entire day yesterday visiting the families of the men on board." His features hardened. "It was an experience I hope never to repeat."

Lacey nodded, seeing the grief and despair once more evident on his face. She also noted a somewhat haggard appearance she hadn't noticed before and suspected the news had been a felling blow to him. Her heart ached for him, and she had to resist the urge to offer him comfort. No doubt he wouldn't appreciate the gesture, and it would only reveal the tender feelings she'd been fighting toward him.

"I imagine this makes your own situation even more precarious?" she asked hesitantly.

He met her inquiring gaze steadily. "I'm very likely going to lose my company. I need that trust money more than ever now; I won't deny that. But don't think I would agree to do this if I didn't believe what I told you. Sebastian is spoiled and childish. And his attitude shows no signs of improving. If he doesn't decide to grow up soon, I'm afraid he'll make a terrible mistake that could ruin his life. And despite how this may appear, I still consider him my best friend."

"And yet you're willing to help me?"

"I'm willing to go along with the introduction we discussed in an effort to make Sebastian jealous. Beyond that you're on your own. I consider myself a good judge of character, and I don't think Sebastian will fault me if he should marry you."

He studied her earnest bearing and shook his head. "No, I'm not concerned for Sebastian. On the contrary. If your plan succeeds, it is you I fear will live to regret this alliance."

The carriage jolted once again, jostling Lacey against the side and disturbing her straw bonnet. She righted it, facing her unlikely partner on the opposite seat.

"Must we go so fast?"

Garreth's lips thinned. "It was the only carriage available. I apologize."

She nodded. "Why do you think I will have regrets? Is Sebastian Avery a brute?"

"Not at all. But I told you he is spoiled and selfish. A man used to getting his own way. If I may be frank, he is also something of a ladies' man. I like to think marriage to you would improve him, but I wouldn't bet on it." He grinned, wondering if the mention of another wager would remind her of the kiss they'd shared in his office. Her pretty blush told him it had.

He stared at Lacey and again his body stirred to life as he considered it himself. Heat spiraled out in every direction from his loins. Again he wondered why she had responded so ardently to him. Had she only been trying to convince him to help her? Or had she felt the immediate attraction he'd been overcome by the moment he took her in his arms?

Garreth concentrated on anything but the memory of Lacey pressed tightly against his body, her sweet lips parted, answering his need. It did no good. He couldn't forget the passion that had nearly knocked him over. Nor could he keep his eyes from returning once more to those delicious lips with a hungry gaze.

Lacey felt a flush creep up her neck. Tilting her head so the beribboned bonnet hid her face, she stared out the window of the closed carriage.

"Nevertheless," she said shakily, "I accept your help. Francie could have managed an introduction, but I truly need you to secure Sebastian's

interest. Don't worry, I considered the consequences of my decision long and hard before
ever coming to you. I can live with whatever an
alliance to Sebastian Avery might bring. Provided I succeed, that is."

A pregnant silence filled the carriage. Neither
spoke as they raced pell-mell through the streets
of Mobile. Garreth silently vowed to throttle
Crazy Larry if they made it back to the Thomas
house unscathed.

Uncomfortable with the quiet, he finally asked
the question that had continued to plague him.
"How did you find out about the wager, Miss
Webster?"

She glanced toward him, then back at the
scenery. "I can't tell you."

"I thought perhaps Francie had told you, but
that's impossible. My own mother knows nothing of that bet. You must understand if I'm curious where your information came from."

"I've already explained that I can't tell you.
Please let it go."

The carriage rocked again and Lacey muffled
a groan as she slammed against the side. Shaking
her head, she straightened.

Suddenly Garreth reached across the carriage
width. Lacey gasped, pressing her back against
the smooth red leather of the seat.

"Relax," Garreth said, a smile spreading easily
across his features. He took Lacey by the shoulders and slid her across the seat to the center of
the carriage. He leaned back and propped his
booted feet on either side of her hips, bracing her

against the rocking conveyance.

The feel of Garreth's boots against her hips brought another stain of pink to Lacey's cheeks. Her arms burned where his hands had held her. The man was bold, too bold. He exuded a restless kind of energy Lacey could feel from across the meager distance separating them. The silence lengthened and Garreth turned his attention to the view out the window.

With his face turned away Lacey took the opportunity to watch him for a long minute, remembering the kiss they'd shared. It had been hot and wicked and had made her stomach do somersaults. He'd enjoyed it, too, she'd thought, for when they'd finally parted his eyes were whiskey dark. However, he hadn't agreed to help her until after his latest misfortune, so maybe she was wrong.

Garreth's boot tips brushed her hips once more and she found she liked the feeling. He glanced up suddenly and she blinked in surprise as he caught her staring. Quickly she looked away, hoping he hadn't seen in her eyes the embarrassment she felt. Why was she reacting this way to a man she barely knew?

"Lacey?"

Lacey jumped and the point of Garreth's boots poked her beneath the ribs. She winced and faced him.

"Yes?"

"You are a very beautiful woman." His words were whispered. His gaze, soft as a caress, slid over her figure. "You shouldn't have to resort to trapping a man into marrying you."

"Trap? I have no intention of trapping Sebastian Avery into anything. I've told you, I'm not taking this decision lightly, Mr. Armstrong. I need Sebastian Avery's money to help my mother and brother, that's true. But I wouldn't even attempt something like this if I didn't think I could make him a good wife."

Garreth felt his blood race through his veins and settle between his outspread legs. He had no doubt she'd make any man happy. Just thinking of her lips against his, her slim body folded into his arms, made him hungry. Damn, what was it about her that had him wishing she'd set her cap for him instead of Sebastian? Of course, that was folly. He had nothing to offer her, as she so obviously knew.

"Well, you were right about one thing: if he thinks I'm interested you'll have his undivided attention. Since we first noticed girls Sebastian's obsessive rivalry has always gotten the best of him. He can't resist trying to woo away every girl I've ever shown an interest in."

"I'm surprised your friendship has survived."

He shrugged. "I was never very interested, I suppose, or it might have made a difference."

"Perhaps, but the important question is will he want to marry me?" Her wide blue eyes were full of the uncertainty she'd previously kept hidden. "Oh, Garreth, you don't know how important this is to my family."

Garreth swallowed hard. Her pleading made him want to promise her anything. The soft vulnerability in her eyes tore at something buried deep in his chest. He thought it was his heart, but he couldn't be sure. He'd been so busy with the company he hadn't had time to pursue emotional attachments in a long while.

"I think I do understand how important it is to you that we succeed. Don't forget, my own situation strangely parallels yours. Besides, I suspect you wouldn't have attempted such a scheme if you'd had any other choice. Coming to me was your last hope, wasn't it?"

"Yes," Lacey whispered, studying the tiny pearl buttons on her dove-gray gloves. "Father left us in quite a fix. Oh, I'm sure he meant to pay the loan off somehow; he just didn't get the chance." She staunchly defended her father, not wanting Garreth to think badly of him. "Now, with Mother ill, it's up to me to do whatever I have to."

Such a heavy load for shoulders so small, Garreth thought again, leaning back against the padded seat. He closed his eyes briefly and let the rocking of the carriage soothe his troubled mind.

Lacey Webster deserved to be treated gently. She shouldn't be worried about mortgages and foreclosures. And with her beauty she shouldn't be desperate for a husband. Why weren't the men of Mobile lined up at her door, waiting for the chance to court her?

But Garreth knew the answer to that question. Money. Those who had a great deal of it married within their own financial station. Unless Lacey could bring a sizable dowry with her, most men would look elsewhere. Only a select few, Sebas-

tian among them, could afford to marry without
financial consideration. And even then, most
would not choose an impoverished bride.

Such a mercenary custom, but one still actively practiced. Even by his own mother, he
thought with distaste. Hadn't she told him just a
few weeks ago that she'd made inquiries concerning Edith Bishop, an heiress?

At the time he'd dismissed her suggestions. But
he'd had to reconsider them. Even if Lacey
should succeed and he should win the wager, his
winnings would barely cover his losses on the
Mirabella and keep the company solvent temporarily. Armstrong Shipping would still be in
strained circumstances and he'd need a more
permanent solution.

As the daughter of a nouveau-riche father,
Edith had a sizable sum to settle on her husband.
More than enough to put his company back on
solid footing for good. And all she asked in return
was the Armstrong name, which would assure
social position heretofore out of reach.

The idea had appalled him before, and it still
did. But he knew he'd do anything right now to
save Armstrong Shipping, even marry a woman
he didn't love. Even betray his best friend?

He would do whatever was necessary to save
his business and take care of his mother. Just the
way Lacey would walk with her head high to the
altar and offer herself for her family's sake. The
admission filled him with disgust.

He heard Lacey clear her throat softly and he
opened one eye to peer at her. She watched him

closely and he felt another wave of heat roll up from the pit of his stomach.

"Yes?"

"There is one other thing I am curious about."

For a moment Garreth sat quietly, watching Lacey blush as she twisted her gloves. All her earlier bravado seemed to have vanished, leaving her true nature exposed. Such a shy thing, compared to the woman who'd walked so boldly into his office and bravely subjected herself to humiliation to enter into an alliance with him.

"What do you want to know?"

"I know you and Sebastian were young when you made that bet, but that's a lot of money. How could you just throw it away like that?"

"Ah, good question," he said, unfastening the button of his jacket and brushing it to the side.

Lacey saw the fine lawn fabric of his shirt stretch across his chest, and watched the play of muscle against cloth with interest.

"We were both young, that's true. But more than that, we were spoiled even then. Our fathers were by that time wealthy men in their own right. Sebastian and I both took that wealth for granted. It might have made a difference in my life had I known at the time that my father would eventually gamble away most of that fortune. Then again, who knows? I thought I wanted to be just like him. So Sebastian and I would spend our free time thinking of outrageous wagers, and money would exchange hands regularly."

Garreth glanced down at the carriage seat and lost his train of thought. Lacey's skirt was tangled around his boots and trouser legs and the sight brought a sudden knot of desire to his gut.

"But why the aversion to marriage?" she said, surreptitiously following his gaze to see what had caused the tense lines across his forehead.

"What? Oh, that." He sighed, glad to have found his voice again. "A rumor had spread through the Academy that one of our classmates had been caught in flagrante delicto with the dean's daughter. The man arranged a hasty wedding to save his daughter's reputation, which we all knew to be somewhat tarnished already. Suffice to say we thought it a terrible price for the fellow to pay and we vowed never to be caught in a similar snare should we find ourselves head over boots for a female."

"And have you?" Lacey asked softly, eyeing Garreth across the carriage. Shadows lengthened and his features were no longer clear. He seemed to be watching her, but she couldn't be sure.

"No, never," he told her firmly.

Lacey felt disappointed at his admission and immediately chastised herself. Had she thought she'd affected him in some romantic way? What a foolish notion. Garreth Armstrong probably had lady friends who were sophisticated and flamboyant, not shy, stammering young women who made outrageous propositions.

Another long silence followed. Lacey considered how she would get Sebastian Avery to propose when the time came. How did one go about dazzling a man who'd been dodging husband-hunting females since he was in short pants?

She tried to remember the talks she and her mother used to have. Katrina Webster had been a heartbreaker in her youth. That thought reminded her of Thaddeus Stone and his nefarious plot. She still couldn't believe he meant to marry her mother and break up her family. No, she'd never let that happen. No matter what she had to do.

Brushing aside thoughts of Stone and her predicament, she focused on what she'd need to know to accomplish her goal of marrying Sebastian Avery. Katrina had also recited fairy tales to Lacey like the wonderful memories of her courtship with Victor Webster. Lacey had always dreamed of meeting a man like her father. A man who could take her breath away with a mere glance. Inadvertently her gaze went to Garreth, but she quickly looked away.

Tears threatened as she pictured her father, so vibrant and alive right up to the end. His gentleness, his love had always come through. She remembered his assurances the day Georgie was born that her baby brother would be all right, no matter what the doctor said. And his determination to keep that promise. Now Stone's ominous vow jeopardized even her brother's sanctuary.

From the shadows Garreth watched with interest the emotions playing across Lacey's face. Sadness, joy, pain. She would never make a successful gambler: her eyes told everything she was feeling.

He wondered again how he'd ever thought their blue depths were ordinary. Lacey Webster had a dangerous appeal, and Garreth almost felt sorry for Sebastian. The old boy didn't stand a chance against the package of feminine delight sitting across from him.

Without warning the carriage jerked to a stop, tossing Lacey indelicately between Garreth's outstretched legs. He reached to grab her as her body thrust tightly against him. He groaned, more in pleasure than pain, as her slender hips met his own. The feel of her cradled against him in a parody of lovemaking, combined with the rocking of the halted carriage, succeeded in bringing an instant tightness to his loins.

Lacey's eyes widened as she felt the hardness press into her pelvis. She knelt, frozen in place by the wildly careening emotions inside her. Her breasts tingled and her stomach clenched involuntarily. Garreth's grip on her upper arms held her steady when she thought she might sway.

Slowly Garreth slid her up from the carriage floor, their bodies fused together in a most intimate manner. Lacey could feel herself blush, but she also felt a thrill of excitement.

"If we're going to pretend to be smitten, we should rehearse our act."

When his lips came down to meet hers she savored the damp, warm feel of them. His hands left her arms to settle on her back, where he gently stroked her shoulder blades. His legs tightened, imprisoning her within their grasp. He clutched her to his chest with a fierce possessiveness, capturing her mouth in another mind-numbing kiss. Lacey went eagerly into his embrace, answering his need.

A flash of fading sunlight streamed into the carriage, and Garreth thrust Lacey abruptly into her seat.

"I beg your pardon, sir," Crazy Larry said with a wicked grin splitting his haggard face. "We're back."

Chapter Four

"Come in for tea," Francie invited, rushing out to meet them as the carriage door swung open.

If she noticed the way Lacey and Garreth scrambled to right themselves her face didn't give away her thoughts.

"Thank you," Garreth said, climbing down and assisting Lacey. "But I really must go. Mother's expecting me; she's made plans for dinner."

Francie trilled a knowing laugh. "Yes, I know. Edith has been talking about it for days."

"Edith?" Lacey asked, not recognizing the name as one of Francie's usual chums. As she straightened her skirts, she prayed Francie hadn't seen the intimate embrace she'd shared with Garreth. Oh, how could she have been so foolish? Why did she seem to lose all her good sense whenever he touched her?

"Edith Bishop," Francie clarified, a slight twist to her mouth hinting at displeasure. "You haven't met her yet. Her father made a fortune a decade ago in the railroad, but for all his money he's as uncouth as a longshoreman."

"Francie!" Lacey chastised, blushing as she saw Garreth hide a wicked grin.

"It's the truth, I swear!" Francie cried, clasping one hand to her breast. "They're having a big party Saturday night to publicly welcome Edith back from school in North Carolina, but the real reason is to find her a husband. That's why they've finagled the invitation to Garreth's for dinner. They're obsessed with Anglomania and hope Garreth's name will give them the entree to society they've never been able to achieve."

Now it was Garreth's turn to flush crimson. He'd forgotten how outspoken—and well versed—Francine Thomas was about Mobile society. Again he wondered if she could be Lacey's wellspring of information. Perhaps she'd versed her friend in some areas, but Lacey's knowledge of the bet remained a mystery, since he was certain Francie knew nothing of that.

However, she'd managed to hit the nail on the head with her assessment this time. He wished she hadn't announced the bald facts to Lacey Webster, though. He tugged at the tail of his coat and cleared his throat.

"I'd better be going," he said, stepping out of Francie's reach. "Miss Webster, it was a pleasure. I'll be in touch soon."

"Thank you, Mr. Armstrong," Lacey said, allowing Francie to lead her away from the carriage as Garreth pulled himself up into the conveyance. A frown marred his features, and she wished Francie had shown discretion while discussing his private affairs. She could tell he'd been discomfited by the woman's revelations.

"'Bye now," Francie called as the carriage pulled away. "Hurry, Lacey," she said, dragging her friend up the walk, through the open front door, and up the stairs to the second floor.

She swept through the sitting room, taking a lemon drop from the crystal candy dish atop the Playell piano. Lacey reached for one of the treats to relieve her dry mouth and remove the lingering taste of Garreth's lips from her own. Too bad she couldn't as easily remove the memory branded into her brain.

"I want to show you my latest piece." Francie closed the bedroom door and motioned Lacey into the chair before the dressing table. Lacey sat down, shifting the tart candy in her mouth.

Francie went to the cedar traveling case on her dresser. Bypassing the sewing drawer and jewelry tray, she removed the portable writing desk from the bottom.

"Here, tell me what you think."

She handed Lacey several sheets of coarse paper and sat on the slipper chair as she eagerly watched her friend's expression.

Lacey read the headline. BLOOD CARRIED OUT IN PAILS, SAYS WITNESS TO THE SELMA QUADRUPLE MURDERS. She winced and read on. The rest of the article was as vivid and colorful as the headline, and she cringed as she read of the terrible tragedy.

"It's very well written," she admitted, passing it back to her friend. "But I can certainly understand why you keep your writing a secret. Your mother would faint if she knew her daughter was Phillip Truman, reporter for the *Mobile Press Register*."

"Hah, that's putting it mildly," Francie said, all traces of her feigned frivolity now gone. The girl perused the article, made one final correction with a thin, gold pencil, then folded the page and placed it back in the traveling case.

"Of course, for that matter, so would most of Mobile. Flighty Francie Thomas, a newspaper reporter? No one would believe my never-ending questions and unquenchable curiosity are talents I've picked up while searching out stories. Instead they're satisfied to think I'm simply a nosy busybody."

"Why don't you at least tell your family? How can you stand to carry on this pretense all the time? You're really very good. I would think you'd be proud of all you've accomplished."

"Lacey, most of this country isn't ready to accept a woman reporter. And the South—well, they may never be able to accept such a thing. My own dear family among them. No, Col. Rapier is right. Truman wouldn't get near the respect he does for his work if everyone knew he was really a she."

Francie's nose for news got the best of her and she leaned toward Lacey, her ears almost twitching with eager delight.

"Now tell me," she demanded. "How did it go with Garreth? I nearly fainted when I saw him arrive after you told me what a disaster your meeting with him turned out to be." She grinned slyly. "I thought when I heard the news about the *Mirabella* that he'd have a change of heart. He did, didn't he?"

Lacey had told Francie the truth about her father's debts the day she arrived in Mobile, careful not to hint at Stone's threats—for Francie's own protection. She'd also told her friend of her father's plans, and the papers she'd found from the banker, a friend of her father's, detailing the wager between Garreth and Sebastian.

Sensibly, Francie had insisted marriage to an indecently wealthy man would be Lacey's only salvation. Together they'd come up with the scheme Lacey had put into action. Later Lacey had confessed the details of her disastrous meeting with Garreth, omitting only the kiss they'd shared.

She and Francie had been friends since finishing school, and kept in touch regularly even though Lacey rarely came to town. Lacey knew all of Francie's secrets. And up until now, Francie knew all of her secrets as well. But could she tell anyone about the kisses she'd shared with Garreth?

How could she explain, even to her best friend, the way he'd made her shiver with desire she'd never known herself capable of feeling?

* * *

Garreth paused in front of the Italianate-style house with its red-brick exterior, lavish iron-lace facade, and ruby Bohemian glass framing the front door.

It was a beautiful house, a welcoming home. Yet Garreth always felt a certain dissatisfaction when returning to it. That was the main reason he'd taken to staying in the rooms above his office these last months. His feelings of discontent grew out of the knowledge that his mother now hated the house. If not for her animosity he'd have been completely content to remain living in the handsome town house.

He traced the renaissance design on the iron-work; four figurines featuring the seasons of the year. The detail was the finest craftsmanship Mobile had to offer. No expense, no matter how great, had been spared when his father had had the house built. At the time money had been no object, and his mother had been satisfied with the finished product.

However, she was now quick to compare the smaller residence unfavorably to their larger, more extravagant country estate in Springhill. And after they'd been forced to sell the country house, she'd come to despise the town house. It represented their declining finances, his father's bad business decisions, and the lack of the wealth she'd grown up accustomed to. In a word, it epitomized their dire situation.

To Garreth the town house would always be his favorite. He'd never much liked the practice of retiring to the hill during the hottest part of the year. But having dual residences signified a position in society his mother had always enjoyed. Only a select few citizens had the depth of pocket to afford a place in Springhill, away from the heat and pestilence and threat of epidemic that ruled the city in the peak of summer.

He let himself in, shaking off his morose thoughts. He'd just have time to change before dinner.

"Garreth," a voice called from the front parlor as he closed the door.

"Yes, Mother."

He removed his hat, hanging it on the hall tree. Loosening his collar, he tugged the stiff fabric away from his neck.

"You're going to be late," his mother said, coming into the hall to meet him. Her still-blond hair was tucked securely into a tidy bun at her neck and her evening dress of lavender silk was the very height of good taste. Lines had begun to show around her eyes and lips, but she still retained much of her beauty.

"I have plenty of time," he told her.

"Where have you been? You should have been here over an hour ago." The parentheses bracketing her mouth tightened sharply in displeasure.

Garreth only smiled, bussing her cheek, and proceeded to the cantilevered staircase. He knew he was late but didn't intend to explain his actions to his mother. Another reason he'd moved to the waterfront. Despite his 32 years, she still treated him like a small child in need of constant supervision.

"I'll be down in fifteen minutes," he called back, unbuttoning his shirt as he went.

In his room he shrugged out of his coat and shirt, tossing them onto the black horsehair sofa against the far wall. There was warm water in the pitcher on the washstand, and he rinsed off before donning a clean shirt and a dinner jacket.

After brushing back his hair, he crossed the upper gallery to the study. With a few minutes to spare, he poured himself a glass of brandy and sat in the leather-covered barrel chair near the window, allowing himself a moment of quiet relaxation to replay the tumultuous events of the past few days.

His first interview with Lacey seemed like a lifetime ago. So much had happened since then. The disappointing meeting with Sebastian and the terrible news of the *Mirabella*, followed by the horrendous task of confronting the unfortunate men's families.

The last thought brought the stinging grief back with painful clarity, and he called Lacey Webster's lovely face to mind in an effort to erase the stricken faces of the wives and children of the *Mirabella*'s crew.

He sank back, savoring the image of his unlikely partner. She was certainly beautiful. But more than that, she was courageous and devoted to her family. He wouldn't have thought himself attracted to that particular kind of woman before. However, when she'd stood beside the equally lovely Francine he'd found himself unable to take his eyes off Lacey.

And his body had testified to his immediate and fierce desire. Why had he felt so strongly attracted to her? Despite his better judgment he hadn't been able to resist that final kiss. He told himself he'd done it to see if they were truly as good together as he remembered, or if he'd somehow exaggerated their first embrace in his mind. He hadn't.

His social life was full. And the kind of entertainment he avoided with the debutantes he could easily buy on Queen's Row. But one would have thought he'd been celibate for months the way he'd reacted to Lacey Webster's sweet kisses and soft body.

The sound of a carriage drew his attention to the window and he looked out in time to see the Bishops' arrival. As the daughter emerged from the elaborate rig, Garreth breathed a heavy sigh.

At least she wasn't unattractive, he thought, taking in her blond hair and reed-thin figure. He couldn't see her face clearly from this distance but he knew it didn't matter. Even if Lacey succeeded, and he must admit it was a long shot, his winnings would only be a temporary solution.

He would need the alliance with Edith Bishop to ensure his company's long-term success. With the loss of the *Mirabella*, Armstrong Shipping teetered on the brink of destruction. And Garreth knew the company was the only thing standing between him and poverty.

Even though he knew he could accept that reduction in status, his mother could not. She was pressing him into the alliance with Edith Bishop to improve their financial situation, and she didn't even realize the true extent of his father's debts. How ironic, he thought, that his situation should so closely resemble Lacey Webster's.

Setting aside his glass, he prepared to go down and meet their guests. Once more he paused to think about the deal he'd made with Lacey Webster. He still thought the best thing he could do for her would be to talk her out of it as soon as possible.

Not that Lacey wouldn't make a wonderful wife. She was beautiful, passionate, loyal to family, and dependable. And, as she pointed out, skilled in all the social graces.

But it seemed contemptible, somehow, all this marrying for money. And he felt worse knowing he stood to profit not only from an agreement with Edith Bishop, but from Lacey's union as well.

But Garreth knew he couldn't bow out of their agreement now. As distasteful as it would be he might convince Bishop to front him the money to save Armstrong Shipping if he were engaged to Edith, but where would that leave Lacey? After all, she had been desperate to come up with such an absurd proposition in the first place. Would she try something even more bizarre?

No, he couldn't back out now. Besides, he had only agreed to pretend to be taken with Lacey Webster. What was the harm in that? It wouldn't even be a lie, actually. He *was* interested in Lacey Webster. Very interested.

* * *

Garreth watched his mother's face in the chaperon mirror above the fireplace mantel and fought a grin. It would take every ounce of social etiquette she possessed to keep her from throwing the ill-mannered guests out as soon as dinner was over.

Money be damned, the Bishop family had not spent a cent on deportment lessons.

Howard, the old man, bellowed when he spoke, sending his mother's delicate ears into her shoulders. He'd even removed a cigar from his obviously new dinner jacket as though he intended to smoke it at the table.

Garreth mentally shook his head. He'd thought his mother was going to have apoplexy. Thankfully the daughter had seen Gladys Armstrong's reaction and forestalled her father's blunder.

Edith was lovely, with her pale good looks and trim figure. He hadn't missed on that account. But Garreth couldn't help comparing her to Lacey Webster. Where Lacey was genteel and graceful, Edith seemed uncomfortable in her skin, unable to relax within the constrictions of her surroundings. Or perhaps it was that she feared another error from her unrefined father.

Myrtle Bishop, not to be outdone in ill manners by her coarse husband, had been openly studying the ruby crystal water glasses and Baccarat chandelier.

"I want one like that, Howard," she announced finally, as though making an important decision.

"Would you consider selling it?" she asked Garreth's mother.

Her face a rare puce, Gladys's fork fell to her plate and a strangled sound escaped her throat.

With Edith's attention focused on her mother, Garreth saw Howard reach inside his jacket once more. Deciding to rescue his distraught parent, Garreth rose. "I wouldn't mind one of those myself," he said, smiling at Howard Bishop. "Shall we retire to the salon? Mother has an aversion to smoke. If you ladies would excuse us."

"You betcha," Bishop boomed, scraping his chair back from the table. He shot his daughter a superior look and drew out the cigar. Garreth barely managed to get him into the salon before he was puffing away on the expensive tobacco.

"Fine cigar," Howard bragged, twirling the dark cylinder in his blunt-tipped fingers. "Want to know my secret?" he asked Garreth, leaning toward the younger man conspiratorially.

Garreth opened the humidor on the Baccus liquor cabinet and took a less-expensive smoke for himself. Lighting it, he nodded with interest as he poured two brandies, handing one to his guest.

"Potter's Bargain House," Bishop whispered, nodding. "Cheapest place in town for fine cigars. You go to the tobacconist and he wants to charge you for his fancy setup." He winked smartly. "Didn't get where I am today by throwing good money away on frippery."

Garreth raised his brows a notch and tried to force an enthralled expression. He knew about

Potter's Bargain House. He also had reason to hunt a low price when possible. However, he knew Potter to be a niggardly lickpenny who treated his help more like slaves than employees, so he refused to patronize the man's establishment.

"Care for one of mine?" Bishop offered in a questionable gesture of generosity.

Garreth accepted the proffered cigar with an appropriate look of appreciation, all the while wondering why the man had made the munificent presentation. He didn't have long to wait for an answer.

"You can't afford too many of these lately if the talk around town is to be believed."

Garreth felt the acrid smoke from his cigar go down the wrong way, and his lungs burned as he forced himself not to cough. "I beg your pardon?" he choked out.

Howard slammed him twice on the back and let out a rude, bellowing laugh. "I never pussyfoot around, boy. Remember that."

"Then perhaps you should get to the point," Garreth suggested firmly, finding his own benevolence had deserted him.

"Rumors are flying about you being near bankruptcy."

"Rumors are always flying, and there's generally no truth in them," Garreth hedged, feeling his hackles rise at the man's boorish intrusion into his business affairs.

"Nonsense, I've found rumors are usually based in fact," Bishop said, his narrow eyes thinning to slits as he studied the younger man.

For the second time that week Garreth found himself pinned like a bug to a wall as a near stranger perused his financial situation. He found he disliked Howard Bishop's examination much more than he had Lacey Webster's. He also found himself wondering how many others knew of his present difficulties.

Garreth refused to acknowledge the state of his business to this man. He merely shrugged in reply.

"I thought as much," Bishop said, nodding and grinning with satisfaction. He patted Garreth on the shoulder. "Shall we sit down, discuss possible ways we can help each other? You see," he said, removing the damp nub of the cigar from his heavy lips, "I've got a little proposition for you."

Oh, God, Garreth thought. Not another one!

Chapter Five

Lacey was careful to hide her portmanteau behind the door of the parlor before going in to see her mother and Georgie. It wouldn't do to let them know she was leaving again so soon. It could only unbalance their precarious hold on reality.

Georgie sat at the piano, his fingers gently playing over the mother-of-pearl keys. Such beautiful music he played! If only he could communicate with her the way he could an instrument. He didn't even read music; he played strictly by ear. Yet in all his life he'd never uttered her name.

How could anyone threaten such a beautiful, precious child? Somewhere inside Georgie was a fragile heart which would shatter if he were ever forced from his home.

"Oh, Georgie," her mother sighed, reclining on the velvet chaise, "you move me to tears."

Lacey moved into the room and took the small petit-point stool at her mother's feet. She smiled at Katrina, touched by the dampness in her mother's eyes.

"When he plays like that I know without words how much he loves us," her mother said. "The way I could read your father's thoughts just by looking into his eyes."

"Of course Georgie loves us, Mother." She thought of her father's costly mistakes, and her own heart ached painfully. "He knows we love him," she whispered, both for Georgie and her father. Their faults and failings didn't matter beside the love they shared.

"Yes, of course you're right, dear," Katrina murmured, patting Lacey's hand.

Lacey was glad to see her family in such a relaxed, untroubled mood. It would be easier on Tess when they realized Lacey was gone. If only she didn't have to go, she thought. She dreaded the party, and her plot against Sebastian Avery. Even more, she dreaded seeing Garreth Armstrong again. Could she hide the feelings she'd begun to have for him? Would he see the longing in her eyes?

She couldn't let that happen. Humiliated beyond belief by her wanton behavior in the carriage, she refused to let him think it was anything more than her desire to win his compliance. As she was sure his actions stemmed from his need to assure himself she could charm Sebastian.

Had she enticed Garreth even a little? She thought she had. Hadn't she felt proof of his desire when he clutched her between his outspread legs and drew her into his encompassing embrace?

Lacey knew men could feel desire without experiencing true feelings of love. So Garreth had been aroused by her nearness, by her body pressing into his. What man wouldn't be? It probably meant nothing.

But what if it didn't? What if he felt a measure of the yearnings she had? It still meant nothing, she told herself. She'd planned, plotted, and schemed to marry Sebastian. That was the whole purpose for this dreadful trip to Springhill. And whatever she felt for Garreth was irrelevant.

"I'll be right back," she whispered, touching her mother's strumming fingers.

She went into her father's study, hoping to bolster her determination by rereading the papers Thaddeus Stone had left for her. They never ceased to propel her into a state of terror, rekindling her motivation to succeed.

A strange smell assualted her nostrils as she entered the room. Cigar smoke? But the room had been aired weeks ago. Who would dare smoke in her father's study?

On the corner of the desk was a carved onyx ashtray, the remains of a cigar butt resting on the side. An icy finger of fear tiptoed along her spine as she studied the chewed end with revulsion. It couldn't be. Stone wouldn't dare come to Emerald Oaks while she was away.

Lacey shook her head and scoffed at her ridiculously naive thoughts. Of course he would dare anything he liked. Especially when she was away. Her family was vulnerable and at his mercy without her to protect them.

But what of Tess? She would never have let the odious man into the house. Of course, Tess had her day off, which wouldn't be hard to determine if Stone took time to watch the house. She also did the shopping. Yes, there were times when he could gain access to her mother. If he were determined.

If? Hadn't he shown exactly how determined he was where her mother and Emerald Oaks were concerned? The fear blossomed into horror, and she roused all the anger she could incite to fight off the wave of terror. Damn the man. He wouldn't win. He couldn't. She refused to let it happen.

Gathering her tattered thoughts, she chastised herself for acting like a foolish ninny. After all, she couldn't be sure it was Stone who had left the cigar butt.

Still, there was no need to read the terms of the mortgage now to bolster her resolve. Just the thought of Thaddeus Stone with her mother and Georgie was sufficient incentive to send her racing for the train station, Springhill, and Sebastian Avery.

The train for Springhill left the Royal Street station at ten o'clock weekday mornings, according to the new schedule posted on the door of the Gulf Mobile and Ohio Railroad Station.

Garreth pulled his watch from his pocket and pushed the stem, releasing the catch and springing the cover open. 9:43. Where could she be?

A hundred times in the past few days he'd told himself he shouldn't go through with their scheme. Sebastian was his friend. It was devious and unfair to try to arrange a match for him behind his back. Besides, it probably wouldn't work anyway.

He'd argued every excuse over and over in his mind. But when it came down to it he knew he would see it through. He had no choice. Lacey was counting on him, and he needed to win that bet. And since the disastrous end of the *Mirabella* he'd need every cent he could get his hands on.

Still, the guilt he felt almost had him turning around and going home.

But home reminded him of his mother. And thoughts of his mother had him remembering the dinner party with the Bishops. They would have been considered outcasts, except they had acquired the funds necessary to buy their way into the good graces of Mobile society. Bishop made it clear he wanted an alliance between Garreth and his daughter; a union that would ensure her a high social position.

Yet another arranged marriage. First Sebastian, whose ill-fated affair had his mother searching for a proper match. Then Lacey, her need for wealth driving her to find a deep-pocketed prospect. And now himself and Edith. Both considering a mutually agreeable arrangement in a loveless match for the sake of money and position.

And Garreth knew he would have to entertain the man's offer seriously. His mother expected it. Bishop let it be known he was counting on Garreth's compliance. And Armstrong Shipping's very existence depended on it.

His business troubles continued to plague him, but they weren't what had his mind in a whirl today.

No, in fact Bishop had sweetened the pot by offering Garreth first chance at a lucrative business deal. Come summer, if Garreth didn't lose Armstrong Shipping to bankruptcy before then, Bishop wanted him to travel to the East Indies and negotiate for a shipment of jade. The offer was just the sort of venture Garreth had dreamed of to get Armstrong Shipping back in the black. One endeavor and he'd be on solid ground again. But he knew that avenue of salvation would come too late if he didn't get the money from the wager to hold him over.

Across the platform he saw Francine waving to him and he knew it was too late to back out. He lifted his hand to her in greeting, still scanning the crowd for Lacey.

"Good morning, Garreth," Francine greeted, waving her servant ahead with her cases.

Garreth saw the man struggling beneath the two large portmanteaus and wondered why Francine needed so much luggage for a three-day trip.

"Have you already checked your bags?" she

asked, straightening the scarlet braid on the bodice of her navy traveling suit.

Garreth motioned to the medium-size carpetbag at his feet.

"That's all you've brought? Good heavens, what do you intend to wear the rest of the weekend?"

"If I run out of suits I'll borrow something from you. It looks as though you brought enough for a month."

"Don't be snide, darling," she said, patting his cheek. "I only brought the necessities."

"God help us if the rest of the females do likewise. We'll be lucky if there's any room in the house for the guests."

"We are in a foul mood today, aren't we?" Francine guessed, watching him yank his watch out and peruse it once more. "She'll be here."

"Who?"

Francine chuckled. "Who, indeed."

Across the sea of people milling about inside the massive station Garreth spotted a familiar-looking straw bonnet. He watched Lacey Webster approach. Wearing the same gray suit she had at their first meeting, she hurried toward the platform, a frown marring her otherwise flawless features.

"There now," Francine whispered close to his ear. "Didn't I tell you?"

She brushed past his arm and rushed forward.

"Lacey," she cried, waving her arm in the air. "Over here!"

For a brief second Lacey's eyes darted past

Francine and met Garreth's gaze. He stared at her, stunned. He had almost convinced himself she couldn't be as lovely as he remembered. He thought he must have romanticized her beauty in his mind. But he hadn't. If anything, she was lovelier. With an effort, he forced his gaze away, breaking the connection between them.

"Where have you been?" Francine demanded, clutching Lacey's arm.

"It's a long story. Suffice to say if I had needed any reassurance that I was doing the right thing, my mind was surely made up for me this morning."

"As long as you made it, darling. That's all that matters. Your reluctant partner has been fidgeting on the platform, thinking you'd bowed out."

"Oh, if only I could," Lacey said ardently, remembering the panic she'd felt sitting in her father's study.

Upon Lacey's return to the parlor Katrina roused herself enough to ascertain that her daughter was leaving again. Georgie, sensing his mother's dismay, had had a spell. That alone would be enough to wear Lacey's nerves to a frazzle, if they hadn't already been that way due to the mysterious cigar and Stone's threats.

Everything depended on her success, and her mother's and brother's behavior this morning had once more brought the fact clearly to the forefront of her mind. She had to get Sebastian Avery interested in her as a suitable wife. She couldn't even bear to think what would happen to her family if she failed.

And, her merciless brain reminded her, it didn't help that the man she'd set her sights on didn't even want a wife, as far as she knew. She drew an exhausted sigh and bolstered her courage. Her work was definitely cut out for her this weekend.

"Your bags?"

"They're already loaded," Lacey said, her glance going back to Garreth. He stood with his back to her now, in conversation with an attractive-looking couple. The pair were both blond, similar in age and build, and she guessed them to be twins, or at least brother and sister. "Who are they?"

Francine turned to look and an excited spark lit her eyes. "Alexander and Andrea Fitzpatrick. They'll be traveling with us."

Lacey saw a faraway expression cross Francine's face and she glanced again at Alexander Fitzpatrick. Could her friend have romantic ideas of her own for this weekend? Lacey wondered.

Francie called to them in greeting and she and Lacey hurried over to join the group.

As Francie made the necessary introductions, Garreth took up his position next to Lacey. Suddenly she felt his arm slip unobtrusively around her waist. Stiffening, she looked up at him, a question in her eyes.

"Might as well get into the part," he whispered close to her ear. "It will make it more convincing when we meet Sebastian."

"Oh, Lacey, look at the scarfpin Sandy purchased in Huntsville," Francie was saying.

Lacey pulled her attention away from Garreth's unnerving attentions and focused on the unusual gold ornament pinned to the younger man's scarf.

The double pin set in rubies and diamonds featured a rose inside a star. In an ingenious maneuver the star revolved in one direction while the rose revolved in the other.

"It's lovely," Lacey whispered, truly intrigued by the piece, but knowing her breathy tone was due to Garreth's nearness.

"Yes, you certainly are," she heard Garreth say, as the rest of the group went back to inspecting the curious pin.

She shot him a startled look and tried to step away, but his hand held her firmly beside him.

"Smile, darling, you've just met your competition for the weekend."

Frowning, Lacey glanced back at the Fitzpatricks.

"Andi is also interested in Sebastian," Garreth spoke softly. "Has been for years. And his parents think she'd make a wonderful wife. If Andi knows I'm interested in you she'll be sure to tell Sebastian, thinking to warn him off. Bless her naivete, she doesn't know she'll be playing right into our plan."

"I see. Does he—um, like her?"

A grin curving one side of his mouth, Garreth said, "Loves her." At Lacey's wide-eyed reaction he added, "Just like a sister."

She smiled up at him and their eyes locked and held. A tingling started in her stomach and fanned out. His hand grew warm against her back and she squirmed slightly as odd sensations coursed through her. Her gaze fell to his mouth and she thought he leaned closer.

For a long minute she relived the kisses they'd shared nearly a week ago. Time had not dulled the memory. Even now she could feel the hot softness of his mouth pressed against hers.

The warning bell rang, announcing the last call for passengers and breaking the spell which had held them in its grip. Garreth cleared his throat and looked away quickly. Lacey turned her attention back to the rest of their party in time to see Francine hide a smile and the twins exchange curious looks.

She knew, for better or worse, their plan had just been put into action.

They arrived in Springhill early in the afternoon. Four other guests had arrived on another train, and Francie introduced Lacey to Daniel and Marshall Sutherland and Patricia and Doris Poe, cousins of the Averys. By the time wagons had been procured for the luggage and buggies for the guests, and the trip to the Avery mansion had been completed, it was teatime.

Sebastian's mother, Anna, met them at the door. "Come in, come in, we are so very glad you young people could come all this way on such short notice," she gushed, her heavy southern accent flavoring each word. "And this late in the season, too. Why, you must have passed half the town going back the other way. I declare, everyone deserts Springhill the last week of September like we had a case of plague here."

The young people laughed courteously and Anna smiled with delight. A beauty herself, she was obviously used to being the center of attention and liked being able to hold the focus of any gathering. Especially young people, Lacey guessed.

"Come along, I'll show you to your rooms so you can freshen up and change. We're planning a wonderful dinner in the south garden tonight with a pyrotechnical display, so I've told the cook to just have tea sent up on trays for now. I hope that meets with everyone's approval," she said, seeming genuinely concerned with whether or not her guests would agree.

They all nodded as she herded them up the massive front stairs. She separated the girls into two rooms and motioned the gentlemen up another flight of stairs.

Lacey found her host to be a delightful woman, but couldn't ignore the underlying tension prevalent among the group. Everyone knew why they had been summoned. Sebastian might be Anna's darling boy, but he'd erred in judgment and she meant to set him back on the appropriate path.

Garreth remained downstairs—almost by design, it seemed to Lacey—and she wondered if he planned to talk to Sebastian. What if he changed his mind? Would he decide they couldn't go through with such a devious plot?

She followed Andi and Francie into a beautiful room decorated in dusty-rose velvet and floral chintz. A huge Malard bed took up one-third of the room, its distinctive egg-shaped carving on the headboard. Beside that was a set of two steps. Lacey knew the bottom step pulled out to reveal a chamber pot. She had a similar piece at Emerald Oaks. A Sheridan sofa was upholstered in rose velvet to match the draperies and, wonder of wonders, there was a huge step-in closet.

"Lord," Francie whispered. "I knew Lawrence Avery had more money than God, but this is incredible," she said, opening and closing the closet door.

"You've never been here before?" Lacey asked, peeking inside the curious portal.

"No, this is my first time."

"I've been here plenty," Andi bragged, shuffling past them and hanging the jacket of her soft blue traveling suit on a peg in the closet. "And if you're impressed by one little closet wait'll you see the rest of this place."

Lacey hated to seem affected by the luxuries but she couldn't help herself. She could see Francie was enthralled as well, and together the three began removing their outer clothing as Andi continued.

"Mr. Avery bought the house from a judge, whose brother was an architect and designed the place. All the interior woodwork is fashioned from heart pine raised right here on the property, and then painted to look like mahogany. The walls are plaster covered with canvas and each of the fireplaces have a different motif carved into the marble. See for yourself," she encouraged, turning their attention toward the fireplace across the room.

Lacey and Francie exchanged curious looks and went to investigate. Their mantel and hearth were indeed marble, white with a flower-basket design.

"They say General Braxton Bragg himself once made a speech from the balcony off the master bedroom, and I don't doubt he did. Why, the whole place simply screams money. Sebastian's father couldn't care less if they tax him on a few meager closets," Andi finished, plopping her hands on her corsetted hips. She'd shucked down to her small clothes and Francie and Lacey quickly joined her.

A maid arrived with their tea and told them they were expected to rest for an hour. When they awoke, she added, their luggage would have been unpacked and their clothes put away.

Lacey still couldn't help getting her hopes up after all the attention the Averys had paid to their comfort. If Sebastian's family were this generous to a guest, a mere stranger they'd only just met, how much more so would they be to their prospective daughter-in-law's impoverished and indisposed family?

Downstairs Garreth found Sebastian in the old judge's law library, a room completely encircled in floor-to-ceiling bookshelves. Standing with his back to the door, he stared out an open jib window, a glass of watered whiskey in his hand.

"Hello, Sebastian," Garreth said, closing the door behind him.

Sebastian slowly turned, a wicked grin splitting his face. "Well, look what the cat's dragged back. You look like hell, you scoundrel."

Garreth held his hands out to the side and shrugged. "Trials of being a working stiff," he complained.

"God, I hope you haven't come back to discuss that blasted company again. I told you, I liked things better when we were both free spirits. I don't know why you don't just hire someone to run that abomination the way your father always did."

Garreth's smile faltered, but he covered the resentment he still felt toward Sebastian's unreasonable spite. "Strictly a pleasure trip this weekend."

"Good. Can I get you a drink?"

Garreth nodded stiffly and Sebastian went to the portable bar and filled another glass before refilling his own. A breeze blew in through the open window, billowing the Belgian lace sheers and drawing attention back to the view of the clear blue lake across the back lawn.

Sebastian's gaze locked on the shimmering water and a meditative grimace crossed his face. Then he seemed to snap out of his musings and he turned, handing the drink to Garreth, who sipped it slowly as he worriedly considered his friend's pensive mood.

"Still pining over the Cajun?" he asked cautiously. When Sebastian didn't respond he gingerly went on. "You said she wasn't special to you."

A sudden, forced lightness came to Sebastian's face and he chuckled. "No, it was nothing like that," he said, waving his hand. "She's the daughter of my father's overseer at the plantation house upriver. We met when I went up there last month to check on things."

He sipped, and his eyes lit with the fire of remembrance. "She's certainly a beauty, though. And we did have some grand times together during those two weeks." The glint of remembered fondness faded from his eye, replaced with the hard edge of bitterness. He continued, his tone sharp. "But, as my father so baldly put it, she's a Cajun. Good enough to work for you, especially since her father is so damned good at keeping things running up there, but definitely not the kind of girl for an Avery," he repeated harshly.

He downed the whiskey, neat this time, and Garreth wondered how much he'd already had. The girl was bothering him more than he let on. Suddenly Garreth felt contemptible for what he planned to do. If Sebastian really cared about this girl...

"Enough of that," his friend said, rousing him from his recriminations. "I saw the little cutie with Francie. What's the story on her?"

Forcing aside his guilt, Garreth prepared to relate the tale he'd practiced all week.

"Her name is Lacey Webster. She and Francine were school chums a few years ago. She lives about ten miles out of town, a place called Emerald Oaks."

"Yes, I've heard of it. Just recently actually." He rubbed his forehead as though chasing an elusive thought. "Someone mentioned it at the club, I believe. It used to be a real showplace, but apparently the old man sold off most of the land before his death. Just as well, no one to tend it now, I suppose."

"Right. The mother hasn't been seen publicly since the old man died. There's a brother, younger than Lacey, but no one seems to know much about him."

"She's a real looker. How come we haven't seen her around before?"

Garreth shrugged, sipping slowly. "She had her debut while we were abroad. After that, she faded out of the social picture." He shook his head. "The reason for that remains a mystery to me. But apparently she visits Francie occasionally."

A wry grin slipped over Sebastian's handsome face. "Sounds like you've done some checking. Interested?"

"Don't get any ideas," Garreth warned, hiding his guilty expression behind his glass as he nursed the whiskey. "I saw her first."

Sebastian threw back his head and laughed. "You always did have an eye. I should have known you wouldn't miss one like that." He eyed Garreth closely. "Anything serious between you two?"

Garreth meant to look displeased, hoping Sebastian would read his expression for jealousy. However, when he thought of Lacey with his charming friend, he found he felt a twinge of real resentment. Had she gotten under his skin? No doubt he'd been affected by her beauty, but could it be more than that?

Refusing to consider such a thought, he carefully masked his features and shook his head, continuing with the plan. "We've only just met," he said dismissively. Hoping Sebastian saw his remark for the lie it was, he raised the glass to his lips once more.

"So, the field is still open?"

Garreth tightened his mouth and narrowed his eyes. It was getting easier to play the grudging would-be suitor. "Yes," he slowly admitted. Then added with a challenging grin, "As if that mattered to you."

Sebastian smiled and held his glass up to Garreth's. "Just like the old days, eh? Well, let the games begin. And may the best man win."

Chapter Six

Flashes of brilliant red, blue, and white lights colored the sky. Lacey, awed by the stunning display, stared up in wonder. Blankets had been spread around to accommodate the guests, and containers of camphor oil had been lit to drive away the insects.

Anna wasted no time making her decision known. She paired Lacey and Sebastian off at lunch, ignoring Garreth's brooding look as she teamed him with Andi. In all the years Sebastian had known Andi he'd never shown a romantic interest in her and Anna obviously saw no reason to continue her arguments in that direction.

Lacey, both beautiful and suitable, was a more likely venture. Garreth scowled his displeasure enough to light a fire in Sebastian's gaming blood. The chase was on.

Garreth watched guilt flash across Lacey's face as she saw Andi's disappointment. He quickly turned Andi away from the couple, whispering cozily in her ear.

Francie steered toward Sandy Fitzpatrick, but Marshall Sutherland beat a path to her side and remained there steadfastly.

They were served a feast of stuffed, blackened fish, seasoned veal chops, cold shrimp, several varieties of fresh fruits and vegetables, four breads, and, for dessert, flavored ices.

Now they lounged, watching the exhibition as they sipped pots de creme—a chocolate drink served with whipped cream—and crisp cookies. The stays of Lacey's corset cut into her sides, but she'd never enjoyed a meal more.

"Would you like another drink?"

She glanced over at Sebastian, reclining on his elbows as he watched her.

"No, thank you. I shouldn't say this, but I'm so full I can barely breathe."

He laughed and took her hand, quickly rising to his feet and drawing her up beside him. "Come on, we'll stroll around the lawn. You'll feel better."

She glanced back to see Garreth deep in a conversation with the Fitzpatrick twins and Francie.

Lacey had been surprised and a little dismayed by her first meeting with Sebastian Avery. He was handsome, and charming in a careless sort of way. An air of easy nonchalance hung about him. And despite what she'd expected, he proved to be a truly pleasant host. Again her guilt smote her.

"Maybe I will have that drink after all," she said, not ready to face the moment alone with him. He bowed graciously and strode toward the refreshment table set up across the lawn.

Lacey wrung her hands as she stared out across the water. The fireworks reflected on the smooth surface, and she thought how truly dangerous the beautiful display could be. Much like the situation she'd gotten herself into. Seemingly harmless on the surface, but fraught with perils. Sebastian could be hurt by their ploy. She could fail, and her mother and brother would suffer. She thought of Garreth and panic gripped her. The biggest danger of all right now was the very real possibility she could lose her heart to the wrong man.

"Lacey?"

She spun, gasping as Garreth's hand closed over her arm.

"Garreth, you startled me. I was waiting for Sebastian."

He scowled, and she thought he was taking his part of the jealous suitor a bit far.

"Not a good idea," he announced.

"What do you mean? I have to get him interested."

"He's interested," he quipped cryptically. "But you can't make it too easy for him. Remember, it's my interest in you that will force his hand. You see?"

She gazed across the lawn and saw Sebastian

eyeing them warily. She couldn't miss the close perusal he gave her. The impotent guilt she'd felt was replaced by a quiver of hope.

She turned back to Garreth and couldn't help comparing the two men. Though both attractive, Garreth's good looks seemed more sophisticated, more developed. His charm was in his earnestness, while Sebastian's seemed almost boyish in comparison.

All in all, she knew her attraction to Garreth held the potential for disaster.

He glanced around, then took her hand. "Come on."

Lacey realized they needed to make it look as though they were infatuated with each other. And although she was more than a little apprehensive about being alone with Garreth again after their previous two encounters had ended with his kissing her, she reluctantly let him lead her away from the group.

As they walked she tried to pull her hand out of his grasp, surprised when he continued to hold it firmly. Without looking at her, he started across the plush grass of the backyard. She thought they were strolling idly until she saw the white, ghostly glow of the gazebo up ahead.

"Did you speak with Sebastian earlier?" she asked, knowing he'd gone in search of his friend when they'd first arrived but unsure how the conversation had gone.

"Yes," he said, glancing up as another elaborate spangle lit the sky. She watched the colors arc to the ground and fade out.

"How did it go? Were you able to convince him we were..."

"Infatuated?"

He nodded.

Garreth wondered how much he should reveal to Lacey. He hesitated to get her hopes up in case Sebastian had merely been ribbing him.

But even in the dim moonlight he could see the hope struggling to surface in her eyes, and the trepidation she couldn't hide. Everything she had was riding on their wild scheme. He decided to proceed cautiously.

"He said you were cute."

Lacey laughed dryly. "Not exactly over-whelmed, I guess."

Hiding the rush of irritation he still felt when he remembered Sebastian's callous challenge, he added, "And he asked my intentions."

Her eyebrows rose and she shot him a questioning look. "Intentions?"

"Well," he said, glancing off to the side to hide the pang of jealousy he feared still remained on his face, "my interests, anyway."

Lacey felt her heart race with sudden desire. She wished, just for a moment, Garreth *were* interested in her. She bit her lip, and squelched the ridiculous notion. What good could it do either of them now?

Embarrassed to voice her next question, but nonetheless determined to know, she asked quietly, "What did you tell him?"

"I let him know you'd caught my eye. Implied I'd like to get to know you—better." All of which was painfully true, he thought, despite their pretense.

"Oh," she said.

She was unable to hide her flush of discomfiture at his leading statement, and Garreth closed his eyes at the alluring picture she made.

"If I had said more he might have been suspicious. So I let him know I was intrigued, but indicated that we were not in any way committed. He offered a challenge. I accepted. Of course I pretended to be unhappy at the prospect of competition."

He forced out the lie, admitting—only to himself—he *had* been disturbed by Sebastian's goading. Again he wondered if Lacey had gotten to him in more than a physical way. He shook off the ridiculous notion, assuring himself his aversion to the idea of Lacey with Sebastian stemmed exclusively from his continued feelings of guilt at their machinations.

They reached the gazebo and climbed the steps. Padded benches lined the octagonal walls of latticed pine, and Lacey sat down, straightening the folds of her powder-blue silk dress around her.

The dress was one of her favorites, although a fashion left over from last season, and she'd worn it because it showed her coloring to best advantage. She hadn't been disappointed at the appreciative stares she'd received from both Garreth and Sebastian as she'd entered the parlor before dinner.

Francie had taken pains with Lacey's hair and

even now the mass of chestnut curls—obtained with the heated rod—draped over her left shoulder and cascaded across the bare skin of her neck.

Garreth turned toward the opening of the small building, staring silently at the group still gathered across the lawn, their attention focused on the fireworks.

"Is something troubling you?"

He made a groaning sound deep in his throat and propped his boot on the bench before him. His head rolled forward, his chin coming to rest on his chest. Then, slowly, he faced her.

"Yes."

In his eyes she could see the inner battle he fought. Apprehension feathered along her spine. "Is it our agreement?"

He furrowed a hand through his hair, hesitating. Finally he nodded. "Yes."

"But all you're doing is pretending an interest in me so Sebastian will notice me and, hopefully, try to win me away. And it's already working. That isn't such a terrible thing, really."

When he didn't reply, she swallowed the hard knot of fear threatening to cut the air off in her throat and offered softly, "But if you want to call the whole thing off, I'll understand."

Garreth watched her face in the bright illumination of yet another colored explosion and saw the anxiety she couldn't hide. Rubbing his hand down his jaw, he shook his head.

"No. It's too late for that. I made sure he saw me steal you away just now. He's probably furious, thinking I've brought you here to steal a kiss."

"Oh," she breathed, her air restricted now for a far different reason. Her stomach fluttered nervously as she rose to her feet. Smoothing down the skirt of her gown, she stepped forward.

"I suppose I should at least try," he said, stepping toward her. "In case he's watching from where he is."

"That might be dangerous," Lacey whispered, her pulse pounding so loud she feared he'd hear it. His eyes dropped from her face to her bare shoulders and he reached out to finger one of the sausage curls lying there.

"Oh, indeed, it could be very dangerous."

A knot of desire constricted her chest as something intense flared between them. The hot, moist air of the September evening closed in around her and she shuddered with a ragged sigh.

"I meant it might deter him. It would look as though our relationship had progressed."

"I agree, we would be taking a chance. But not for the reason you think. No, in fact I feel certain the ploy would still be effective. Maybe more so," he said, lowering his face toward hers. "Sebastian hates to lose. Anything."

His lips came closer: his breath fanned her cheek. She felt herself leaning in, her hands moving of their own accord to his shoulders.

"I thought I'd find you here," a voice echoed behind his shoulders. Lacey and Garreth sprang apart, turning to see a dark form leaning negligently across the opening to the gazebo.

"I should have known you wouldn't have the good grace to admit defeat," Garreth goaded.

"Tsk, tsk," Sebastian said, stepping through the opening, out of the shadows. He was wearing a wide grin, his thumbs tucked into his vest pockets. "After one day? Not bloody likely. Now if you'd care to step aside and give me back my date."

Garreth moved toward his friend and scowled. He'd meant it to be a feigned reaction, but realized he was more perturbed than he should be under the circumstances. Speaking so only Sebastian could hear, he said, "It's not over yet, old friend."

He ignored Sebastian's chuckles, knowing his plan had worked. Sebastian had seen them slip away together and had obviously decided to step in before Garreth had a chance to romance Lacey. Almost certainly Sebastian would make his first move now.

"Father is looking for you," he told Garreth, his gaze steadfastly on Lacey's moonlit features. "You go on ahead. I'll keep a close eye on Miss Webster."

Garreth watched the nervous anticipation cross Lacey's face. This is what they'd hoped for. Better than they'd dreamed possible in so short a time. Sebastian was playing right into their hands. So why did Garreth find himself hesitating? Why did he long to clutch Lacey's hand and personally see that she was not left alone with Sebastian for a minute?

Eyes wide, she silently urged him to go. He stared at Sebastian's easy grin. He'd done his part; she didn't want him to ruin her chances now that Sebastian was showing an interest.

Looking back at Lacey he put his finger to his lips. Forcing a light tone to his words, he said, "It was almost a pleasure, Miss Webster." His words brought a scarlet flush to Lacey's cheeks and elicited another robust laugh from Sebastian. With that, he turned and left the pair under the cover of the gazebo.

"Shall we?" Sebastian said, holding his arm out to Lacey.

She took his elbow and together they stepped out of the shadows. She glanced up into his face and saw a spark of amusement mixed with the fire of triumph. He couldn't resist besting Garreth. Lacey only hoped his competitiveness held out a while longer.

He slowed his steps until Garreth had gained a distance ahead of them; then he stopped and stared down at her for a long minute.

"It was highly improper of Garreth to bring you out here unchaperoned. Of course, I can't really blame him for trying," he whispered. "I might have done it myself had I had the opportunity first."

Lacey gazed up at him and pretended to be scandalized by his outrageous flirting. "I certainly hope you don't think I would encourage anything untoward."

"Not at all," he assured her. "I can see you're an innocent. He no doubt coerced you."

"Well..." She lowered her lashes and tipped her mouth in a coquettish smile. "I had no idea what his intentions were, but he can be charming."

Her barb hit its mark. Would Sebastian try to turn her favor toward himself now?

A flash of displeasure lit his dark eyes, and his hand covered hers where it rested on his arm. "Darling, you haven't begun to be charmed. Just stick with me."

Their plan was working well, she thought, gliding across the lawn toward the other guests. Sebastian suspected Garreth was interested and he'd already made a play to win her away. She should truly be flattered.

But all she felt was the familiar guilt at their ruse, and intense disappointment that Sebastian had arrived in time to stop Garreth from kissing her again.

Lacey slept little that night, troubled by her thoughts of Garreth and the ever-present fears which had plagued her since Stone's threats. Her worries refused to be appeased, but at least now she was actively doing something to remedy the situation.

Francie, the most petite of the three women, had volunteered to sleep on the slipper couch, leaving Andi and Lacey to share the big bed.

Even this far south the summer heat had given way to the cool nights of approaching fall, and the open windows were equipped with crystal camphor lamps to drive away any insects still about.

Their cases had been unpacked, their clothes pressed and hung in the closet. Pitchers of warm water for bathing were delivered by servants to their door. The three recounted highlights of the previous night's activities as they prepared to go down to breakfast.

No one seemed to have noticed her departure with Garreth, or her return on Sebastian's arm. And both men had been perfect gentlemen the rest of the evening, making her wonder if she'd imagined the intense rivalry they'd shown in the gazebo.

Her mind whirled with the implications of their actions and she longed for a moment alone with Francie to relate all the details. But in a houseful of guests privacy was a scarce commodity.

Downstairs, the buffeteria kept warm dishes of fluffy eggs, ham, hominy grits, toast, and beaten biscuits covered in sugar and cinnamon. Tea and coffee were served by uniformed servants, whistling as they went in and out of the dining room; a customary practice to warn the family of an approaching servant as well as to keep the servants from nibbling the food as they carried it in from the warming kitchen.

By the time Lacey, Francie, and Andi came down, the gentlemen had already come and gone. Patricia and Doris Poe, the cousins Lacey had met at the station the day before, had completed their meal and were sipping tea and chatting about the day's planned events.

"Sebastian's mama told me there are five rowboats they use for races across the lake. That means each gentleman will choose a lady as his partner, making each team a couple. This is going to be so much fun," Doris cooed, tucking a strand of her frizzy red hair back into the untidy chignon on top of her head.

Her sister, blessed with the same rusty tresses, chose to wear her hair in a braided coronet which tamed the wiry strands. Both women had pearly complexions with natural rose splashes on their cheeks and only a trace of red freckles sprinkled becomingly across their noses.

"So who do you want for your partner?" Doris asked, eyeing Francine over her teacup and grinning slyly.

"Anyone except Marshall Sutherland," Francie said, wrinkling her nose as she added a small pellet of sugar to her own cup. "I swear that man could talk a flea off a fat hound."

The girls giggled and she shot them a wounded look. "I'm serious. My ears ache from the inside out. I've never met anyone who could complete a thirty-minute recitation without pausing to draw breath."

"Well, why don't we pair him off with Patricia?" the girl's sister offered teasingly. "Maybe he won't notice that she doesn't say more than two words at a time."

"Fine by me," Francie said, noticing Patricia blushed but offered no objections.

Lacey silently observed the byplay, a nervous tingle vibrating through her. The girls were looking forward to a lighthearted day of flirting and fun. Patricia and Doris would choose from the Sutherlands or Garreth, since Sebastian was a first cousin. Francie would try again to be paired with Sandy Fitzpatrick, leaving Sebastian for Lacey.

Her plan was taking shape, and despite her conscience she felt relief that her hopes might soon be realized. However, remembering the previous night's events, she couldn't stop an unexpected twinge of resentment knowing someone else would be charmed by Garreth today. Would he try to steal a kiss from his boating companion, as he had her? A pang of jealousy shot through her as she glanced around the table at the other ladies and wondered if he would succeed with one of them where he had been thwarted with her.

The men came in, boasting and bragging about the boats they'd each chosen. After collecting parasols and picnic baskets the girls joined them in the large front hall.

Francie smiled at Sandy and he moved to her side, thrusting an approaching Marshall off toward the Poe sisters. Garreth stepped toward Lacey, as though to choose her for his partner, but Sebastian was watching his approach and quickly swept her against his side before Garreth could get a word out.

"You'll do me the honor of being my partner, won't you?" he asked, shooting his friend a triumphant smile. "I plan on being the winner and I want the prettiest girl by my side when I claim victory." His words held an obvious double meaning.

Lacey looked from Garreth's scowling countenance to Sebastian's mischievous grin, and forced a reluctant nod. "Of course, I'd love to," she said, her eyes lingering on Garreth another long moment.

He quickly turned away and was met by Doris Poe, the only lady left without a partner. Graciously, he took her hand and bowed over it. "We'll show them a thing or two, won't we, Dory?"

The girl blushed, her vivid pink cheeks clashing horribly with her fiery red hair, and smiled broadly. "Yes, indeed."

The Averys' cook had prepared each girl a picnic basket equipped with enough food and supplies for her and her escort. The gentlemen carried the baskets and led the way across the lawn to the edge of the lake, where the five small boats bobbed impatiently.

"Listen up," Sebastian called, silencing the chatter of the group. "The rules are simple. The men row across the lake to the markers, row back to the markers on this side and across the lake again to the shore where we'll have our picnic. However," he added, a wicked grin tipping his full lips, "the ladies must take the oars and maneuver around each marker."

The men groaned and laughed good-naturedly and the ladies began to protest their abilities. The gentlemen naturally encouraged them and boosted their confidence as each team climbed into its waiting boat.

"I'm counting on you, Lacey," Sebastian whispered close to her ear as he handed her carefully into the rocking vessel. "With your earnest approach we should easily win the day."

Lacey frowned at the praise, not sure she liked his opinion of her. Had she appeared too grave? Could he suspect she was not here for a gay weekend? She would have to try to lighten her demeanor or he might begin to suspect her motives.

Forcing herself to giggle softly, she tidied the skirt of her yellow poplin day dress across the seat. "I hope you won't be too disappointed in me, Mr. Avery," she said, looking up at him through her lashes the way she'd seen Francie do on many occasions. "I have never directed a boat in my life."

"Call me Sebastian," he told her, patting her hand gently as he piled on the charm. "And don't worry about a thing. We're sure to prevail. After all, this is my home and I know this lake better than anyone."

Lacey noticed there was no tingle where his hand touched hers. Sparks didn't shoot up her arm and center in her chest the way they did when Garreth touched her in a like manner. Why couldn't she feel the pang of desire with Sebastian she did when she was with Garreth?

She glanced over and caught Garreth's gaze on her. His brow furrowed and his lips thinned in a frown. He looked angry. At her? she wondered. She couldn't imagine why. Their plan had worked. He could easily bow out now and say he'd done his part. So why did his features look as black as storm clouds?

The boat swayed as Sebastian untied the tether and pushed them off. Lacey forced her attention back to her partner as he gave the shout for the race to begin. The men took up their oars, plying them through the calm waters of the lake.

In the next boat Garreth and Doris Poe stayed adjacent to them. Sandy Fitzpatrick and Francine had jumped to the lead. Daniel Sutherland and Andi Fitzpatrick, in the far boat, had fallen into last place.

The boats sped across the lake, the couples shouting encouragement to one another and good-natured insults to their opponents.

Lacey, caught up in the excitement, wiggled on her seat. The boat swayed and Sebastian laughed as Lacey clutched the sides of the boat and squealed.

She urged him on, shouting the positions of the other boaters. As they neared the marker on the other side of the lake, Sebastian spun the boat about and handed Lacey the oars. She shrieked, fumbling for the smooth wooden handles, and settled herself more firmly on the seat.

"I can't do this," she cried, trying to control the drifting boat. She struggled with the momentum the little vessel had achieved, trying to turn it around the marker. The water on this side of the lake was deep and thick with undergrowth and she cringed as she looked over the side into the dark depths. Sebastian laughed and settled back against the bow.

Next to them Garreth and Doris Poe approached at a steady pace. Garreth lounged back casually as Doris expertly maneuvered their craft around the marker.

"Put some muscle into it, Lacey," Doris called, her own thin arms straining as she paddled.

"I'm afraid I haven't got any," Lacey cried, finally getting the boat faced in the right direction. The men laughed at the women's antics, even as they shouted encouragement.

Lacey continued to struggle. The boats drew closer together. Garreth's gaze caught Lacey's and she saw fire leap from the hazel depths. Her breath caught; her grip faltered. Desire arced between them as they passed, the sides of the small boats touching briefly.

"Come on, darling," he urged Lacey softly as they passed each other. "Show these fussy females what a real woman can do."

Doris completed her part of the trek and Garreth reached for the oars as if he hadn't just sent Lacey's world spinning. There had been something besides desire in his look this time. Pride, affection? The strong emotions she'd read on his face reverberated through her. Vaguely she realized she'd stopped rowing. The smooth wood of the oar slipped from her hand, and Sebastian's shout of alarm yanked her from the insensibility that briefly held her in its grip. She grabbed for the oar, but it fell into the lake.

With a cry of dismay she lurched forward to retrieve it before it could float away. In her haste, she tipped the boat and it listed dangerously. Sebastian saw Lacey sway toward the water and he jumped to catch her.

Lacey realized her mistake too late. She cried out as her arms flailed the air. Her slippers skidded across the slick bottom of the boat. Sebastian's sudden movement sent the hull over, succeeding in capsizing the boat. He dove away from the vessel as it thrust him out, landing some feet away.

As the boat flipped, tossing her into the chilly water, Lacey felt the heavy wooden side catch the top of her forehead. Fighting off the wave of blackness, she tried to kick her legs, but the skirts of her voluminous dress tangled about her. The water sucked her down and she called out to Garreth, her mouth and nose filling as the lake enveloped her.

Chapter Seven

Garreth shouted Lacey's name and thrust the oars roughly at Doris. Without pausing to consider his actions, he dived over the side of his boat into the lake. He swam the few feet to where Lacey had gone down, but he couldn't see her anywhere in the water.

Diving, he searched the deep water for some sign of her. Reeds and grass obscured his vision and clutched at his clothing. He shucked off his lightweight summer jacket and tossed it away. One shoe fell free and he quickly removed the other, desperate for every ounce of buoyancy he could summon.

Again, his burning eyes searched the deep water. Finally, with a burst of relief, he saw a flash of yellow sinking toward the bottom of the lake. Swimming deeper, he managed to grasp the back of Lacey's dress. But her sodden skirts pulled them both down.

His muscles clenched and he fought to retain his hold. Struggling, he hauled her slowly toward the surface. His arms ached and his lungs burned as he fought the lake for its victim.

Finally his head broke the glassy surface and he sucked in great gulps of air. With his arms clutched tightly around Lacey's waist, he lifted her up until her face was out of the water.

Briefly he noticed the other boaters shouting with joy. Sebastian, whose dive had propelled him toward the middle of the lake, had surfaced some distance away and was frantically searching the water where Lacey had gone under. He paused midstroke as he saw Garreth make for the opposite shore, successful in his search.

Marshall and Patricia turned around and rowed toward Sebastian, finally drawing close enough to pull him into their boat. Doris followed behind, her face flushed with exertion.

Garreth felt Lacey slipping from his grasp and he tightened his grip. They were no more than five yards from the shore. The other boaters had rounded the marker and headed back in the opposite direction when Lacey and Sebastian capsized. It would take them several minutes to get turned around and gain the shore on this side. He couldn't wait that long. He'd have to try to get her safely to shore on his own.

The cool air on her face revived Lacey and she came to, kicking her feet frantically. She tried to scream but only a gush of water escaped her trembling lips, followed by a fit of coughing.

"Easy, love," Garreth whispered soothingly. "I've got you."

She relaxed in his arms and he quickly closed the distance to shore. Hefting her onto solid ground, he crawled out beside her and they both collapsed side by side behind the dense thicket of brush edging the bank.

"Are you all right?" he gasped.

Lacey nodded, coughed up more water, and finally managed a weak "Yes."

Garreth rolled to his stomach and looked down at her. Her hair had come unbound and the wet curls clung to her face and neck. His eyes hastily scanned her from head to foot. Her breasts rose and fell with her harsh breaths and the yellow poplin did little to hide her figure beneath the soaked fabric.

Their gazes locked and he saw the fear in her blue eyes slowly fade away. His fingers reached out and touched her damp cheek and she turned her face into his palm. A last shiver of panic rippled through her body and he felt her tremble.

"My God, I don't think I have ever been so terrified in my life," he admitted, feeling himself shudder now that the urgency of the moment had passed. Cupping her cheek, he absorbed the feel of her skin against his hand, and tried to calm his careening emotions.

"Neither have I," she said, her own hand closing around his. She pressed her trembling lips against his damp flesh and closed her eyes as a shaky sigh escaped her. "Thank you."

His hands bracketed her face, his lips lowering to press a hard, quick kiss against her cold lips.

He drew back, gazed at her, then stood as he heard the sound of oars frantically splashing through the water at the edge of the lake.

"Garreth..."

He glanced back, a hard glint in his gold-green eyes as the other couples spilled forth, racing toward Lacey and Garreth.

"Is she all right?" Sebastian asked, dropping to his knees beside them. His attention was focused on Lacey. He didn't seem to notice the awkward silence that followed his question.

"She's fine," Garreth finally answered, his voice rough with suppressed emotion. Furrows marred his brow as he saw Sebastian clutch Lacey to his chest.

"Thank heavens," his friend exclaimed. "I thought I'd killed you."

Lacey forced a weak chuckle and gently pushed out of Sebastian's crushing embrace. She knew it was the perfect excuse to let him hold her for a moment, but she couldn't abide his touch with the taste of Garreth's kiss still on her lips.

"Lacey, are you all right?" Francie cried, shoving past Sebastian to drape a shawl around her friend's shoulders. Lacey clutched the ends of the wrap and drew it across her bosom.

"I'm fine," she said, announcing it loud enough for the others to hear her. "Only my pride is wounded."

"Not your pride alone, I'm afraid," Sebastian

said with a worried frown, reaching out to brush the tangled strands of hair away from her brow. "That's a nasty bump you've got there."

Reaching up, Lacey touched the hard, protruding knot rising along her hairline. She winced as her fingers probed the injury.

"Let's get you back to the house. Mother will fix that goose egg right up. She always managed to put me and Garreth back together after our adventures. Isn't that right, Garreth?"

Suddenly Garreth rose to his feet, mumbling a reply as he quickly strode toward the boats. Lacey watched him go, his angry movements confusing her.

Was he angry at her clumsiness, or were his actions a delayed response to his fear for her safety? Or could he be feeling something more for her than the idle attraction she'd seen thus far?

Immediately she dismissed the crazy notion as a result of her head injury. He hadn't indicated he felt anything at all for her. Except maybe a measure of disdain for getting him involved in her scheme.

"Come on, dear," Francie was saying, taking Lacey's hand and drawing her to her feet. "We'd better get you back and into dry clothes."

"Here, let me carry you," Sebastian offered, slipping his arm around her back.

"No, thank you," Lacey protested, forcing her gaze from Garreth's retreating form. Even if he did feel something for her, their situation would be impossible and she'd do well to remember that fact.

"I insist."

She faced Sebastian, the man she would marry if she succeeded. His expression was kind and genuinely concerned. It occured to her then that she should use the circumstances to further her plan. The thought repulsed her, but she knew it was the perfect opportunity.

Once more her gaze went to Garreth and she stifled the longing she felt for his reassuring presence. She ached for his arms to hold her again, comfort her.

Unaware of her wild thoughts, he approached the boat being rowed by Doris. The redhead fussed over him as he stepped in beside her and took his seat without a single glance in Lacey's direction.

"All right," Lacey finally whispered, covering her distress. She meekly allowed Sebastian to sweep her into his arms.

Someone had righted their boat and towed it to shore. Marshall held the bow as Sebastian settled Lacey onto the bench seat. With the oars lost, they would have to be towed across the lake, so he sat beside her, keeping his arms around her for warmth.

"Are you certain you're all right?" Francie asked, her pretty mouth turned down in a frown.

Lacey smiled stiffly. "I'm fine," she said.

Francie nodded toward Sebastian and she shot Lacey a conspiratorial look. Her eyes danced with mischief and she fought a grin.

"Don't you let her get a chill, Sebastian," Francie called out, backing toward her own boat with a knowing wink for Lacey.

"Take this line and I'll give you a tow," Sandy said, handing Sebastian the end of his tether.

Lacey's smile disappeared as soon as the group got under way, her misery so great it was almost a physical pain. Doubts assailed her as she shifted uncomfortably in Sebastian's embrace. His were not the arms she longed to feel around her. His was not the face she wanted to look up and see.

But in spite of her regrets, he was the man she desperately needed to marry. Thaddeus Stone had left her with no choice. There was no other option for her, or Garreth.

It didn't matter how either of them felt about the situation; feelings played no part in their futures now. Money. That was the all-important motivation. The thought brought on a wave of nausea. How low she had sunk for the sake of her mother and Georgie. She couldn't even afford the luxury of wondering how her decision would affect Sebastian's life. Stone had robbed her of any choice when he detailed his blueprint for revenge.

The others had their picnic on the lawn while Lacey rested, at Anna Avery's insistence. She didn't mind being separated from the others for a few hours. In fact, she needed the time to clear her thoughts. She'd let herself become infatuated with Garreth Armstrong; she had to admit the truth if only to herself. And that would surely bring her pain in the end.

Sebastian was the one she should direct her feelings toward. True, he was spoiled and self-centered, but he was the one she had to marry.

Besides, he'd shown he could be kind and considerate. Lacey had no reason to doubt he'd help her family when the time came. It wouldn't be easy to convince him to give up his freedom, but her desperation, her determination to stop Stone was on her side.

She had to get Sebastian to propose soon. And in order to do that, she would have to put aside the hopeless infatuation she'd developed for Garreth. He was not the one for her.

Her head continued to ache dully, but the bump had already shrunk and only a colorful bruise remained. She rose and dressed for the afternoon's activities, which Anna told her would include a treasure hunt.

Donning a gown of gold satin trimmed in black braid, she piled her curls into a loose chignon on top of her head, pulling a few free to frame her face. Time was running out. Stone hovered over her shoulder, waiting to pounce on her mother and Georgie with his cold brutality. She had sparked Sebastian's interest, but that was a far cry from a marriage proposal.

Downstairs she found the others gathered in the formal parlor. A wave of excitement rippled through the gathering as they discussed the upcoming game.

"Lacey," Francie called, sweeping to her side

in a rose silk gown with an antique lace overskirt. "I'm so glad you're feeling better. We're going to have such fun."

Lacey smiled and stepped forward into the room. Her gaze met Garreth's across the room. She smiled, but he turned his attention back to Andi Fitzpatrick.

"We've all drawn names from Mr. Avery's top hat," Francie told her. She leaned forward. "I'm paired with Marshall, drat it all. We can't possibly win: he'll be too busy talking to search for the treasure."

"I hope you don't mind," Sebastian said, coming to her side with a smile. "We're partners again. I promise I won't allow anything to happen to you this time, though. I plan to keep my eye on you every minute."

Lacey forced a flirtatious smile and touched his arm. "How are we supposed to find the treasure if you're busy watching me?"

He took her hand in his and she resisted the urge to draw away. "I think I have already found the treasure," he said, a twinkle in his dark eyes.

Francie gasped and took Lacey's arm, shooting Sebastian a scandalized frown. Their host merely laughed and sipped his drink. Francie led Lacey to the table loaded with refreshments.

"Mustn't make it too easy for him," she whispered. "We don't want him getting suspicious or, worse luck, losing interest."

"Yes, you're right," Lacey agreed, secretly pleased to be away from Sebastian. She felt horrid about the plans she'd made. More than anything she wanted to call off the whole farce and go home to her family. Only the knowledge that she'd soon have no home or family to go back to kept her from leaving.

"I suspect Mama Avery has wasted no time in giving her blessing to Sebastian's interest in you. Besides their horror at his interest in the Cajun, she claims she was impressed by the way you handled that whole messy business with the boat accident. I think she feared you'd scream the house down about her son's clumsiness."

"Nonsense, it was my own bumbling that caused the whole thing. If I hadn't dropped the oar—"

"Nevertheless, she was favorably impressed by your graciousness. I saw her and Sebastian with their heads together a while ago. After his recent bad judgment she isn't taking a chance on him picking another unsuitable girl. Probably decided to do the choosing herself. And since she and Mr. Avery still hold the purse strings I imagine Sebastian will go along with whatever they want. That would certainly explain his boldness a moment ago."

Forcing a pleased look, Lacey glanced toward the object of her machinations. He'd refilled his glass and she saw him down half of it in one gulp as Marshall bent his ear about something or other. His gaze was overbright, his laughter loud.

Was he drunk? she wondered. And did he make it a habit to imbibe heavily? Could she tolerate a husband who drank to extremes?

What a foolish question, she thought. It

wouldn't matter what faults Sebastian Avery possessed: she still needed to marry him. And she would do her best to make her plan succeed, no matter how horrible his flaws turned out to be.

He saw her and winked, raising his empty glass in a salute. Lacey frowned and turned around, crashing right into Garreth.

"Why the frown, pretty lady?" he asked, and she smelled the liquor on his breath as well. "You're about to get exactly what you came after. I would think you'd be celebrating."

"What are you talking about?" she asked, silently wondering if all the men in the room had taken leave of their manners.

"Sebastian told me his mother has taken a very sudden, special liking to you. She's already hinted that you'd be the perfect girl to take his mind off the unfortunate incident with the Cajun girl."

"She really said that?" Lacey gasped. At Garreth's sardonic nod, she pressed her hand to her pounding heart. "But the woman barely knows me. Why would she say such a thing?"

"Oh, don't underestimate your charms, Miss Webster. You're beautiful, well bred, genteel. What's not to love? Besides, I think she's desperate to get him settled quickly. This weekend was probably invented so she could encourage a match between him and Andi Fitzpatrick, but when she noticed his interest in you, she altered her strategy."

Lacey couldn't fail to recognize his sarcasm and she wondered what she'd done to anger him.

He'd been in a foul temper since the boat accident. Or rather, she amended, since the impulsive kiss he'd given her on the shore afterward.

She'd been assailed by the now-familiar desire she always felt when he touched her, but she hadn't thought he'd noticed. Perhaps she was wrong. Had he read the longing in her eyes? Did he think her loose-moraled for succumbing to another man's attentions while scheming for an alliance with his best friend?

Even to her own ears she had to admit the whole thing sounded sordid and vulgar. And she couldn't forget the story he'd told her about the dean's daughter, the one who'd precipitated his wager with Sebastian. With a wave of shame she realized her own manipulations might be construed as equally contemptible.

"Garreth, maybe we should just forget this whole—"

His impatient wave cut her off, but she realized it would have been useless to speak her thoughts aloud. She couldn't tell him how she truly felt about him. It would only make them both more uncomfortable. Andi called his name and he strode away without another word.

"Those two are going to be pie-eyed before the game even begins," Francie scoffed, coming up behind Lacey. "I've never known Garreth and Sebastian to be such elbow-benders before."

Mirroring Francie's confusion, Lacey couldn't help wondering what had caused Garreth's ire. The plan was going much better than they'd ever dreamed. And now that she had Anna Avery's assistance, he could pull out of their agreement whenever he liked.

Imagine having the gentleman's own mother give her nod of approval! He should be singing with joy. Glancing around the room, she frowned. Sebastian's joviality looked forced. Garreth's eyes were stormy and hard. Her own heart felt as though it had sunk to the pit of her stomach. They all appeared miserable.

"Attention, everyone," Anna Avery called brightly from the doorway. The group turned, their chatter dying to silence. "I've hidden the treasure, along with clues to point you in the right direction. There are five clues, hidden in various places throughout the house. Each clue will lead you only to the next clue, not to the treasure. You must find them in order. Mr. Fitzpatrick was generous enough to donate his charming scarfpin, the one he was wearing when he arrived. That is the treasure, young people. Now go, search, and have fun."

Lacey almost giggled at the woman's melodrama. You'd think they were hunting the queen's own jewels! She was thankful at least that Anna's excitement seemed to have put the group into a cheerful frame of mind. Garreth and Andi Fitzpatrick had their heads together, plotting their strategy. Marshall was bending Francie's ear, her friend nodding and looking attentive. Sebastian set aside his crystal tumbler and came toward her.

"Shall we begin?" he asked, holding out his arm for her.

She took his elbow and smiled. "You have our first clue?"

"Absolutely," he said, patting his coat pocket. "And I have the inside advantage, as this is my house."

"You said the same thing about the boat races," she reminded him with a feigned look of alarm.

Laughing, he tapped the end of her nose. "How rude of you to remind me of that," he teased, his breath heavy with the alcohol he'd consumed. "Come, let's begin."

Garreth and Andi Fitzpatrick were mulling over the piece of stationery their clue was written on. As she and Sebastian passed, Garreth lifted his head and their eyes met. His cool demeanor chilled her: then he turned back to his own partner.

Francie tried to focus Marshall's attention on their clue, but he'd begun a story about his latest success at the Bayside Park driving club. She rolled her eyes heavenward as Lacey glanced her way.

In the main hall Sebastian removed the sheet of linen stationery from his pocket and unfolded it. The clue read, *The lion wins the day.*

"Too simple," he said, tucking it back into his pocket.

"Simple? I haven't a clue what that means."

"At last, the lady sees the advantage of my presence. There are three fireplaces in the house carved with a lion in the motif. One is in my room—even Mother wouldn't dare send us in there unchaperoned. One is in my father's study,

139

and so is my father, so that is likely out. The last is in the warming kitchen. A harmless dwelling, even this late in the year, as no one in their right mind would linger in its oppressive heat for long."

"Let's go," Lacey said, forcing herself into a festive mood.

Taking her arm, Sebastian led her through the main hall, past the dining room, and into a servant's hall that led from the dining room to the warming kitchen. Food was cooked in the main kitchen, a separate building set back from the house. But everything was brought in before meals and kept warm and at hand.

On the black marble fireplace was indeed a lion's-head carving. And in various niches in the marble were small folded pieces of paper. Sebastian waved his hand and Lacey stepped forward and drew one out.

This clue led them to a crystal tulip tieback accenting the rich red velvet draperies in the dining room. They heard Andi Fitzpatrick's cry of triumph from the warming kitchen and knew Garreth and Andi were right behind them in the search.

The tulip clue sent them upstairs to a linen press situated at the end of a dark, narrow servant's hall.

Sebastian brushed against her closely as he reached for their third clue. She felt the nap of his coat lightly caress her breasts through the thin fabric of her gown and she sucked in her breath sharply.

Clue in hand, he turned toward her. They stood face-to-face in the shadows of the hall.

"Mother certainly didn't consider the possibilities to be found here," he whispered. "I could kiss you and no one would be the wiser."

Lacey decided she had better make it clear to Sebastian right away that she wasn't interested in anything less than an honorable proposal. She backed up against the wall, straightening her spine and forcing a small distance between them.

"You wouldn't dare take advantage of a lady in your mother's house, would you?"

He chuckled and leaned toward her, pressing his hands on the wall beside her head and grinning at her startled expression. "Where have you been, Miss Webster? I have a reputation for just that sort of thing."

"Oh, then you mean I'd be just another dalliance to you?"

His eyes cleared and he studied her face, the graceful line of her neck exposed to his view.

"No," he said, his voice rough. "I don't think you could ever be that to anyone."

He pressed his lips lightly to hers and Lacey forced herself not to shrink away. His kiss was nice, warm and comfortable. Not too demanding.

She waited, but it didn't bring on the sensations she'd felt when Garreth kissed her. There was no fire, no heat coursing through her. He didn't touch her with any part of his body save his lips. His hands remained flat against the wall, his legs carefully kept away from hers.

Though brief, to Lacey the contact seemed to go on interminably. She fought the urge to fidget, to drag her mouth away.

Only when they heard a high giggle behind them did they finally part.

"Oh, my," Andi gasped, covering her mouth with her fingers. Her amusement died. She blinked rapidly, trying to hide her shock and dismay. "We didn't mean to interrupt, did we, Garreth?"

Lacey's gaze flew to Garreth's and her breath lodged painfully in her throat. His frame stiffened dangerously and his eyes narrowed and darkened with anger.

Chapter Eight

The smoke from his cigar burned his throat as Garreth inhaled deeply. He savored the pleasure-pain, using the stimulation to clear his thoughts. He'd been in a muddle since that cursed treasure hunt. Or rather, since he'd stumbled upon Lacey and Sebastian.

Morning crept onto the upper gallery. Dressed in nothing but his trousers, he slumped against the wall and watched the tip of the glowing red fireball tease the horizon.

Why couldn't he put the picture of them from his mind? He tried to tell himself it was of no concern to him. He should be pleased their plan was going so well. They even had Anna Avery's endorsement, something they couldn't have planned on.

But it did no good to tell himself how he should

feel. He knew the truth, and the truth was he was jealous. Grass-green, fists-clenched jealous. Jealous of a woman he barely knew. Resentful of his best friend.

He'd been haunted by the image of Lacey and Sebastian since he'd retired. An ulcerous cramp gripped his stomach every time he thought of them together. Unable to fathom how it had happened, he finally admitted, beneath the pink fingers of dawn, that he'd fallen in love with his unlikely partner. And it didn't seem to matter they'd known each other so short a time.

She was just the sort of woman he'd assumed he'd one day find and settle down with. Intelligent, loving, gentle, yet strong. A lady whose love of family overshadowed everything, even her own happiness. Sensuous, with hidden fire and passion waiting to be tapped. Passionate, with desires only he could satisfy.

Only he wouldn't be the one to fulfill her needs, he reminded himself sharply. He had nothing to offer Lacey. That same family loyalty that he admired would prevent her from seeing him as anything but a convenient way to get to Sebastian.

And although he wished they could put aside their financial considerations and see what might develop between them, he knew that was impossible.

The entire situation had quickly gone from sorry to contemptible. He felt his dark mood grow blacker by the minute.

With a whispered curse, he tossed the cigar to

the ground and watched until the glow faded from its tip. Returning to his room, he shucked his trousers, dropped across the bed, and fought for sleep.

Breakfast the next morning was to be a casual affair. A buffet had been set up on the back veranda and the guests came down at their convenience. When Lacey arrived, Anna Avery sat alone, sipping tea.

"Good morning," she greeted Lacey enthusiastically. "Come, sit with me. There's plenty of food in the warming dishes. Unless, of course, there's something special you'd like."

Lacey tried to force a smile to her lips, but the effort fell short of the mark. She took in the bright light of excitement in Anna's eyes and felt like the unsuspecting fly being lured into the web by the beautiful—but dangerous—spider. What caused her feelings of disquiet, she wasn't quite sure.

"No, thank you," she said hesitantly. "I'll just have tea this morning."

"How are you feeling, dear? No ill effects from your spill in the lake, I hope?"

Lacey poured herself a cup of tea and sat across from Sebastian's mother. "None at all," she assured the woman. "In fact, I don't know when I've felt so well. Your home is lovely. And it's very peaceful out here."

"Yes, I do enjoy getting away from the city for a brief respite. But I must admit I'm ready to return to Mobile."

She sipped her tea slowly, her smiling eyes continuing to watch Lacey over the gold-trimmed edge of the ivory French china cup. "We've decided to accompany your group back on the afternoon train, you know. The servants will close up the house and follow."

Hiding her surprise, Lacey slowly nodded, unsure whether a reply was expected or not.

"I think this weekend has served its purpose," Anna continued sagely.

At Lacey's wide-eyed stare, she hurriedly went on. "Don't get me wrong, dear. I'm not really as bad as I must seem to you. But I love my son more than anything, and his happiness is my only concern."

She took a sip of the pale liquid and set the dainty cup aside. The guilelessness had left her gaze and she met Lacey's eyes with a frankness previously absent in the congenial woman. "You're a bright girl, you understand what I'm trying to say. I believe in fate," she confessed, watching her guest closely. "And I think it's fate that you're here this weekend."

Astonishment rippled through Lacey and she set her cup in the matching saucer with an abrupt clank. "Fate?" she choked.

Anna smiled, and Lacey couldn't feel animosity toward the woman, even if her efforts seemed calculating. "I'd like to speak candidly if I may."

Again Lacey could do no more than nod in stunned disbelief.

"Good, I knew you were sensible the moment I laid eyes on you. And lovely, too. Just the thing to offer Sebastian proof of something his father and I have been telling him." Leaning in, she smiled conspiratorially.

"What's that?" Lacey asked, realizing she'd bent closer as though about to hear a secret.

"It's as easy to fall in love with a suitable girl as it is an unsuitable one. And so much more pleasant in the long run."

Her hands trembled violently and Lacey was thankful she'd set aside the beautiful and expensive china cup. She swallowed the shock she felt at Anna Avery's remark. A new thought occurred to Lacey, adding to her feelings of guilt and confusion.

Sebastian must have loved his Cajun very much, for the Averys' fear certainly was evident. It seemed they'd do anything to ensure he married what they considered the right girl. Even going so far as to ratify their choice overtly. She strongly suspected Anna Avery had purposely lingered over her breakfast just to give Lacey her nod of approval face-to-face.

Suddenly Lacey wasn't sure she could go through with her plan. She had always believed in love and its ability to triumph over any adversity. Her parents' marriage was proof love matches could be as successful as arranged ones. What if Anna Avery was wrong about what was best for Sebastian? Could she be the one to stand in the way of his happiness? Especially if he truly loved the Cajun girl?

With a shock, Lacey realized something else. She wanted a love match for herself. She didn't want to spend her wedding night in the arms of a man she didn't love and who possibly loved another. She wanted completeness in her union.

"Lacey? Have I said something to upset you?" Anna queried anxiously, touching Lacey's hand.

Lacey jerked herself out of her contemplation, shaking off her doubts. She couldn't afford to be sentimental, she reminded herself harshly. Her situation demanded she act quickly and unemotionally. For surely if she let her feelings rule the day it would be Garreth she longed for and not Sebastian. And under the circumstances, that would never do for either of them.

"No, of course not."

"I know it seems callous to discuss this as though it were a business deal, where emotions have no place. But I assure you I'm thinking of Sebastian's best interests. And yours as well. No matter what he thinks, he needs an intelligent girl who understands the social duties that will be required of her as an Avery. Do you understand what I'm trying to say?"

Unfortunately, Lacey did. She nodded, pushing aside her cold tea.

"Yes, but how can you be sure Sebastian is ready to marry anyone?" she asked, her feelings running the gamut between despondency and cautious excitement.

"Sebastian is a good sort, really. But he's more than a little spoiled, as I'm sure you've noticed. Of course, he doesn't claim to be otherwise, so mostly people accept him the way he is. And up until now we've left him pretty much to his own devices. But in this one area, his father and I will not relent. We have made it clear to Sebastian that the time has come for him to seriously consider marriage. And nothing less than a commensurate match will do. You do understand?"

"Yes, I do," Lacey whispered.

"Good," Anna cooed. "I knew you were a bright girl. I've instructed Sebastian to bring you to the town house for dinner as soon as we're settled. You will come?"

This was the moment of truth, Lacey thought wildly. If she accepted, it was as good as putting her stamp of approval on Sebastian's courtship. She wished Garreth were here now to advise her.

But she didn't need to see his face to know what he'd say. This is what they came here for. More than they'd hoped to achieve! She'd be a fool to refuse. A heaviness filled her heart as she met the expectant look in Anna's eyes. She swallowed her scruples and nodded. "That would be very nice. I'll look forward to it."

Sebastian's mother beamed. "Wonderful. Now if you'll excuse me, I need to see about the last-minute arrangements for our trip this afternoon."

She swept from the room, leaving Lacey in a clouded daze. She tried to tell herself it wouldn't have mattered if she'd refused. The Averys' minds were made up. Sebastian was being pushed to settle down, and he wouldn't be allowed to marry the Cajun. If she declined Anna's offer, the woman would simply move on to her next choice.

Besides, she had been kidding herself. She had no choice but to marry Sebastian Avery as soon as possible. Love, affection, emotions played no part in her predicament. And as repugnant as that was, she could no longer ignore the truth.

She might fancy herself falling in love with Garreth Armstrong. But with Anna Avery's help, she would marry Sebastian.

"I can't do this!" Lacey breathed, clutching Francie's arm frantically.

Around them people strolled along the shaded walkway of Church Street. Ahead she could see the bright-colored umbrellas of the open-air cafe which had been their destination when they left Francie's home 15 minutes earlier.

It had been three days since their return to Mobile. Sebastian had come to see Lacey the first day back with the promised dinner invitation. His manner had been impeccable, giving no sign he was there at his mother's command. Lacey had graciously accepted, and tonight she would make her first appearance on his arm. Her nerves were already stretched to the breaking point. Francie's latest scheme only added to her worries.

"You said you needed money now. It won't be enough to save Emerald Oaks, but it will pay Tess's salary with a little left over. Now come along."

"I've changed my mind. I don't think I can do this after all."

"We're just going to have tea with the man.

You'll do fine," her friend insisted, dragging her along.

"But a job!" Lacey cried, her voice breaking sharply. "My mother would have a stroke if she knew I'd taken employment."

Francie pulled her over to the side of the walkway beneath an overhanging magnolia tree.

"Your mother has no idea the fix y'all are in, Lacey. And besides, no one is going to find out."

"I'm involved in all the subterfuge I can handle, Francie. What if I slip and say something? The whole thing will be out. And I'm afraid I'll ruin your secret as well."

"Pish," Francie snorted. "What do I care if anyone finds out I've been writing for the *Register*? Maybe it would be for the best."

"No, it wouldn't. You said yourself no one would accept a woman reporter. It'll ruin everything."

Francie dropped Lacey's arm and plopped her hands down on her hips. "You're not going to be writing about murders, for goodness' sake. 'Trifles Light as Air' is a society column. It's nothing more than social gossip."

"But I'm not a writer," Lacey argued.

"You're a very intelligent woman, and no one knows more about the social graces than you do."

"But, Francie..."

"But nothing. Come on. Col. Rapier is waiting. And remember, it must appear to be a chance meeting."

Lacey allowed herself to be swept along the

walkway. Up ahead she could see couples sitting at the umbrellaed tables sipping tea and talking. Several businessmen held heated discussions at other tables over coffee or something stronger.

Francie clutched her arm and leaned close. "Look happy, dear, we're supposed to be having a good time."

Lacey forced a smile as they walked forward. A waiter approached, preparing to seat them. Instead, Francie suddenly waved her arm.

"Col. Rapier," she called, startling both Lacey and the waiter. "There's a friend of my father's," she explained. "He seems to be sitting alone. I think we'll join him," she told the waiter, sashaying through the clustered tables. Lacey shrugged and followed.

"Hello, Francine." The older man rose and nodded to the waiter. He took Francie's hand and held her chair as she sat beside him. He came around and seated Lacey and then returned to his chair. "How is your father?"

"Daddy's just fine. Busy as usual."

"And your dear mother?"

"Very well," she said, smiling as the waiter held a framed slate up next to the table with a menu listed in chalk.

Francie placed their order and waited for the man to leave before she said, "What do you have for me?"

Col. Rapier slid an envelope across the table. "It's all in there. Nothing exciting, I'm afraid. It's been a slow news week."

Lacey could see the disappointment in her

friend's face and she shifted uncomfortably in her chair. Both heads turned in her direction and she froze.

"This is the lady I was telling you about. She would be perfect for the 'Trifles' column."

"I don't—"

"How do you do?" he cut in. "Francie gave you a glowing recommendation. And I confess, I'm in something of a spot. You'll need to start right away. I had a gentleman doing the column but he left for a better offer without notice. You only have three days to get something together. I hope you can manage it in such a short time. The ladies depend on their bits of gossip, you know."

The waiter arrived with their tea, cutting off Lacey's reply. The editor jumped to his feet, dropping enough cash on the table to cover their bill.

"It was nice seeing you again, Francine," he said politely, loud enough that the guests closest to them could hear him. "Tell your parents I said hello. Nice to meet you too, Miss..."

"Webster," Lacey mumbled, realizing the man didn't even know her name, yet it seemed he'd hired her on the spot.

"Of course, Miss Webster. I'm afraid I must get back to the paper. Good day."

He bustled off as Francie poured two cups of tea from the little porcelain pot.

"Congratulations," she said, lifting her cup in a semblance of a toast. "You are now gainfully employed as a writer for the *Mobile Press Register*."

Funny, Lacey thought, it felt as if she'd been run down by a heavily loaded wagon.

Chapter Nine

"TRIFLES LIGHT AS AIR" FOR THE LADIES OF MOBILE

Since this is my first column, I would like to say how delighted I am to be bringing the ladies of Mobile all the latest news of fashion and events. I hope you enjoy my little tidbits of information. I am here to inform and entertain. To start, I have it on good authority that the unseasonal boating party at the splendid estate of Lawrence Avery and his beautiful wife, Anna, was a knockout success....

Garreth tossed the paper aside and stared out his office window at the docks of Mobile Bay. The trip to Springhill had indeed been a success. A disastrous success. Disastrous because of Lacey's accident and the Averys' reaction to it. Successful because of Lacey's accident and the Averys' reaction to it. She'd immediately won their compassion, along with their favor. And he'd seen firsthand Sebastian's attempts to charm her.

The jealousy born in Springhill had quickly become his constant companion. He called himself a fool, but he knew for certain he'd fallen in love with Lacey Webster. Now he'd have to watch—no, help—her marry another man.

Stroking his chin, he wondered how he'd ever be able to keep his feelings a secret. Would Sebastian see the desire in his eyes when he looked at Lacey? Would she read the anguish on his face as he watched her take the arm of his friend?

Drawing his watch from his vest pocket, he pushed the stem and stared at the face. Six-thirty. He'd have to hurry to be on time for the evening's festivities.

Sebastian was wasting no time. He'd invited Lacey to dine at the Averys' home last night and now he'd arranged for the two of them to escort Francine and Lacey to the opening of the Mobile theater.

Garreth pushed to his feet and closed the ledger on his desk. Lifting his coat from the rack by the door, he rolled his shirtsleeves down and slipped it on.

"Good night, Gramb," he said, passing the

secretary on his way through the outer office. The man muttered a reply but Garreth barely heard him, steeped in dread of the night to come.

"This is perfect," Francie said, arranging her hair in a fashionable Marcel wave, the ring of curls framing her face. Her gown was a pearl-trimmed green silk with gigot sleeves, her gloves ivory lace to the elbow.

"I have to admit I was surprised when Sebastian sent the invitation asking us to accompany him and Garreth, tonight of all nights."

"Like Anna said, it's fate, dear Lacey. You were meant to marry that man, and that's all there is to it. Your plan has proceeded better than we ever dreamed."

"Yes, that's true. But to the very showing of the comedy by the 'U & I' company that I'm to write about, it's almost eerie."

Francie laughed as she fastened the buttons up the back of Lacey's pink polonaise dress. Lacey donned her long white gloves and carefully covered her topknot with a white cashmere beret.

"You'll get your assignment in ahead of schedule *and* have another opportunity to charm Sebastian Avery. What could be better?"

Lacey forced a smile as they collected their matching cabas, which held pencils and notepaper along with the usual handkerchief and pin money.

She told herself she should be happy her plot

to marry Sebastian was going so well. She really should. But somehow she couldn't help wishing she were Garreth's companion tonight, and wondering how she'd get through the evening in his presence without her newly discovered feelings showing through.

The bell rang as they descended the simple staircase. A servant opened the door to the gentlemen, both dressed in black frock coats, black trousers, and white vests. The men were handsome enough to turn every lady's head at the theater. But Lacey's gaze was for Garreth alone. He smiled warmly and her heart flipped over in response. For a long moment they stood, their gazes locked. She could almost believe he nurtured the same feelings for her she did for him. Then the smile vanished and he stepped to the side, making room for Sebastian's approach.

"You look ravishing," her date said, taking Lacey's gloved hand and touching it to his lips. "I will be the envy of every man there."

Lacey flushed, shyly drawing her fingers out of his grasp. But she couldn't stop her eyes from searching out Garreth's reaction. She read the look of distaste in his expression and thought he was once more wishing they had never begun their ploy.

Garreth helped Francie with her cape, all the while complimenting her appearance. She twittered flirtatiously, even batting him with her fan as he leaned in and whispered something close to her ear.

Lacey watched, a heaviness filling her chest. Why, oh why, couldn't Garreth have been the one with the fortune she so desperately needed? It would be no hardship giving her heart to Garreth, and the devotion she exhibited would be genuine.

"We've brought the carriage, but it's a beautiful night, if you ladies would rather walk."

Lacey stared at Sebastian, with his dark hair carefully parted and brushed into order. His eyes twinkled like dark gems, his joviality shining through. He was a handsome man; she could certainly understand how he'd gotten his reputation with the ladies. She'd be the envy of Mobile if he proposed to her. Still, she felt nothing but despair as he tucked her hand into the crook of his arm.

They agreed to walk the two blocks to the theater, where Sebastian had reserved a box. Lacey experienced a moment's panic as she saw the four seats aligned in a row. Francie took her seat, followed by Garreth. Sebastian waved his hand for her to proceed him, and the frenzy of emotions she'd held so closely in check threatened to fly out of control.

How could she sit beside Garreth, their seats touching, through the entire night? How would she bear being able to smell his shaving lotion and the pomade he wore on his hair? From a distance she heard a pounding and realized it was the beat of her heart slamming against her rib cage. She pressed her hand to her stomach.

"Lacey?"

Sebastian's voice seeped through her hysteria. She glanced up and caught the frown creasing Garreth's brow. His mouth tightened in warning and she cleared her throat, as well as her mind.

"I'm sorry," she whispered, slipping into the seat.

Sebastian sat beside her and she prayed the evening would go quickly.

The play was the first of the season. The overture began at eight o'clock. The four sat through the first act of the three-act comedy chatting and sharing an occasional outburst of laughter. Lacey realized her fears had been unnecessary.

Sebastian held her attention through the entire first half. Between his prattle and her trying to concentrate on what she would say in her article, she had little time to dwell on Garreth's closeness.

At the first intermission, she and Francie excused themselves to go to the ladies' room, where they made notes on what they'd seen. Afterward, the talk in the lobby was all focused on the new theater. Lacey disappeared to the lounge once more for another round of frantic scribbling. She quickly caught the fever for reporting, and found she rather enjoyed putting her thoughts and observations down on paper.

As she exited the ladies' lounge, she saw Thaddeus Stone coming toward her. Frantic, she glanced around and saw Garreth watching her. She felt herself go pale. Garreth must have seen her startled reaction. He strode toward her, closing the distance in a few steps and reaching her side a second before Stone.

"Lacey, dear," Stone said, his oily voice dripping false affection. "How are you?"

She glanced quickly at Garreth and saw his lip curl as he studied the man. She had to get away before Stone said something to alert Garreth to her plight.

"I'm, fine, Mr. Stone." She turned as though to walk away.

"And how is your dear mother?" he asked, stopping her in her tracks. "I've been meaning to go visit her for some time. Maybe this would be a good chance, since you're tied up in town."

Slowly she turned to face him once more. Her rage flamed to life and she knew hot spots of color had flooded her cheeks. "My mother is just fine, Mr. Stone. In fact, we're all exceedingly well. However, I really don't think a visit right now would be a good idea. I appreciate your—concern, but I'll be home before you know it."

He quirked a brow at her challenging statement, and she could see the confusion on Garreth's face as well. But she didn't care. She wanted Stone to know she wasn't just going to lie down and let him destroy her family.

Garreth apparently sensed her dismay. He stepped close and took her arm. "Shall we get back, Lacey?"

She nodded, ignoring Stone's amused chuckle as she walked away.

Garreth eyed her with a troubled frown, but he didn't question her about the odd encounter. She went back to her seat eagerly, determined to put the whole episode from her mind.

At the end of the play Sebastian suggested they go to the open-air cafe for a late supper. The ladies agreed, and together the four of them strolled down Church Street past the fire station.

"Oh, we should climb up and ring the bell," Francie said, pausing in front of the brick structure which housed the engine for Station Number Six. It had always been a lark to the youth of Mobile to climb the metal stairs in back of the building, cross the roof, and ring the bell. Since the bell rang continuously during an actual fire, no harm was done by ringing it briefly.

"Don't you think we've outgrown that bit of mischief, Francie?" Garreth asked, pushing aside the flaps of his frock coat and stuffing his hands in his trouser pockets.

"Oh, pooh," Francie said, her eyes shining with excitement. "You may have turned into an old stuffed shirt, Garreth Armstrong, but the rest of us still know how to have fun. Come on, you two."

Sebastian laughed heartily, and it was evident he saw no reason not to go along with Francie's bit of mischief. Lacey would have none of it, though. Her mood had remained pensive following her brief meeting with Stone.

"No, really," she said, drawing her arm from Sebastian's hold. "You go ahead. I have a bit of a headache."

"All the more reason to indulge in a little harm-less fun."

But Lacey continued to refuse, despite Sebas-tian's flirtatious coaxing. She was in no mood for the childish prank. Her thoughts were on bigger concerns.

"Fine," Francie finally said, her tone exasper-ated. "You two go on to the cafe and get us a table; we'll catch up. Just remember when y'all hear that bell that we're having fun, while y'all are stuck with your boring, stodgy ways. Come on, Sebastian."

Francie clutched Sebastian's hand and they turned down the side street that ran behind the fire station.

"Come on," Garreth said. "We'll wait for them at the cafe."

"I can't believe the things Francie does sometimes," Lacey said, making an attempt at small talk now that they found themselves alone together. She'd carefully avoided a situation like this all night, only to fall into it the minute they left the theater. But not even to avoid Garreth would she go along with Francie's foolish prank.

Garreth frowned. "She's too flighty, even for a society miss."

Lacey glanced up, surprised at the caustic comment. How could anyone think Francie was flighty? She held a position no woman had ever held before, reporting every tragedy and scoop in the city no matter how heinous or scandalous. Most society women weren't even allowed to read the articles by Phillip Truman—Francine Thomas.

But of course, she reminded herself, Garreth had no idea Francie was Phillip Truman. No one knew that except herself and the editor of the *Register*. For the first time Lacey understood why Francie acted so addle brained in front of other people. It hid her real self so well no one would guess the truth.

They fell into an uneasy silence as they walked along. Lacey could think of nothing but Stone's veiled attempt to reinforce his threats.

Her reckless heart reached out to Garreth, and she worried that he'd see the newfound love in her eyes, so she avoided his gaze. He seemed likewise tense, his shoulders taut with strain. As they passed the Farley house on Church Street, the branches of a huge live oak extended across the walkway.

Lacey shivered in the coolness of the tree's silhouette, aware of Garreth's nearness and the security his presence represented. She replayed the moments she'd spent in his arms and felt her blood warm.

Warily she took another step away from him, trying to put a safe distance between them. Before she realized her mistake, her slippered foot dropped off the side of the brick-covered walkway and she stumbled.

"Oh!" she cried.

Garreth reached out and steadied her, his hands holding her firmly.

"Are you all right?"

Lacey looked down and by the light of the gas-lights saw the scuff marring the soft leather on the side of her shoe. Feeling foolish, she straightened and said, "Yes, I'm fine. Embarrassed at my clumsiness, is all."

She shifted her weight to her ankle, thankful it held without pain. Nothing was injured.

After a moment she became aware of the large, warm hands still gripping her shoulders. Her gaze slid up the buttons of Garreth's vest to his stiff collar, jaw, and finally his eyes. They stared at her boldly, darkened by a hunger she could no longer doubt.

She swallowed hard, but refused to look away. Tired of blushing and stammering, she determined to look desire straight in the face, if only this one time.

His eyes proclaimed his longing, and no matter what, she couldn't help the thrill it sent through her. Fate had led her to him, this man she loved. It had also put him out of her reach.

But right then, standing in the warm puddle of muted light, she knew if there had been any way for them to be together, she'd have already succumbed to the feelings she held steadfastly in check.

She couldn't have him. Thaddeus Stone had cheated her of that possibility. But she longed to let Garreth know how she felt. She needed to know if he felt the same, even if it could never be. Her flesh ached for his touch; her lips longed for the feel of his mouth covering hers as they had that first day in his office. She wanted him to take her in his arms with abandon the way he had twice before.

For a brief time, she wanted to forget her family and their needs. Her own needs were too great at that moment to be denied.

Neither spoke, but Garreth read the acceptance on her face. He turned and drew her against the trunk of the massive oak, shielding their bodies from the glow of the lamp. He pressed her back against the tree and let his mouth claim hers.

The kiss, gentle at first, turned desperate. He plunged his tongue between her teeth and ravished her mouth. His arms gripped her so tight she could feel the echo of his heart beating against her own. His thighs flattened her skirts on either side of her legs as he bowed over her.

Drawing back a fraction, he met her startled gaze. His expression was almost angry and she shivered.

"Sebastian may have all of you in time, but, by God, I will have this tonight."

Once more his mouth descended and the flames of desire exploded within her. Heat suffused her body all the way to her fingertips and toes. A sheen of sweat broke across her lower back beneath her corset as their passion blazed.

Never had she done anything so improper! The streets were quiet, but not completely uninhabited. She struggled for control, knowing she should push him away. But, like Garreth, she wanted to sample the pleasures they could have known if things were different.

After a long moment he released her. His breath came out raggedly in the silence of the night, as did hers. Her lips felt bruised, swollen, but sensitized like never before. She reached up to touch them, wanting to imprint his kiss on her lips forever.

"I should apologize," he said, tugging at his vest.

She met his eyes and her hand fell to her side. "Are you sorry?"

"Not one damned bit," he admitted with a dry chuckle. "If only I could accept that you must marry another."

"Garreth—"

"No, don't say anything," he cut in. "I've tried to tell myself my feelings for you don't change anything. You need to marry Sebastian. I have nothing to offer you. Even my business is nearly done for if I can't get my hands on cash fast."

She knew he was right. The memory of her mother and brother that she'd held at bay came flooding back to haunt her. They needed her, were depending on her whether they realized it or not. She couldn't throw away her only chance to save them from Stone's scheme. Especially when things were going so well.

"Then we'd better go," she whispered, turning away and stepping into the puddle of light beneath the street lamp. "Francie and Sebastian will be along any moment."

As he nodded they heard the sound of the fire

bell split the stillness of the night. The humorous situation was lost on Garreth and Lacey as they slowly strolled toward the cafe, a safe distance now between them, in both body and heart.

Chapter Ten

"Come in, Lacey," Col. Rapier said, rising from his desk and walking toward her. "Your articles for the 'Trifles' column were excellent. I'm very pleased Francine recommended you."

"Thank you, sir." Lacey sat in the chair opposite his desk. "You have another assignment for me?"

"Indeed. As you know, we do the 'Trifles' column three times a week. I'd like you to write all the articles."

Heart racing, Lacey sat forward on her seat. "You would?" she asked, unable to keep the surprise from her voice. Francie had told her the article she did on the opening of the theater season was good, but Lacey had doubted her ability to be a real writer. A surge of pride coursed through her, making her want to laugh with the thrill of accomplishment.

He passed an envelope across the desk and Lacey looked inside. Her eyes flew wide at the amount of the check. Her first payment! A soft gasp escaped her. It would never be enough to save Emerald Oaks, or even keep Stone at bay, but it was enough to allow her to continue paying Tess. And Lacey knew the woman needed the money no matter what she'd said.

"Your next assignment is in there as well. I hope you won't have any trouble. If you should, let me know. Perhaps I can help."

"Thank you, Col. Rapier."

"Thank you, Lacey. You really came through when I needed you. We didn't have a chance to get acquainted at the cafe, but I have some time now. Why don't I show you around the operation? We can get acquainted and you can get a feel for the way we do things in the newspaper business. You can even see your article go to print. Since your name won't be appearing on the actual columns, perhaps that will help."

Hoping the diversion would take her mind off the impending threat for a brief time, she nodded. "I'd like that."

Lacey followed the editor out of his office and down the hall. They came to a large room filled with bustling workers running around frantically. He shouted to be heard over the whine of machinery.

"It's always like this before deadline. News is a minute-to-minute business."

Nodding, Lacey surveyed the frenzied activity.

Col. Rapier led her to a tall black iron machine across the room. She saw a man working with a circulating brass matrix.

"This is our new Linotype machine," the editor explained. "Our operator can set seven lines of print per minute with this beauty," he bragged, clapping the man on the shoulder and offering a proud smile. The worker paused for less than a second and went back to his feverish task.

Lacey saw every stage of the process involved in putting out the daily paper. It amazed and fascinated her. Like most people she never thought of the work involved in getting the news out in a timely manner. She gloried briefly in the knowledge that she was now a part of the procedure.

She left the *Register* some time later with the envelope clasped tightly in her hand. As she strolled down Government Street there was a slight bounce in her step. For a fleeting moment the problems of the last few months disappeared beneath her newfound self-esteem.

She, who had always counted on her father to handle all of life's important details, had managed to take care of this one on her own. Knowing Tess would be able to stay, looking after her mother and Georgie while she continued her mission in Mobile, brought Lacey a moment's peace.

She crossed Government and walked on down Church Street to Francie's house. She'd planned to leave this evening for Emerald Oaks. Even Tess, with her infinite patience, needed a break once in a while. But on Monday she'd be back, ready to begin her new article.

The lightness vanished from her stride as she turned the corner. Sebastian's carriage sat outside the Thomases' house. Slowing her step, she continued up the walkway.

Francie had been watching for her and she opened the door as Lacey approached.

"He's here to see you, Lacey; tidy yourself quickly. I've got him waiting in the informal parlor."

"Where are your parents?" Lacey asked, glancing around at the quiet house. Usually the Thomas family bustled in and out constantly.

"Mama and Papa are at a meeting at the Relief Hall, and Jeannie has gone off to her friend Sarah's house for a tea party or some nonsense."

She rushed off again, leaving Lacey standing in the main hall in stunned silence.

Her heart raced uncontrollably. Was Sebastian at last going to further their relationship? Her desperation grew with every passing minute as the deadline for the mortgage payment drew closer.

Sebastian had been an attentive escort, and the dinner with his parents pleasant enough. But otherwise their association seemed to have stalled. In fact, she hadn't spoken to him since the night of the theater opening a week ago. He hadn't been in touch since and she could only wait until he made the next move or risk appearing too eager and arousing his suspicions.

She stuffed the envelope with her check and

assignment into her caba, and dropped it on the petticoat table by the door. Looking in the hatpin mirror she removed her tiny straw bonnet and tucked her hair back into place. Her cheeks were flushed from the brisk walk and the cool fall breeze off the bay. Her eyes still sparkled from the joy she'd felt at Col. Rapier's compliments. Removing her gloves she went to greet her guest.

As she entered the parlor Francie swept toward her, a mischievous grin on her face.

"I'll go and tell Cook to prepare us some tea," she said, making a quick exit and leaving Sebastian and Lacey alone together in the room.

"You look lovely," Sebastian said, coming forward and taking her hand. He bowed over it, then held it as he led her to the forest-green settee.

"Thank you," Lacey murmured, seating herself beside him on the small sofa.

"Mother has sent me with another invitation. She would like for you to come to the town house for Sunday supper, and bring your mother."

Jerking her hand from his grasp, Lacey rose to her feet. "I'm sorry," she said, smoothing the folds of her skirt nervously. "My mother isn't well. She isn't accepting any invitations at this time."

Sebastian slowly stood. "I apologize. I meant no harm. Mother only wanted to meet your family."

His smile died briefly, but then he resumed a good-natured boyish mien. "You must know we were all enchanted by you in Springhill."

"I appreciate the offer and I'm pleased your mother liked me. I liked her very much, too. But it's just not possible."

This was a complication Lacey hadn't considered. What would Anna Avery think if she saw her mother now? And Georgie. God, she knew people thought he was touched; that was why she'd quit socializing. Visitors disturbed her brother. She hadn't wanted him hurt or upset.

Anna thought Lacey was the answer to all her prayers after Sebastian's unfortunate infatuation with the Cajun. But what would she think if she was faced with the truth? Would Lacey be able to convince the woman there was no reason for her to be concerned over the peculiar mental state of her family?

"I'm sorry if we've done something to upset you," he said, glancing down at her tightly clenched hands.

"No, of course you haven't. Please thank your mother for me and tell her I'm flattered. But I must return to Emerald Oaks this evening and I won't be back until late Monday."

"Then let me at least escort you to the station."

"That isn't necessary, but thank you again."

"I insist," he said, smiling as he stepped tentatively toward her. Lacey forced herself not to back away. This was the man she planned to marry. And she'd promised Garreth she would make Sebastian a good wife when they discussed their agreement. The least she could do was grant him this small courtesy.

"All right," she conceded, forcing a polite

smile. "I'm taking the last train. It leaves Royal Street at five o'clock."

"I'll be here at four-thirty sharp," he promised, bowing over her hand once more. This time his lips touched her flesh and she felt the tingle of warmth glide along her nerve endings.

"Good day."

Francie arrived with the tea and Sebastian made his excuses as he passed her on his way out. She rolled the tea cart into the room, one eyebrow climbing upward toward her hairline.

"What was that all about?" she asked.

Lacey sank into the corner of the settee and blew a ragged sigh, lifting the strands of hair from her damp forehead.

"His mother wants to meet mine."

"Oooh," Francie cried, abandoning the cart and rushing to her friend's side. "This is wonderful. You arrived at the prime moment. The Averys are intent on marrying Sebastian off to an acceptable girl before he changes his mind about giving up his Cajun. And you are going to be that girl, Lacey."

Lacey shook her head, panic threatening her control. "No, it's terrible. What am I going to do? Mother can't meet Anna Avery. Not now. And I can just see Sebastian's mother's reaction to Georgie."

"Nonsense. Your mother is suffering from grief; that's not only understandable, it's commendable. And Georgie—well, the doctor assured y'all his defect was caused by his difficult birth. The Averys can't find fault with that reasoning."

175

"They forbade Sebastian to marry a girl just because they considered her unsuitable! What will they think of my menagerie of troubles?"

"Stop this. You're being silly. You are going to be Mrs. Sebastian Avery, I tell you. I'm certain of it!" she crowed.

Lacey swallowed the bile filling her throat as Francie hugged her enthusiastically. Was Francie right, was this finally the culmination of her plans? She should be happy. She should be, but...

After walking the two blocks from the railway station to Emerald Oaks, Lacey felt the oppressive weight of responsibility resettle on her shoulders. Occasionally she experienced fleeting moments when she could almost forget how dependent her mother and brother were on the success of her plan. But when she returned home to Emerald Oaks it became all too apparent once more.

Just another reminder of the importance of pressing Sebastian's suit. But she wasn't experienced at wooing a man with her wiles and she couldn't think of another thing she could do without seeming brazen.

Again her heart sank at the thought of refusing his offer. What would he do when he found out her mother had had a mental breakdown? How would he feel when he saw Georgie? She should have told him the truth.

No, she couldn't. She had to marry Sebastian Avery.

Stopping to stare at the overgrown foliage surrounding Emerald Oaks, the urgency of her plight pressed even closer. The azalea hedges needed trimming, as did the matching gardenias flanking the long drive. Huge oak and magnolia leaves littered the walkway and fell relentlessly into the now-dry fountain. Sounds of hammering could be heard from the area behind the garden, where a cottage was being built on what had recently been their back lawn.

Time was running out, and each visit home cost her precious days. But she had to relieve Tess occasionally, and she loved her mother and Georgie too much to stay away for long. A gripping melancholy embraced her as she reminded herself that once she married she would, of necessity, see far less of them than she liked.

Tess met her at the door, lines of fatigue and tension etched on her wrinkled brow. Lacey knew that meant the week had not gone well without her. Tess needed help with her charges, but there was no money for more servants. All had been let go save for Mamie the cook, and a part-time maid. Tess's days were full just catering to Katrina's and Georgie's needs.

"Have yourself a bite to eat before you go up. She's in a fine temper."

"I saw the cottage going up. I thought she'd be upset."

"Upset?" Tess cried, throwing her hands into the air. "She's absolutely raging."

Lacey shook her head slowly, the weight on her shoulders growing heavier with every moment. "I'll go on up," she told the exasperated woman.

"You'll get no break again until she's down for the night. Better take some nourishment first."

"I'll be fine. Thank you, Tess. I don't know what I'd do without you."

There had never been a truer statement. Without Tess, Lacey would never get away from Emerald Oaks. There'd be no hope of arranging a marriage, no hope of a future at all outside her duties here. She clutched her reticule, relishing the knowledge that her new assignment lay within it, waiting for her to bring it to life as she had the theater opening. The pride sustained her as she ascended the stairs to her mother's room.

"Lacey," Katrina cried as she came through the door. Her mother hurried to embrace her. Immediately she whirled back to face the jib window standing open across the room. "Have you seen that atrocity? What are you going to do about it, Lacey? I tell you, I won't have it."

Lacey looked out the window where her mother was frantically pointing. "I saw the cottage, Mother."

"Cottage? It's nothing more than a dogtrot," her mother said. "They have four rooms downstairs, laid out like a checkerboard. And nothing upstairs except a loft. A loft, Lacey, for those half dozen little ragamuffins I've seen running about. It's disgraceful, not to mention unhealthy."

"I don't know what you think I can do."

Katrina's tone took on a wheedling quality as she faced her daughter. "I know it's a heavy burden to place on you, but you must stop them, dear. Without your father these interlopers think they can just move in and take over our property. You must get rid of them."

A pounding started behind Lacey's eyes and she wished she'd taken Tess's advice about having something to eat before facing her mother's wrath. She felt unprepared to handle this well-worn subject.

Taking a deep breath, she went to the window and stared down at the square building being built less than 20 yards from the edge of her mother's garden. That alone was proof of her father's desperation. Given a choice he'd have never sold that portion of land. He must have known it would break Katrina's heart to see strangers so near her favorite place.

"We've been through this before, Mother. Remember, I told you they're not trespassing. Father sold them the land and they have every right to build any kind of house they like, anywhere they like on it."

"Don't talk that nonsense to me, young lady. Your father never would have sold off pieces of Emerald Oaks. He loved every inch of this land. His heart and soul lives in every grain of dirt."

"He had no choice, Mother. I've tried to explain to you the circumstances Father was in before he died. I'm sure he meant to tell you himself...."

"Hush!" Katrina demanded, clapping her soft white hands over her ears. The lace-edged sleeves of her dressing gown settled against the mahogany hair now streaked with silver. Her gray eyes shot fire. "I will not listen to such lies about your father, Lacey. I cannot understand how you could turn on him like this. He loved you so much," she said, tears coming to her eyes. She dropped her hands to her sides and turned back to watch the workmen finishing up for the day. Hard lines of anger drew her wrinkled mouth into a frown. "He loved us all."

Despair cloaked Lacey. How could she make her mother understand their dire predicament? She refused to come out of the fantasy world she'd retreated to since her husband's death. Thinking of fantasies, Lacey closed her eyes tiredly. "I'm going to see Georgie, Mother. I'll be back soon."

She escaped her mother's room and walked slowly toward the nursery. Inside, her brother sat cross-legged on the rug in the dusty ray of sunlight slicing across the floor. His hands reached for invisible particles only he could see in the fading light.

"Hello, Georgie," she whispered, knowing he wouldn't look up or otherwise acknowledge her presence. He continued to finger the air absently. She sank down beside him on the floor and brushed the reddish curls from his forehead.

"How have you been?" He wouldn't respond— he never did—but she talked to him often and she sometimes thought her voice soothed him.

Lacey needed some comfort herself and she drew on the memories of her surprise success at the *Register*. "I've had the most amazing thing happen, Georgie."

She propped herself on her elbows, ready to tell her secret to the one person she knew would never tell. "I've begun writting articles for the *Mobile Press Register*. They're only society pieces, but it feels wonderful to be doing something worthwhile. And I admit I get a chill just thinking of all the people who will be reading the words I write, Georgie."

As the emblazoned sun sank below a huge oak, her brother turned away and picked up a small wooden clock. He could take it apart and put it back together again without pause. All the intricate wheels and sprockets were a simple puzzle to him, one he'd done so many times he could accomplish the feat in record time. His mechanical abilities never ceased to amaze Lacey, when he'd never spoken so much as a word in his life.

His interest in the clock soon waned and he began to rock methodically back and forth. A low humming came from deep in his throat, but nothing of meaning had ever passed his lips.

"Had a bad week, huh?" she asked, picking up a small cedar music box she used to play for him when he was a baby. She wound the key and let the soft tinkling of the chimes fill the silence in the room for a long moment. Georgie's swaying slowed but didn't stop. She could tell when he was agitated, and the music usually helped calm him.

"I saw the cottage. I know mother has been in a regular snit about it. I wish she could understand there isn't anything I can do. When Father sold the land he had to have known the buyers would build on it. I've met this family, Georgie. They're nice people. But it won't matter. As long as Mother remains the way she is, living next to them peacefully will be impossible, I'm sure."

Rising, the little boy went to the window. He picked at the high sill, carving into the half-moon indentation already there with his thumbnail. Splinters fractured away from the sill and fell to the floor. Lacey went to the window and silently directed her brother away from the tedious task. She handed him the clock and immediately he began disassembling it once more.

Fatigue settled over Lacey as she placed a kiss on top of the boy's head and left him alone in the private world he lived in. She couldn't reach him. He didn't know she tried. Sometimes the grief she felt was almost more than she could bear.

In her own room, she washed and changed her clothes. She released her hair and ran the bristles of her silver brush through it until the throbbing in her head subsided. Repinning the coil, she caught a glimpse of her face in the mirror. Touching her fingers to her lips, she relived Garreth's kiss for the hundredth time. Her whole being ached for his presence. She longed for a glimpse of him. Closing her eyes, she could still smell the scent of his shaving soap and hair tonic.

Their private moment beneath the huge oak replayed itself in her mind. Never had she felt so moved. The world changed for her in that instant, and she feared it would never right itself. Garreth was the man for her. The one her heart would love forever.

But he was not the man she would marry. And

she had to accept that. The sooner the better, she admitted, feeling the pain pierce her chest. A tightness closed her throat, but she forced back the emotion.

Needing something to take her mind off her impotent feelings for Garreth and the ever-present pall of Stone's threat, she went to fetch her reticule from the hall table. She'd read the assignment Rapier gave her at least a dozen times, and each time it managed to give her battered spirits a small lift.

She descended the stairs, crossed the checker-board marble of the front hall, and collected her bag from the cherry table. The pendulum clock marked the seconds as she opened the clasp and drew out the envelope. She carefully read each word that Col. Rapier had written, though she could have recited them by heart.

> *Have obtained membership for you in the Pixley Social Club. Third annual meeting and election Thursday night. Drago's string band scheduled to accompany wagons of members on serenade. Enjoy!*

Lacey wished things were that simple.

Chapter Eleven

"TRIFLES LIGHT AS AIR" FOR THE LADIES OF MOBILE

It seems the chill of fall is being warded off by the promise of love in the air. Several local ladies have been seen regularly in the company of the same young men, making this reporter wonder if next June the reverend will be busier than usual. Among the more unlikely twosomes are dashing Sebastian Avery and a newcomer to Mobile society, Lacey Webster....

The wind off Mobile Bay took a chilly turn. Lacey visited Emerald Oaks for a week at Thanksgiving, but she returned to the city eager to get back to her pursuits. She couldn't forget for an instant Stone's vulturous presence hanging like a black cloud over her life and the lives of her mother and Georgie. She'd seen him twice since the theater opening and he never missed an opportunity to taunt her with the powerful hold he had over her.

Anna had arranged for Lacey to be seen on Sebastian's arm several times over the past weeks, enough to start the gossips speculating. Lacey hoped it would be enough to assure Stone that she had not given up her plans to pay him off before the deadline.

Francie had heard through Mobile's gossip grapevine that Anna Avery was speculating on her son's nuptials being in the near future.

As Lacey sat in the upstairs parlor of the Thomas house, her mind was filled with troubling questions.

Sebastian had been attentive, but their relationship seemed to be stagnating. He was a perfect gentleman, an excellent companion. They had fun together. He took her to the theater again, a few social events, and even the races at the Bayside Park driving club. All of which she later wrote about in the hopes Stone would see the articles and understand the significance.

But he seemed to have no interest in furthering their relationship. Sebastian seemed content to go his way, escorting her when the occasion called for it. And Lacey was only too aware that time ticked on toward the destruction of her family.

Francie seemed to think it was only a matter

of time before Sebastian proposed. Lacey wasn't so sure. Usually his joviality covered the pensiveness, but recently she'd become aware of a certain coolness in his manner he couldn't hide. More and more lately she grew frantic, aware that they could go on in this state of limbo forever.

She had no time to shift her interest to another man now, even if she could find one who was willing to marry an impoverished woman with a mentally unbalanced mother and a simpleton for a brother.

Her thoughts were harsh, but she had to constantly remind herself how others would view her family. There was no one willing to take them in. And anyone who heard of Thaddeus Stone's offer to marry her mother and secure a safe haven for her brother would consider him a saint. Only she would know the truth. Only she could stop him.

Since she'd thrilled to the feel of Garreth's arms around her, his lips bringing hers to life with a single kiss, she'd wished for more than a match of convenience. She wanted to feel something for her husband, and that knowledge chilled her. Stone had robbed her of that opportunity, but he couldn't stop her from dreaming.

She desperately wanted to feel the sweet heat of desire for her husband that Garreth had aroused in her. Sadly she suspected she never would.

Garreth had gone back to spending most of his time at his shipping office. She rarely saw him at the functions she attended. When they did chance to be in the same place, he nodded a brisk greeting and went his way. She knew he was avoiding her purposely so she might accomplish her goal without further complications. Nevertheless, she missed him terribly.

And she suffered great spasms of jealousy when she knew he was spending time with Edith Bishop. As he'd done last night.

Garreth cradled the glass tumbler of whiskey and studied the diamond droplets of rain chasing one another down the windowpane. The dismal day befitted his mood.

He remembered the unendurable evening he'd spent the previous night and a shudder of disgust ran through him. It had been an arduous task getting through the episode while keeping everyone's benevolence intact.

His mother continued to push for a union between him and Edith Bishop, despite her obvious loathing for the ill-mannered family. She had her heart set on another Springhill residence and saw Bishop's money as the means to her rather self-serving end.

Bishop himself was no better. He'd railroaded Garreth into the meeting last night and even suggested he take Edith for a stroll alone in the garden after dinner; something no man of quality would have allowed, much less sanctioned. But Bishop wanted Garreth to propose immediately, and he hadn't been subtle in affording him an opportunity.

Likewise, his daughter had a similar lack of finesse. She'd taken his arm, pressed her body close to his, and even pretended to stumble in order to get into his arms.

Unfortunately, her ploy had only reminded him of the moment Lacey had stumbled on the sidewalk after the theater opening. He couldn't forget the feel of her in his arms, the taste of her lips on his tongue. Edith's deception seemed a parody of the fierce emotions he'd read in Lacey's beautiful blue eyes that night.

Finally he could no longer ignore her overtures and he decided to approach her with honesty.

"Do you know your father is expecting me to propose tonight?" he'd blurted.

Edith had only laughed, the twangy, nasal sound chafing his taxed nerves. She appeared not the least disturbed by his announcement.

"Of course he is. And I must say, you're taking your time about the whole thing."

He frowned, grasping her slender arms and turning her face toward the moonlight so he could make out her expression.

"You know?"

"Of course I know. You don't imagine he concocted all this without any help, do you?"

"And you're in agreement? I mean, about the whole thing? The engagement?"

"It was my idea, silly," she told him, again pressing her chest to his. The white half-moons of her breasts pushed dangerously against the low neckline of her gown. Despite his revulsion at her brazenness he didn't look

188

away. She saw his regard and laughed again, the pitch causing him to cringe.

"I know what people think about my parents," she said, a note of hauteur in her tone. "They don't like them because they don't use the right fork, or speak the King's English properly. And therefore they snub us even though we have more money than any of them. I wasn't born into society, so if I want to become part of the upper crust, I must marry someone who is accepted. And that is precisely what I intend to do."

"What of love?" he asked.

Her eyes turned cold and hard. "Love can't give me what I want. I don't give a damn about such senseless sentimentalities. I intend to be someone of importance in this town. With or without your help. There are others who could use a dowry the size my father is offering, but you were my first choice."

The fervor in her eyes almost made him step back. Position, that was all that concerned her. It was an obsession. But Garreth understood that level of determination. It was the same sort of preoccupation he had for preserving Armstrong Shipping.

"And you don't care that I have no real feelings for you at all?" The notion still left him cold, but his desperation kept him from turning away in disgust.

"I couldn't care less about feelings, real or otherwise. It's your name I want. The Armstrong name will guarantee me admittance into every social gathering in Mobile. And I promise you, that is worth more than a fleeting moment of passion."

Again, Garreth remembered the feel of Lacey in his arms. Edith was wrong. That kind of pleasure was worth more than gold.

But he couldn't have Lacey. She needed something he couldn't give her. Even if she could accept him as he was, he could never ask her to sacrifice her family to be with him. She'd eventually grow to hate him for whatever hardships his penury brought them to.

He loved Lacey Webster. He'd readily admitted that, if only to himself. But he could never have her. And he didn't think he'd ever be able to love anyone else the way he loved her.

So what would it matter who he married. Wouldn't it, in fact, be better to marry someone who also sought gain from the union instead of a hopeless romantic searching for a lover and a helpmate?

He had stared at Edith for a long time as he debated what to do. Finally, for better or worse, he made his decision.

The sound of footsteps on the stairs drew Lacey's attention back to the present and she quickly slipped the article she was working on beneath a tome of Shakespearian plays, pretending to read.

Francie peeked into the parlor and then stepped inside and slid the double doors closed behind her. Her pale face was tight, her mouth turned down in a frown. Lacey sat up expectantly.

"What is it?"

"I met with Col. Rapier to get my new assignment," she said, fidgeting with the silver clasp on her reticule. "He asked me to give this to you." She held a cream-colored envelope with white-knuckled intensity.

Lacey recognized the *Register* stationery. Her heart fluttered, racing with anticipation. She still got a thrill out of every assignment. But she met the bright gaze of Francie's eyes and apprehension seized her.

"I know what your assignment is, Lacey. And we've got to do something to stop it."

Rising abruptly, Lacey hurried forward and took the envelope. She ripped the seal and nearly tore the heavy parchment in her anxious rush to read the contents. Her eyes scanned the words and a harsh breath lodged in her throat. Her hand fluttered to her chest and she sank back into her chair.

"I didn't think he'd do it. I felt certain...."

"He can't go through with it, Lacey," Francie cried. "He'll ruin his life."

Lacey could only shake her head, rereading the assignment. She still couldn't believe what her eyes saw. "We knew this was a possibility."

"No!" Francie said, flouncing across the room and back again, her carefully trimmed nails under assault from her small white teeth. "I suspected Howard Bishop was after something like this. But I never thought for a moment Garreth would accept. That man—that family, they're horrible, Lacey. He can't do this."

"Apparently he has no choice," Lacey whispered, seeing the knuckles of her own hand pale as she gripped the page, despair rendering her immobile.

Francie's high drama was nothing compared to what she felt at that moment. But her emotions went too deep for mere exclamations of protest. She was stunned speechless.

She didn't want to think about this assignment. She couldn't do it. Francie was horrified by the news because she considered Garreth a friend. Lacey had her own reasons for the trembling she felt moving up her legs.

How could she possibly fulfill this duty? Her column was filled with light gossip and frivolity. How would she ever write an article about the engagement party of Garreth Armstrong and Edith Bishop without her unqualified misery showing through?

Sebastian's appearance in Garreth's office was so unexpected Garreth jumped to his feet in startled surprise. Gramb followed Sebastian into the room, an apologetic frown on his face.

"I would have announced him, sir...." the man began.

Sebastian scowled at the secretary. "He knows who I am," he barked. "He doesn't need you to tell him."

Garreth waved the anxious man away and Sebastian slammed the door behind him. "What the hell do you think you're doing?"

"Hello, Sebastian." Garreth sat back down, forcing a cool smile to his lips.

"Don't act as though you don't know what I'm talking about," his friend raged, waving a peach card embossed with raised black lettering. "Tell me this is a mistake and you haven't agreed to marry that chit."

"It's no mistake."

"Damnation!" he thundered, slamming the card down on Garreth's desk hard enough to rattle the crystal globe in the lamp.

Garreth stared down at the invitation, his eyes narrowing. The Bishops hadn't wasted any time getting the word out. Of course, that was more his fault than theirs. He'd insisted on a short engagement, to be announced as soon as the arrangements could be made.

His name jumped out at him from the pastel card, along with the date. A week from Saturday. Eight days, and he'd be bound to Edith Bishop as surely as if they were already married. Bitterness rose in his throat, but he pushed the feeling aside. He'd made his decision; there was no use covering the same ground again.

"Well, I don't believe for a minute you actually love that ill-bred churl." He sank onto the seat in front of Garreth's desk, his anger spent for the moment but still simmering just beneath the surface.

"Love has nothing to do with marriage in most cases," Garreth said, absently pushing the expensive invitation farther away. He didn't want to read the carefully calligraphic phrases.

"Maybe not, but why Bishop's daughter? And why now?"

"Because Bishop has included me in a very lucrative venture."

"What kind of venture?"

"Jade. He wants me to go to the East Indies at the first sign of summer and bring back a shipment of jade. He's offered me a share of the profits, which promise to be substantial."

"And the offer comes with the price tag of marrying his daughter? Dammit, is this what your precipitous visit to Springhill was about? Are you so desperate to save this damned company you'd marry a horse-faced hoyden you care nothing about?"

Garreth stiffened in defense. "I can see you've never met Edith Bishop. She is far from horse-faced. Quite attractive actually. And she was schooled back east, so she isn't quite the wretch you seem to think her."

"I've heard she talks through her nose and snorts when she laughs."

Garreth rubbed the bridge of his nose where a pounding headache was taking root. He wished he could tell Sebastian the rumors about his fiancee were untrue, but the sound of Edith's grating voice and her irritating nasal laugh still rang in his ears.

His mercenary motives didn't sit well with him either, and he disliked Sebastian's airing them in detail. It made him seem contemptible.

Then again, he thought, why should it? Edith felt nothing for him. She had her own reasons for wanting the match: his name and the social position it would afford her.

God, the whole thing made him feel as though he needed a wash.

"Call it off," Sebastian urged.

"No. I won't go back on my word."

"Dammit, I will never understand your obsession with this company. Why can't you let it go?"

"Because it's all I have left," Garreth shouted, his patience extended beyond endurance. He rose to his feet and leaned across the desk. "This company and the house in town are all that's left of Father's fortune."

Sebastian went white beneath his tan and he slumped back in the chair.

"What are you saying?"

Garreth shook his head in disgust. "I'm broke, dammit. Why else do you think I came to you?"

"My God, you can't be serious." He studied Garreth's tightened features and his dark eyes widened.

"The money from Edith's dowry will assure the survival of the company, and the East Indies job is just the coup I need to make Armstrong Shipping lucrative again. It'll mean my salvation. That is, if it comes in time."

"Dammit, Garreth. Why didn't you tell me any of this?"

"I tried. You refused to listen to anything concerning Armstrong Shipping. What would you have me do, beg?"

"God, I had no idea things were so bad. But this is your life we're talking about. Don't do this; we'll work something out."

"It's done."

"It can be undone. My God, this is all my fault." The horror on Sebastian's face would have been comical at any other time. Garreth had never seen him contrite about anything in his life. But unfortunately, this was too serious a matter for him to take lightly and he couldn't allow his friend to assume the burden of guilt.

"No, it's my fault. I let pride stand in the way of good sense. But I've come to my senses now and I know this is the right thing to do. It's the only way."

He could see Sebastian's genuine distress and it went a long way toward dissolving the remaining resentment he'd harbored at his friend's hasty dismissal.

"Don't look so guilt ridden," he added, his own guilt getting the best of him. What he had done was far worse. He'd schemed to entrap Sebastian into a loveless match much the way he felt trapped by Bishop.

He forced a lightness to his tone he was far from feeling. "I had hoped you'd find a woman to wed, thereby affording me a little more time. But you don't seem to be in any hurry, and unfortunately I am."

Sebastian frowned, not comprehending Garreth's comment. "I don't understand."

"The wager," Garreth said, bitterness welling in him once more. That money would have kept him from bankruptcy, and Sebastian didn't even remember it.

"The wager!" Sebastian cried, sitting forward. "That's the solution. We'll go to that lawyer, what was his name, and tell him we're dissolving the wager. He'll return your money and you can call off this whole fiasco."

Already Garreth was shaking his head. God, he'd have given much to hear those words a few months ago. Before the wreck of the *Mirabella* the wager would have been enough to sustain him. Later it would have kept him solvent until another venture came along. Now he'd need every penny just to hold on to the company. Besides, he'd given Bishop his word. "No."

He picked up the invitation to his engagement party and numbly handed it back to Sebastian. "It's much too late for that now."

Dressed in a lavender silk dress with black lace covering the bodice and gathered over her rump, and with a black felt hat adorned with a soft purple feather, Lacey strolled into the engagement party on Sebastian's arm.

He'd invited her to the event and she'd accepted, putting aside her misery for the sake of her pursuit of Sebastian and her commitment to Col. Rapier. She needed to encourage Sebastian, and she'd accepted an assignment to write a 'Trifles' column about the highlight of the social season. She prayed she could get through the evening without her despair showing.

As they entered the German Relief Hall, Sebastian's arm stiffened beneath her fingers. He'd been tense and withdrawn since he'd called for her and she'd wondered at his strange mood.

Now, following his gaze, she felt her heart slam into her ribs with enough force to leave her breathless. Garreth stood arm in arm with a pretty blonde. The girl's overloud laughter reverberated through the great hall, sending a shudder through Lacey. But she knew it was Garreth's expression that had Sebastian's spine stiffening.

Garreth looked miserable. A sadness filled the hazel eyes, all but obliterating the bright green specks that usually glowed with fire. Two furrows bracketed his mouth, which was turned down and hard edged. It soon became apparent why he looked so ill at ease.

Edith Bishop paraded him around the room like a prize, glorying in her newfound status and ogling all the important guests present. She curtsied dramatically before the mayor and his wife as Garreth performed the introductions.

Sebastian and Lacey awkwardly avoided the couple as long as they could, then strolled casually in their direction.

"Garreth."

At Sebastian's greeting, Garreth turned to face the pair. His eyes went directly to Lacey and lingered. She tried to appear friendly, but the bitterness in his eyes grasped her heart and she found she couldn't look away. She wanted to soothe the frown from his face, erase the abject desolation from his features. They stood for a long moment drinking in the sight of each other.

It had been weeks since they'd stood this close. She could smell his hair tonic and aftershave, and the scent spun her back in time to their heated embrace beneath the overhanging oak. A pang of desire twisted her insides until she felt herself leaning toward him, seeking his touch once again.

"Well," a high-pitched nasal voice intruded, "aren't you going to introduce me?"

Garreth snatched his gaze from Lacey and stared at his partner as through he'd forgotten her presence. The hard glint in her eyes plainly said she didn't appreciate the slight. She gripped his elbow and leaned in close to his side.

As Garreth's voice swept over her, Lacey fought to control the pain of loss which racked her insides. Garreth had made his choice, and clearly he meant to stick by his decision. She forced a tight smile for Edith Bishop.

After the introductions, Sebastian led Lacey toward the refreshment table, which was straining beneath the array of lavishly prepared foods laid out for the guests. Howard Bishop had pulled out all the stops for his daughter's big night. Lacey tried to focus on the items she'd report in her article and not on the way Edith's hand lingered on Garreth's arm, or the way she pressed her lips close to his ear each time she spoke to him.

Finally the evening drew to a close. The formal announcement would be made soon, along with the date for the planned nuptials. All the details would be given, and Lacey knew she had to stay and listen to each item decribed. But the thrill she usually felt on writing an article didn't come tonight. She felt only a black void of depression. She wanted to close her ears so she wouldn't have to hear how many bridesmaids Edith would have or what Paris designer would devise the one-of-a-kind gown.

She excused herself and ducked behind a large potted tree. Removing her spectacles and note-pad from her reticule, she poised herself to write every detail.

"Hello, fellow colleague," Francie whispered behind her.

Lacey jumped, the round glasses slipping down the bridge of her nose. She tipped her head back and focused on her friend. Glancing around, she looked for Sandy Fitzpatrick, Fran-cie's date for the evening. She spotted him across the room in conversation with a group of busi-nessmen.

"I see you've managed to secure the only dis-creet nook in the place," Francie said, nudging closer.

"Are you writing about the party as well?" Lacey asked, pressing against the wall so Francie could slip behind the plant.

"Not this time. While I'm sure there's a juicy story here somewhere, I don't think I'd like to be the one who writes it."

"Why is that?"

Francie quirked her brow and a sympathetic smile tipped her lips. "My headline would read, 'HEARTS BREAK AS GARRETH ARMSTRONG IS LED

TO THE GALLOWS OF MATRIMONY.' And since your heart is the one most affected, I'm certain my objectivity would suffer."

Pushing her glasses back in place, Lacey turned away. "Don't be ridiculous, Francie. You know I've set my cap for Sebastian."

"Yes, and I know why. Which has nothing to do with what we're discussing."

"Which is?"

"The fact that you're in love with Garreth Armstrong."

Lacey froze, her heart jumping into her throat. She opened her mouth to deny Francie's words, but the lie died on her lips. A tear broke her resolve and she faced her friend.

"My God, have I been that transparent?" she said, certain her plot to marry Sebastian had just been extinguished.

"Only to me, darling," Francie told her, touching her shoulder lightly. "I'm a reporter, remember. I notice things other people don't. And I've noticed how your eyes light up when you look at Garreth. I've listened to you try to avoid asking about him these past weeks, but never quite succeeding. And I've noticed something else."

"What?" Removing the spectacles, Lacey dashed away the lone tear.

"He's in love with you, too."

A rush of joy flooded Lacey's heart and she felt it take flight and soar in her chest. She couldn't stop her pulse from pounding or her breath from rushing out. But then she glanced toward her heart's desire and the joy crept away, beaten down by the undeniable reality.

Garreth would marry Edith. And she would go on with her plan as though her life depended on it, as it did.

"I didn't say anything before because I knew you needed to marry Sebastian. But I can't keep quiet any longer. You're both in agony over this. And you're a fool if you let Garreth marry that woman. Stop him, Lacey. Tell him you love him. You deserve some happiness. Both of you."

She shook her head. "I can't do that," she whispered. "I can't think of myself. How could I be happy at Mother and Georgie's expense?"

"Can you live a lie? Can you marry another man now that Garreth holds your heart?" Francie pleaded.

Sliding the spectacles back into place, Lacey shook her head. "I'll make Sebastian a good wife," she vowed. "He'll never lack anything it's in my power to give him, I promise you that. Besides," she said, "I have no choice." Not as long as Stone was around. Again she considered her decision to remain silent about the man and his threats. But she knew she had to; he was too dangerous to underestimate.

Howard Bishop took his position on the dais where the band played. The soft strains of music faded slowly. The guests pushed forward in their eagerness, closing ranks around the couple they'd come to honor.

Lacey supported herself against the wall and began to write, blinking her eyes to focus through the sheen of tears.

Chapter Twelve

"Only two events remain and then I can go to Emerald Oaks for the holidays," Lacey said, fussing over her jade-green satin gown. She tucked a loose strand of hair into the coronet of curls pulled back from her face.

"Thank goodness," Francie said, slipping her stockinged feet into her kid slippers. "It's not that I won't miss you, but you're beginning to look like a refugee from Ellis Island."

"I have lost a little weight," Lacey conceded.

"A little? That dress had to be refitted twice. And Garreth has only been engaged for three weeks."

"Tess will take good care of me when I get home. If I can just get through the play tonight and the annual Christmas ball on the twenty-third, I'll have a little time to recuperate."

"Eat extra mince pie while you're there. When you come back for the New Year celebration I want to see some color in your cheeks."

Her tone was light, but the worry remained in her green eyes as she watched Lacey. With good reason, Lacey knew. Francie was aware of the threat of poverty hanging over Lacey and her family, even if she knew nothing of Stone. And time was dwindling too fast, like sand through an hourglass.

Her anguish over Garreth's sudden engagement was an added strain on her nerves. Now feelings of grief and loss had been heaped on top of her constant fears and ever-present confusion.

She and Sebastian had developed a unique friendship over the weeks, but his romantic indifference only added fuel to the fire of her incessant worries. Should she press for a more profitable relationship? Would it only ruin their friendship and chase him away?

Maybe tonight would prove different. Perhaps he would indicate a growing interest that would offer her a small flicker of hope.

Forcing a smile for Francie's sake, Lacey collected her beaded bag and together they went down to meet Sebastian and Sandy, their escorts for tonight's assignment.

All during the play Lacey felt distracted and out of sorts. She'd glimpsed Garreth and Edith as they arrived, but their seats were farther back, so she'd been spared the agony of watching them together.

Occasionally she felt a hot tingle on the back of her neck and couldn't help wondering if Garreth's eyes had sought her out in the crowd-packing Mobile theater for the first showing of *Everybody's Friend*, being performed by the Palmer Dramatic Club.

Or, worse luck, was Stone again present? He had attended a few of the events she'd been to lately, and he never missed an opportunity to drive home his threat. Was he here tonight? And if so, was he waiting for another chance to torment her with his malice?

During the third act her restlessness had her fidgeting in her seat. Sebastian glanced over and frowned. Smiling, she tried to remain still. But her nerves burned with the effort.

The theater held a sold-out crowd and the furnace billowed heat to combat the chill off the bay. The combination soon had Lacey feeling as though she couldn't get her breath. The close quarters didn't help. Every time she moved Sebastian noticed. The music of the overture seemed thundering; the gaslights wavered until she felt nauseated and light-headed. Finally she couldn't sit still another minute.

"I need some air," she whispered frantically, rising and pushing past Sebastian before he could stand aside or offer to go with her. Francie leapt to her feet and clutched Lacey's arm as she broke into the aisle.

"What's the matter?"

"Nothing. I just need some fresh air."

"I'll come with you," Francie said, reaching for

her reticule. A harsh whisper sounded behind them and they lowered their voices.

"No, that isn't necessary. I'll only be a moment," Lacey assured her, dashing up the incline before Francie could argue the matter further.

Forcing her eyes to lock on the double doors at the end of the aisle, she fled the theater without searching out Garreth in the crowd.

The brightness of the lobby caused her to squint, but she pushed forward toward the glass doors lining the front of the theater. Half blind from the harsh glare, she stumbled toward the exit, and right into a man standing between her and escape.

"Excuse me," she mumbled, pushing the heavy door open. The cold December wind whipped off the bay, reminding her she'd forgotten to collect her cloak.

Darting around the side of the building, she ducked behind the brick facade that extended on either side of the theater. The corner was private and secluded, and the brick cut the wind.

Lacey slumped against the wall and took a deep, shuddering breath. How had things gotten so far beyond her control? Her life had been incredibly simple before her father's death; now every single aspect bore unbelievable complications.

And when had her love for Garreth become so all-encompassing she couldn't deny it? Her chest ached, and she clutched her arms around her middle for warmth and for the sense of security it brought her.

"What are you doing out here?"

Stifling a startled gasp, she whirled to see Garreth standing in front of her.

"Garreth," she whispered, wondering briefly if she'd summoned him here with the power of her need.

"Christ, it's cold out here. Come inside."

He took her hand, and a frisson of awareness raced along her arm, centering in her pounding heart. She snatched away from him before he could feel the tremble of desire his closeness caused.

She needed time to calm her raging emotions and find a way to mask her distress before someone noticed the evidence of her emotional turmoil. She couldn't seem to hide her feelings tonight, and she couldn't return to the close confines of the packed theater until she gained a semblance of control.

"I need some air; it's dreadfully hot in there."

He eyed her closely, then casually propped his polished black boot on the bottom of the brick incline. "Mind if I smoke?"

She shook her head and shivered as the harsh breeze whipped around them. He removed a cigar from his jacket pocket and lit it, then shrugged out of the jacket and slipped it around her shoulders.

"No, really..."

"Take it. You already look pale," he said.

The light was dim and she knew he couldn't distinguish her coloring in the dark. Did that mean he'd noticed her, maybe even watched her earlier in the evening when she arrived? The thought warmed her, gripping her insides in a tight knot of longing, even as she told herself his scrutiny meant nothing.

"I hear you're going home to Emerald Oaks for the holidays."

His comment, and the disappointment she heard in his tone surprised her. She glanced up quickly, trying to read the expression in his eyes, but it was too dark.

"Sebastian mentioned it," he added.

Lacey nodded. "Yes, I am."

"You'll miss some very exciting parties. I hear everyone's trying to outdo one another this season," he said, the inane prattle seeming forced and uncomfortable.

Lacey suspected he was trying to keep the encounter casual despite the current of intimacy which arced between them whenever they were this close.

"I've never been much on parties," she said. "I'd rather spend Christmas with my family."

He nodded, lifting the cigar to his mouth.

She watched the red glow from the tip illuminate his face. Lines of fatigue circled his eyes and flanked his mouth.

He looked tired and worried. She told herself it was none of her business, but she couldn't keep from voicing her concern.

"You look a bit peaked yourself. I hope everything is all right with your business."

"As well as can be expected, I suppose. Of course you know better than most the difficulties

I'm facing right now. It'll take time before Armstrong Shipping is back on solid ground."

"Yes, time and money. I understand only too well."

He stiffened at her words, but then his features relaxed. They shared this one problem, and it seemed natural to stand on whatever common ground they could find at this time. Since neither wanted to dwell on their feelings, finances seemed somehow safe.

"I wanted to speak with you before the engagement party," he said, surprising her. "But there didn't seem to be a good time."

"Me? Why?"

"I should have told you my plans beforehand. Things happened fast."

"You don't owe me an explanation."

"No, but since my engagement could affect our agreement, I felt I owed you something." He'd wanted to talk to her, all right, but for far more personal reasons. However, he knew his explanation was at least partly true, and so he continued. "After all, the deal was to get Sebastian to marry first. And now it seems I will beat him to the altar."

"Nonsense. By the time you wed Edith my fate will be decided. The date for the loan payment will have come and gone. Either I'll have succeeded with Sebastian, or I'll have failed. You have to do what's best for Armstrong Shipping. And you have to think of your mother as well as yourself."

"The same as you," he said, dropping the cigar

butt and shredding it beneath his boot heel.

Lacey nodded, sinking deeper into his jacket and absorbing the last of his body heat from the fabric. "Yes, the same as me."

"I want you to know if there had been any way—"

Lacey snapped to attention, her fingers going to his lips before she thought through her actions. His eyes closed as the thin lace of her glove caressed his mouth. For a moment they stood frozen.

"Don't say it," she pleaded. "It's hard enough to feel the way I do without knowing whether or not you feel the same. If I were certain...well, I don't know what I would do. But there's no changing the way things are. You'll marry Edith and, God willing, I'll marry Sebastian. And whatever might have been between us will never be spoken of again. Sebastian is your friend. We must always remember that."

"I wish that I could forget it," he told her roughly, clasping her gloved fingers in his hand. He ran the tips along his cheek, to his jaw, and finally brought them to his mouth. Through the thin, lacy fabric she felt his hot breath warm her. She shrugged off his coat, handing it back to him.

"Hey, here you are," Sebastian's voice called out, and they sprang apart.

"I—I needed some air," Lacey murmured, flushing with heat as she saw Garreth turn away uncomfortably.

"I'd better get back inside," he said, brushing past Sebastian.

"Are you all right?" Sebastian ambled up to Lacey.

"Fine. It was so warm inside...."

"Yeah. But it's damned cold out here."

Silence stretched out uncomfortably between them, broken only by the sound of a carriage slowly passing on the paved street. They both followed the black carriage with their eyes until it disappeared around the corner. Lacey paid it no mind, but Sebastian seemed inordinately interested in its occupant.

"We should get back," she whispered.

He didn't reply, but he took her arm and led her back to the interior of the theater. Neither noticed the black carriage pull to a stop in the shadows across the road.

The fire glowed brightly in the fireplace as Lacey added the finishing touches to the large evergreen tree. The parlor boasted batches of greenery decorated with brightly colored ribbons; the tree held wax tapers, their flickering light gaily reflected in the tin holders.

Beneath the branches packages filled the floor. She'd shopped every day for a week to find just the right gifts for her family and Tess. It meant a lot to Lacey that this first Christmas without her father not be fraught with pain and grief. She'd taken pleasure in her shopping all the more because for the first time in her life she was spending money she'd earned. Her success in this one area always gave her a breath of hope that she might be able to defeat Stone as well.

Dangling a gilt ribbon over the spiny branches, she mused at the turn her life had taken. Never much for the round of parties and social affairs, she'd been happy to spend her time at Emerald Oaks with her family and a few close friends. Now, she'd gained a sense of pride and self-respect she hadn't known was missing in her life from writing about those very things.

It still amazed her that people could happily live such a shallow existence, without real purpose or meaning. But things had been that way so long she suspected they would never change. She had a hard time imagining herself in the role of hostess at such frivolous gatherings, but she knew that was exactly the life she'd be expected to lead as Sebastian Avery's wife.

As much as she'd liked Anna Avery, Lacey could not picture herself hosting an endless round of parties with silly parlor games and superficial socializing.

"How's that?" she asked, forcing her troublesome thoughts back to the present and the joyous task she'd just completed. Stepping back, she eyed the Christmas tree with delight.

"Wonderful, darling," her mother said, looking up from the needlepoint she'd been engrossed in.

On the floor, Georgie's constantly seeking hands had found a long strand of fabric ribbon and he was methodically shredding it into threads.

"What do you think, Georgie?" she asked,

kneeling beside him. As always, he offered no response, not even enough to acknowledge he'd heard her question. Lacey continued. "I think it needs a bit more color. How about it? A few ribbons? That one you have is pretty. I like the way you've frayed it so the colors flow together. Would you like to put your ribbon on the tree, Georgie?"

He didn't look at her, didn't make a sound. But after a moment he rose silently and went to the tree, distributing the tattered strands of the ribbon over the branches with the precision of a doctor doing surgery.

Lacey's heart swelled with undiluted delight as she turned to her mother in amazement. The tears of joy she saw in the gray eyes reflected her own, and for a moment she thought the miracle of the season had visited her home. It had been so long since Georgie had shown the slightest response, and always before it had been with their father.

"Oh, that's lovely, Georgie," she choked out, fighting her emotions for control. He didn't answer, just continued his task, but she felt encouraged.

Katrina Webster stood and took a roll of gilt ribbon. Going to the tree, she pulled off a length of ribbon and fashioned it into a bow. She offered it to Lacey, who took her hand, and together they placed the decoration, as well as several more. Then Lacey stood on a petit-point stool and placed a paper angel on the top of the tree. The women stood back, their arms around one another, and savored the magic of the moment.

*   *   *

The tree was even more beautiful dotted with the colored paper cones Lacey had made and filled with everything from candy and dried fruit to tussie-mussies. She'd bought her mother a silk fan and a new cashmere cape. For Georgie she'd purchased a new suit and shoes, and a Chinese abacus she knew would keep him entertained for hours.

Tess loved her brooch and gloves and gave Lacey a hand-knitted scarf in return. The day was the most pleasant Lacey had spent in weeks and she indulged in the sugar-cured ham, sweet potatoes, and mince pie. A shadow of grief caused by the loss of her father hung over the gathering at times but she struggled to keep the cheerful spirit high.

And as much as she enjoyed spending the day with her family, she was surprised to find she missed being in Mobile with Francie and the others. In her room for an afternoon nap later that day she admitted to herself she missed Garreth most of all. Even a glimpse of him occasionally, though somewhat painful, was better than constantly wondering where he was and what he was doing.

She tried to picture how he and his mother would spend their holiday. His office would be closed, she knew, since the city had declared Christmas a formal holiday the previous year. Would he let the troubles of Armstrong Shipping color his festivities? Or would he put them aside for this one sacred day of celebration? And would he be celebrating with Edith Bishop?

Lacey knew that was the question troubling her the most. She was jealous of every moment he spent with his fiancee. She had no right, she told herself. But it didn't lessen the dark abyss of sadness which, along with her fear of Stone, had become her constant companion.

The days passed quietly, her mother and Georgie soothed by her presence. Tess went to visit her sister in Birmingham for a few days and came back refreshed and ready to resume her duties.

Although bored with the round of parties and socials in the city, Lacey found she was anxious to get back to writing. With a week left until her time at Emerald Oaks was up, she spent as much time with her mother and Georgie as she could without upsetting their routine.

In the afternoons she usually rode or strolled around the sparsely wooded property to the west. She'd just changed into her riding habit when Tess knocked on her bedroom door to announce she had a visitor.

Pinning her small felt hat atop her piled hair, she glanced quickly in the mirror and followed Tess to the formal parlor.

"Sebastian!"

He rose from the brocade wing-back chair and came toward her. His sudden appearance startled Lacey so much she nearly forgot her manners and asked him what he was doing there. Instead, she forced a smile and said, "What a delightful surprise."

With his usual good humor in place, he laughed. "Well, I see I should have sent word first and waited for an invitation."

Quickly recovering, she took his outstretched hand. "No, of course not. I'm sorry. You just startled me. I was about to go for a ride."

"My horse is outside. Would I be a total boor if I invited myself to accompany you?"

"Not at all," she said, blinking away her surprise. "Tess," she said, turning toward the woman who still stood like a sentinel in the doorway, "would you ask Robert to saddle Splendor for me?"

Tess eyed Sebastian curiously for a moment, then nodded. "Certainly, miss." Turning on her heel, she hustled away.

"What brings you out here?" she asked, unable to contain her own curiosity.

"You. I thought I'd come to Emerald Oaks and introduce myself to your mother, since she's unable to travel to the city at this time."

Lacey's face lost all color and she pressed her hand to her fluttering stomach. She couldn't stop her horrified words this time.

"You want to meet my mother?" She gasped.

Sebastian chuckled. "Don't fret; it's just a casual social call. I promise I won't tire her."

Lacey knew there was no such thing as a casual social call in the circles which Sebastian Avery traveled in. Every move, every act was accomplished within the strict blueprint of accepted protocol. The matriarchs of society held to rigid codes of propriety. And a gentleman calling on a lady at her home during the holidays for the sole purpose of meeting her mother would imply serious interest on the gentleman's part.

Once more her heart raced, making normal breathing difficult. Could this be the start of his earnest pursuit? It would seem so. Still, Lacey cautioned herself not to draw unwarranted conclusions.

Besides, how would Sebastian react when he did meet her mother? Not to mention Georgie. She received her answer sooner than she'd thought. Katrina Webster wandered into the parlor in search of her embroidery and stopped short at the sight of Sebastian.

Stunned into silence for a full minute, Lacey could only stare between her mother and Sebastian. Finally she found her tongue and stepped forward.

"Mother, this is Sebastian Avery. Mr. Avery, my mother, Katrina Webster."

Katrina stood rooted in place, her eyes wide and frightened. Sebastian sketched a bow and stepped forward.

"Mrs. Webster, my pleasure."

"Who is this man, Lacey?" she demanded. Turning to Sebastian, she narrowed her eyes and studied him. "And why is he here?"

Flustered, Lacey could only murmur, "Ah, ah..."

"I'm a friend of your daughter's from Mobile. I came to see how she'd enjoyed the holidays and to introduce myself to you, madame."

"Me? Sir, if you have any idea to court my

daughter you should be here to speak with her father, not myself."

Sebastian's mouth fell open and he shot a quick, uncomfortable glance at Lacey. "I thought—that is, isn't your father...?"

Lacey cringed. So much for thinking her mother's condition had improved. Thinking quickly, she took Katrina's arm. "Sebastian and I were about to go for a ride. Mother, would you tell Mamie that we have a guest so she can set another place for dinner? We can all get better acquainted then."

Katrina turned back to look at their guest as Lacey led her from the parlor. Tess came rushing back just then and took her mother's arm and they went off toward the kitchen. The older woman glanced sympathetically at Lacey as she spoke to Katrina in hushed tones.

A heavy silence encased Lacey and Sebastian. Neither knew what to say, how to react. Deciding her only course was to tell him the whole truth, Lacey took Sebastian's hand.

"Come with me," she said.

Chapter Thirteen

Leading him across the hall to the smaller family parlor, Lacey felt her legs tremble beneath her.

At the door she paused, knowing this could prove to be the most definitive move of her life. Her breath caught in her throat and her pulse raced.

Finally she moved forward, stepping aside so Sebastian could see beyond her into the room. Inside, intent on working the abacus, Georgie sat quietly.

"Georgie," Lacey said softly, stepping into the room. "We have a guest. I'd like you to meet Sebastian Avery." The boy remained engrossed in the task, showing no sign he'd heard or seen his sister or the man beside her. She turned back to Sebastian.

"My brother, Georgie."

"Is he deaf?"

Lacey shook her head. "No, he can hear us just fine. He knows there's a stranger in the room—see his hands?"

As they spoke, the small hands moved faster and faster on the beads of the abacus. Their movements became jerky and frantic and finally Lacey waved Sebastian into the main hall.

"Do you see why we don't visit Mobile?" She felt her hopes for a match between her and Sebastian slipping away. His face registered his shock and she feared he'd turn and run from Emerald Oaks. But he didn't.

"What happened?"

She shrugged. "His birth was difficult. The doctor suggested brain damage. My father took him to a number of physicians, but none could offer any hope. They all agreed his condition was tragic and irreversible. He's always been as you see him now, totally self-absorbed and delusional. Georgie lives in a world of his own making. That is his reality," she said, pointing to the parlor door.

She watched the emotions play across his handsome, dark features. Surprise, pity, acceptance.

"Do you still want to go for a ride?" she asked, holding her breath as she waited to see how meeting her family had affected Sebastian.

He blinked, facing her. She could see the alarm in his eyes mixed with what might have been grudging admiration. For a long minute he didn't answer; then a small smile tipped his full mouth.

"Of course," he told her, taking her arm. "If you're sure it's not an intrusion."

Releasing her breath, she smiled. "Not at all," she assured him.

Outside the temperature was still pleasant, the breeze blowing off the bay holding a scent of salt. Robert, husband of Mamie, sometimes helped out at Emerald Oaks' stables. She saw him approach, holding the reins of a melon-colored mare.

Lacey placed her booted foot in his cupped palms, pulling herself into the sidesaddle. "Thank you, Robert," she said.

Sebastian mounted his black gelding and nodded to the older man.

Silently, they led their horses down the shelled drive to the road. Turning left, they followed a path through a grove of massive oaks shading the lane.

Neither spoke for several minutes; then Sebastian turned to face Lacey. "Your mother?"

She had known some explanation would be necessary. Thankful he'd given her time to collect her thoughts, she cleared her throat.

"Most days Mother is fine. She knows Father's gone, and she accepts the fact, though she has never come to terms with his death. Other days, she refuses even to acknowledge he's dead, choosing to hide in a world as far removed from reality as Georgie's."

"I see."

Another pregnant pause drew out uncomfortably. They passed the cottage being built at the edge of Emerald Oaks' declining property and he raised an eyebrow.

"Who does that belong to?" he asked.

She swallowed her bitterness at the blatant reminder of what her father's bad judgment had brought them to. "The Cox family. They purchased the land from my father before his death."

Well, the truth was out, she realized with a hint of relief. Sebastian could put two and two together. Already she could see the wheels in his mind turning. Would he realize her interest in him had been purely monetary? How would this knowledge affect their friendship, which she had come to appreciate?

"I see," he said again. "That explains a few things I've been wondering about."

The path turned south, the stillness of the day broken only by the sounds of the horses' hooves on the packed earth.

Finally he drew back on his reins, a look of startled admiration in his eyes. "You must have had a difficult time of it since your father's death. You're a very courageous lady."

A short, sharp laugh escaped Lacey's lips. "Not at all," she said. "I've been more terrified than ever in my life."

"But you knew what you had to do, and you remained loyal and steadfast to your family through it all. Looking out for their welfare. Ready to defend them from the smallest slight."

"You make me sound like a cross between He-

222

len of Troy and Florence Nightingale. I assure you, my actions are not to be admired. I've done things I never thought I could. Things I'm not proud of." She tried to cover her look of embarrassed chagrin.

He quirked an eyebrow questioningly. Finally he nodded. "Well, be that as it may, I can't find fault with your actions. Especially considering my own of late."

He pulled up beneath a low-hanging oak limb and dismounted. Draping his reins around the branch, he turned and helped Lacey down from her saddle.

"We all do things we must, Lacey. Society demands certain things. Family adds its own expectations. No one understands these complications better than I do now. So shall we discuss a plan of action openly and put aside all this subterfuge?"

Stunned by his frankness, Lacey could only nod.

"My mother adores you. She hasn't stopped talking about you since we were at Springhill. I know why she's been so persistent and I think you do, too."

She nodded once more.

"I was dead set against giving in to her demands that I marry. But recently I had to face the consequences of my selfishness, and I didn't like what I saw. A friend, a good friend, came to me for help. But I was too self-absorbed to see how desperate he was. I don't like to admit that I'd become such a jackanapes, but it's the truth.

I acted like a fool because I hadn't gotten my way about something I thought important, and he suffered for it."

Lacey could see the new maturity in Sebastian's eyes and it surprised her. What had caused him to grow up so fast? And what did this newfound knowledge have to do with his reason for coming here to see her?

"I want to make things right, if I can. For once I'd like to do something my friends and my family can be proud of. I didn't think anyone else's opinion mattered to me, but I find it does. And now, after what I've seen here today, I'm more convinced than ever that my plan of action is the right thing for everyone concerned."

"Your plan?"

"Yes. I've thought a lot about it the past three weeks. I think we can help each other. I don't see anything wrong with that, do you?"

Beginning to feel rather foolish, but still not understanding, she shook her head.

He smiled and nodded. "Good," he said.

Somewhat clumsily, he took her hand. Lacey saw the nervous tremble he couldn't hide and her heart fluttered.

"Lacey, I am no good at romantic declarations, and I won't insult either of us by pretending an undying love for you. But I have put off the inevitable long enough. My parents want me to marry soon, and it appears you wouldn't be hurt any by a hasty union, either. I admire and respect you, and many marriages have started with less. Wouldn't you agree?"

Again she nodded.

"Good. Then if you have no objection, I'd like to announce our engagement immediately after the New Year."

Shock rippled through Lacey's body, her legs trembling, her heart pounding against her breast. Her lungs burned. A split second before she succumbed to the strange numbness gripping her, she realized she wasn't breathing. Sucking in great gulps of air, she struggled not to faint. "The New Year?"

"I'm sorry." He shook his head in disgust. "You must think me a clod, bumbling the whole thing like that. Usually I'm more delicate with the ladies. I fear I've muddled this proposal."

"Proposal?" She felt like a mockingbird, dumbly repeating every word he said. She'd desperately hoped and schemed for this. She'd even involved Garreth in the deception despite his reluctance, and she'd gone ahead with the plot even after she realized her heart would always belong to another man.

But somehow now the coldness, the calculation, chilled her to the bone. She wanted to tear her fingers from his grasp, mount her horse, and ride until she left everything behind her.

Angry, hurt tears threatened behind her tightly closed eyelids. She cursed her own weakness, calling herself a hypocritical fool. Bolstering her strength, she blinked back the betraying moisture.

"What about your mother? How will she feel when she meets my mother and Georgie? Can she accept in-laws with such obvious failings?"

He nodded. "Yes. Fortunately, my mother thinks you're a godsend after the scare I gave her."

Lacey frowned and he forced a dry laugh.

"She hasn't exactly approved of my choice of companions recently. She'll be so thrilled to know I'm marrying a well-bred, socially acceptable young lady like yourself, I'm convinced she'll be more than willing to overlook a few minor blemishes."

Lacey thought her mother's illness and Georgie's infirmity could hardly be called minor blemishes, but she supposed that was Sebastian's somewhat delicate way of indicating the level of prejudice his mother felt for the Cajun.

He waited for her response, but still she hesitated. One word and her fate would be sealed. There would be no going back. Sebastian Avery would make her his wife and hopefully help her family. Though her heart threatened to break, Lacey knew what she had to do.

"I would be honored," she said, meeting his worried frown with a hopeful smile.

The lines eased from his face and he returned her smile. "You accept?"

"I do," she whispered, feeling her heart ache with the pain of her resolve.

"The engagement should be brief, and the ceremony simple, since your family is still in mourning."

She nodded stiffly, fighting the panic that welled inside her when she realized the significance of the bargain they had made.

She glanced down at their joined hands and saw years spent as man and wife, growing old together. Having children. A lump wedged in her throat. Would she grow to care for him? Would he ever love her? Would she ever forget Garreth and the brief, blazing moments of passion they'd shared?

"Lacey?"

"Yes?" Her voice sounded faint, even to her own ears. She swallowed the terror closing off her breath.

"You agree?"

"Yes, whatever you say," she whispered, unsure what he actually had said.

"I'll want to tell my parents as soon as I return to Mobile. Everyone else will know soon enough."

She nodded.

"I assure you this discussion will never be mentioned again," he said. "As far as anyone knows, we are both totally smitten and eager to begin our lives together. Agreed?"

Again she nodded. Being a gentleman, Sebastian would never openly discuss her ploy, but he must be aware of what she had set out to do. He was telling her it no longer mattered. And asking that she not question his motives too closely either. She felt relieved that the deception was finally over. They understood each other. For now, that would have to be enough.

He leaned forward, his lips closing the distance to hers. She knew he was about to kiss her and, even as she felt repelled by his actions, she welcomed the anticipation of his mouth against hers. Maybe he could remove the memory of Garreth's kisses. Now that she has what she'd hoped for maybe everything would work out between them. Perhaps he could drive her love for Garreth from her mind and her heart.

His hands closed around her shoulders and she could feel the heat of his palms through her plaid surah dress. She let his grip draw her close. Her eyelids lowered as he approached, his minty breath fanning her cheek.

Suddenly he stiffened. Lacey felt the tension in his hands, his grasp tightening painfully. His spine grew rigid until his chin reached almost to the top of her head. Surprised, she glanced up, but his attention was focused behind her. She whirled, following the hard glint of his stare.

Across the way, parked on the avenue leading to Emerald Oaks, was a familiar-looking black carriage. She couldn't remember where she'd seen it before, but judging from Sebastian's reaction she felt certain he knew who the conveyance belonged to.

"Who is that?" she asked. The closed carriage faced away from the house, blocking the face of the driver from their view. As she watched, the reins snapped and the horses shot forward. The carriage sped away down the road and out of sight.

"I don't know," Sebastian finally said, his eyes

still locked on the road. The bleakness in the dark orbs belied his words.

At last he turned back to Lacey, but the moment had passed and he didn't try to kiss her again. Instead he helped her mount her horse and they returned to the house in silence.

Sebastian strode into Garreth's office. This time Gramb made no attempt to stop him.

"I've solved the problem," he crowed, slumping into the red leather chair across from Garreth's desk.

Garreth pushed aside the invoices he'd been perusing and met Sebastian's overbright gaze with a frustrated frown. "What are you shouting about?"

"Your salvation! Here," he said, grabbing a sheet of stationery from the wooden box on the corner of the desk. "Write old Bishop and tell him he can find another sucker to marry his daughter."

Garreth shoved the hand holding the paper to the side, his expression black. "Dammit, Sebastian. Are you drunk again?"

Sebastian only laughed, throwing back his head. "Not at all. At least, not much."

"I should have known. Get out of here and let me get back to work. Some of us do take our responsibilities seriously, you know."

"Oh ho, I assume that was meant as a crack? Well, forget it. You can't ruffle my feathers today. Besides, you'll be eating crow soon enough."

"Why is that?" Garreth asked, certain he'd regret the question which could only appear to encourage Sebastian's game.

"Because I've fixed everything. I've undone the mess I made of things."

Garreth met Sebastian's gaze and his frown deepened. While trying to appear jovial, Sebastian couldn't quite hide the downturned corners of his eyes or the ghosts of worry lines which still creased his forehead. He might be smiling now, but he couldn't hide the darker mood still lurking behind his cheerful expression.

"Dammit, Sebastian, I'm in no mood for riddles. What are you talking about?"

"You were always so annoyingly serious. I wonder how we ever became friends."

"Sebastian," he ground out through his teeth.

"Oh, all right. I've just come from Emerald Oaks."

Garreth sat straight. A finger of dread inched slowly up his spine. "You went to see Lacey?"

"Of course I went to see Lacey. Why else would I travel ten miles out of town the day after Christmas?"

"I'm sure I can't imagine."

"Oh, I'm sure you can," Sebastian said with a grin. "I should have suspected something when you admitted defeat so easily at the boating party."

"What are you talking about now?"

"Your little performance at Springhill. The tender moment in the gazebo, the feigned anger when I interrupted. It was a grand plot. My hat's off to you both. And it worked."

"It did?" Garreth murmured, more befuddled than ever. If Sebastian had somehow discovered his pact with Lacey, why was he pretending to be in such a damned good mood?

"Yes, although I'm almost ashamed to admit it. Good Lord, have I been such a reprobate? Don't answer that," he quickly added, holding his hand up. "I know I have. And I enjoyed every minute of it, so I won't pretend to be contrite. But I've turned over a new leaf, so to speak."

"Well, that's good." One golden brow couldn't help jumping into Garreth's hairline quizzically.

"And I'm letting you both off the hook. In fact, I've taken a good look at my life and I've decided to face the music."

"For God's sake, will you quit talking in tired cliches and get to the point. What have you done?"

"I've fixed it so you don't have to marry Edith Bishop."

A fist of apprehension slammed into Garreth's gut, forcing the breath from his lungs. He tamped down the foreboding he felt and forced a reply.

"Leave Edith out of this and get to the point, if indeed there is a point to this folderol you're spewing."

"A point, yes. A very important point. A momentous turn in the direction of my life."

Garreth cursed beneath his breath and made to rise from his chair. Sebastian jumped up and leaned over the desk, forcing Garreth back into his seat. The glint in his dark eyes looked almost maniacal now. A crazed gleam shot from the near-black orbs.

"The wager. I concede. You'll win, and there will be no reason for you to marry Edith."

Garreth gasped and jerked back to better see Sebastian's expression. "What the devil have you done?"

"Exactly what you wanted me to," he bellowed, as though Garreth were the one acting strange. "Don't worry, soon enough you'll have the money from the wager and you can pour it all into this cursed company if that'll make you happy. I don't care. As long as you call off this ridiculous alliance with Bishop."

A foul expletive escaped Garreth's tightened lips and he gripped the arms of his chair until his knuckles whitened.

"You asked Lacey to marry you?"

"Of course I asked Lacey. Who do you think?" Another raucous laugh exploded from deep in Sebastian's chest. "You old rogue, isn't she the very chit you tried to snare me with?"

The color left Garreth's face and he seemed to shrink into the chair. His hands lost their grip and hung limp from the round padded armrests.

"What's the matter with you? I've just saved your hide, old friend."

Sebastian's dark eyes narrowed. For the first time Garreth realized the lengths Sebastian had gone to on his behalf. And all for nothing, Garreth thought.

"You fool," he whispered, shaking his head sadly. "You crazy fool."

"Now wait just a minute...." Sebastian interjected.

"Did you tell her why you were proposing?" he demanded to know.

Sebastian silently stared at Garreth for a long minute, then nodded. "Not all of it, but the important details, yes."

"And she accepted?"

"Of course she accepted; you should know better than anyone the answer to that."

"And you really did it only so I wouldn't have to marry Edith?"

"Well, my mother has been harping on the subject for months now, you must know that. But, yes, I did feel somewhat responsible...."

"I can't call off my engagement to Edith," Garreth snapped. "I explained that to you before. Her family may not have the social position you enjoy, but money equals power in this town. Bishop could ruin me if he wanted to. And even if he didn't, I thought you understood the wager would only sustain us temporarily. It wasn't a complete panacea. So if you asked Lacey to marry you just to ease your conscience, you've made a big mistake."

"No, it's you who have made the mistake. I am merely trying to make it easier for you to rectify the damnable situation. You don't need Bishop's money now. I'm willingly forfeiting the wager. Hell, I'll even double the amount we put into the wager. That ought to salvage this wreck."

Garreth raked stiff fingers through his hair, standing the golden strands on end. His eyes wide with anger and resentment, he knew he must look like a wild man. Indeed, he felt on the verge of going insane. Lacey had what she wanted, and he was being offered more than he'd set out to get. He should be thrilled. He and Sebastian should be lifting their glasses in a toast. Instead he looked at Sebastian's grinning face and longed to put his fist through it.

He should be angry at the trap he found himself in. He *would* still have to marry Edith Bishop. And not just because the trust money wasn't enough. His damnable honor would demand it.

And somehow, knowing Lacey would soon be Sebastian's wife, he found he didn't even care anymore. Still, he had to assure himself Lacey wouldn't be hurt any more than she already had been.

"You know about Lacey's mother? Her brother?"

Sebastian relaxed in his chair and propped his booted feet on the corner of the desk. "Yes, I know it all. I admit I was more than a little shocked. Good God, with the exception of Lacey the whole family appeared to be nutty as this season's fruitcake."

He saw Garreth stiffen and held up his hand. "Don't get riled; I didn't mean to sound crass. I pity the little boy, but it doesn't seem his affliction is anything to worry about as far as bloodlines go. And obviously Lacey dotes on him. Her mother's condition appears to be a temporary state brought about by the shock of losing her husband *and* most of her land in one fell swoop. That is certainly understandable. And I admire Lacey for having the fortitude to accept such a heavy burden on her somewhat frail shoulders."

"There is nothing frail about Lacey Webster," Garreth told him firmly.

"No, I don't suppose there is. She's had a great deal to contend with in the past months. The fact that she has handled it as well as she has only makes me more firm in my decision to marry her."

"But I've told you it's too late for me to call off my wedding. If that's the only reason for your actions it would seem—"

"On the contrary, Garreth. My engagement is beneficial to all concerned."

"How so?"

"Mother loves Lacey; she thinks she's the perfect choice for my wife. And I don't mind telling you I look forward to having her off my back after these last few months of maternal hell. Lacey needs a generous husband who will accept her family and," he added, studying Garreth closely, "possibly assist them financially."

A question mark hung in the air as the two men stared quietly into each other's set features. Garreth was the first to look away.

"Yes, well, as I was saying," Sebastian continued. "My union is fortuitous for all concerned."

"Is it?" Garreth's lips thinned and he fought the rage he felt at Sebastian's emotionless recitation. Knowing jealousy drove him, he couldn't help throwing a barb to see if he could hit a vulnerable spot. For a moment he considered his anger and his motives in provoking Sebastian. Honesty forced him to admit he was doing it for purely selfish reasons. He couldn't bear the thought of seeing Lacey and Sebastian together for the rest of his life.

"Is it fortunate for everyone, Sebastian? What about your pretty little Cajun? What does she think of your betrothal? Oh, I forgot, she meant nothing to you. Isn't that right? Just a quick little tumble? A pleasant little diversion? A good time, but not good enough for a wife?"

Sebastian's face lost all color for a moment, then swiftly went red with rage. He jumped to his feet, his fists clenched at his sides, trembling, Garreth was certain with the desire to bury themselves in his face. Somehow he thought he'd feel better if Sebastian hit him. God, he wished he'd knock him senseless and release him from the images of Lacey and Sebastian together that played across his mind. Images that, God help him, would forever plague him even if he never saw them again.

But Sebastian reined in his temper and turned to go. At the door, he looked back once.

"I think I understand your anger, Garreth. And I can't blame you. But remember, twice now I've tried to help you," he said, his voice impassive.

Garreth felt the coldness permeate the room and he knew he'd pushed too hard this time. After a lifetime of deep friendship seasoned with good-natured rivalry and true affection, he had finally dealt their relationship a fatal blow.

And he'd done it purposely. He'd wanted to end their association in order to save himself the heartache of watching Sebastian with Lacey and knowing he had every right to the love and passion Garreth craved.

Yes, dammit. No matter how he'd hoped for this very outcome, he found he couldn't face seeing them grow old together. The gentleman inside him demanded he call Sebastian back and mend the rift between them. But the man who ached for his friend's fiancee refused to speak the words.

Then it was too late. Sebastian left, slamming the door behind him, and Garreth dropped his head onto the desktop. A sweeping pain engulfed him. He'd lost the only woman he'd ever love, though he knew Lacey had never actually been his. And, most likely, he'd permanently severed all ties with his closest friend.

He'd never felt so alone.

Chapter Fourteen

"TRIFLES LIGHT AS AIR" FOR THE LADIES OF MOBILE

Brr, ladies. January certainly blew in with a vengeance. I hope you've all been to Dunlap's and seen their new line of fur-lined opera cloaks. They've also put on display their elaborate masks in preparation for the Mardi Gras season which will soon be upon us. Rumor has it the Infant Mystics will boast the finest float in the parade. Indeed, Mobile's cream of society are putting their heads together to make this event unequaled in its splendor....

The winds of winter turned the bay dark and turbulent. Ships anchored all along the docks rode the waves, their owners and captains tucked safely in their houses until spring. But inside the empty warehouse on the corner of Water Street and St. Louis Avenue a bustle of activity was under way to finish the float before the upcoming Mardi Gras festivities began.

Francie, Garreth, and Sebastian, as lifelong members of the Infant Mystic Society, had been commandeered to construct the float. With no desire to be in close proximity to Sebastian or Lacey, Garreth had tried to bow out. But the other members were having none of his defection.

After trying to no avail to get out of the awkward situation, he'd given in. Sebastian hadn't been overly pleased with the situation himself, but had relented—albeit somewhat ingraciously.

So resigned, they'd enlisted the help of Lacey, the Fitzpatrick twins, and, of course, Edith Bishop, since Garreth was rarely seen these days without his clinging fiancee, and for the time being all the unwilling participants in this confusing drama were temporarily existing within an uneasy truce for the sake of the festivities.

The vacant warehouse was the property of Alexander Fitzpatrick Sr., and had been donated as a place to assemble the float.

The Order of Myths parade, scheduled for the tenth day of February, had chosen scenes from Waverly novels as their theme. The group in the warehouse had less than two weeks left to finish their project.

The king and queen of Mardi Gras would be

announced at the ball following the Order of Druids parade on the last night of the celebration, but the occupants of the warehouse already knew their names.

Garreth looked over at Lacey, his feelings of pain and loss momentarily mirrored in her eyes. Quickly he masked the telling look, but he couldn't stop himself from drinking in the sight of her every chance he got. What quirk of fate kept throwing them together? he wondered.

His mother's position on the Infant Mystics board could account for him being chosen as king. She'd thrown his name into the running relentlessly since he reached the age of maturity.

But how had Lacey gotten elected as queen? Had Francie's parents, as members of the Mystics board, decided months ago to help Lacey further her search for a husband by exhibiting her before Mobile's most elite and wealthy patrons?

Draped in crepe, she laughed, drawing him from his ruminations and sending a wave of heat straight to his loins. It seemed her attachment to Sebastian agreed with her.

Apparently Anna Avery desired an engagement party, and even though she promised to subdue the occasion out of respect for Lacey's bereavement, she'd begged time to prepare. So Lacey and Sebastian had yet to announce their engagement formally.

The wire in his hands lay forgotten as he studied her. Smiling, she looked even more beautiful than usual. She didn't laugh often—he suspected she'd had little enough reason to since her father's death—and the emotion transformed her face. The seriousness dissipated, replaced by sparkling eyes and high color in her cheeks.

Francie tossed a strand of colored ribbon into the air and it landed across Sandy Fitzpatrick's shoulders. He turned with a scowl and started toward her, setting off a round of shrieking that snapped Garreth back to his task. He bent the wire, shaping it into the form of a lance that would later be covered with papier-mache.

"Daydreaming?"

He looked up and saw Sebastian standing in front of him, his own piece of wire twisted beyond recognition. His shirtsleeves were rolled to the elbow despite the chill of the warehouse and a frown furrowed his brow. Their tenuous truce allowed them to work together on their task, but the closeness they'd once shared was gone.

"How the hell did we get roped into this mess?" Sebastian asked, tossing the misshapen wire aside.

Garreth forced a laugh, motioning to the barrel beside him. Sebastian sat. "We were shanghaied, remember," he reminded Sebastian.

Sebastian chuckled dryly. "Yes, I do seem to recall something along those lines now that you mention it. Well, I'll be more wary next time," he vowed.

"I think it looks all right." Garreth tried to view the float objectively. They'd picked a scene from *Ivanhoe*, in which the black knight, Brian de Bois-Guilbert, jousts against the hero, Ivanhoe. With the thrones for the king and queen in place and the various pennants raised, it didn't look half bad.

"Yeah, I suppose."

A brooding silence came over Sebastian. Garreth had noticed the mood taking hold of his friend more and more lately. It couldn't be his parents this time, Garreth knew. They'd been thrilled with Sebastian's engagement to Lacey Webster, the near-scandal with the Cajun all but forgotten as far as they were concerned.

However, if Garreth's suspicions were correct, Sebastian's memory stretched a bit farther. He escorted Lacey, showed her the respect she was due, and let it be known they were a couple. But the closer the two became the more morose Sebastian seemed. Was he regretting his self-sacrificing efforts now? Garreth wondered. Or was he, like Garreth, just regretting what could not be?

For a moment Garreth thought of the tangled web each of them found themselves in. Four players in a real-life drama. Lacey, forced to sacrifice herself for the sake of her mother and brother, marrying a man she didn't love and who didn't love her. Sebastian, loving a woman he couldn't have and marrying another to atone for past mistakes and childish misadventures. Edith, cold and mercenary in her desire for social position, willing to marry anyone with an influential name. And himself, truly in love for the first time in his life, and unable to do anything but stand by silently and watch as his best chance for happiness faded away for the sake of a failing company.

Good Lord, had they all gone mad? It seemed like madness, the course each of them had chosen. Oh, their reasons were mostly honorable, but how great a price for honor!

Sebastian had matured greatly in the past few months, but it had been a hard-won maturity. The lines on his face and around his eyes testified to the extent he had suffered despite his forced gaiety. Lacey had become a stranger to laughter, so that when she did indulge in any lightness, the emotion seemed foreign on her lovely face.

And the more time Sebastian spent with Lacey, the blacker Garreth's own mood grew. Edith's desperate, almost claustrophobic attentions didn't help matters any. In her zeal to assure her acceptance, she hovered around him until he felt smothered. Already her nasal twang had gone from irritating to unbearable.

She seemed more and more dissatisfied with his efforts to promote her position in society. He wondered more than once if perhaps she had decided someone else would be more beneficial to her outline for the future. He glanced over to see her in close conversation with Marshall Sutherland. She chose her friends with a banker's eye for worth, it seemed.

More than once Garreth had considered delaying the wedding, now that Lacey and Sebastian's impending marriage would assure his winning the bet and temporarily remedy his financial situation. However, knowing Lacey would soon be

Sebastian's wife, he saw no point in delaying the inevitable.

The women began discussing the costumes they would wear on the float, and Sandy Fitzpatrick ambled over to where Garreth and Sebastian sat. Garreth was thankful for the other man's presence as it would hopefully ease the tension which constantly surrounded him and Sebastian since the scene in his office.

"What is that contraption?" Sandy asked, eyeing the wire frame Sebastian had been appointed to make. It looked like it had been run through a bread wringer.

"It was supposed to be the beginning of Ivanhoe's broadsword." Sebastian tossed the wire away with a muttered expletive, his voice sharper than the minor mishap would seem to warrant. "What do you say we make the damned things of wood and be done with it?"

Again Garreth wondered at his friend's deteriorating good humor. Christ, he had everything a man could want. He had Lacey.

Lacey only half listened to the chatter around her, her eyes constantly searching for Garreth in the gathering. She tried to keep her thoughts on their project and away from Garreth, but her heart seemed to overrule her mind these days.

Sebastian caught her glance and she forced a smile for his benefit. He really had been wonderful to her the past month, despite her growing assurance that he still loved the mysterious Cajun. They'd seen the black carriage again, and this time she'd gotten a glimpse of long black hair. Sebastian's expression had been rife with pain, but again he'd denied knowing the occupant.

They attended numerous parties and plays together, enabling her to get fodder for several articles. As a result, *"Trifles"*'s popularity had grown substantially since she'd taken over the column, and Col. Rapier had even given her a small raise.

And although they hadn't made their engagement public knowledge, they had told his parents. The Averys' delight couldn't have been greater, despite the problems with her family, which didn't seem to concern them overmuch, and everything was progressing better than she'd dreamed possible.

So why was she so miserable? Unfortunately she knew the answer only too well.

Between Edith's high-pitched whine and her constant complaining about every detail since they started work on the float, the girl was beginning to grate on Lacey's already raw nerves. Only when she spoke to Marshall Sutherland was her tone honeyed and flirtatious. One would think he was her fiance.

Lacey viciously twisted the piece of ribbon she held. Why was Garreth still determined to marry that woman? He no longer needed her money to save Armstrong Shipping. Sebastian had told her of his generous offer to double the amount of the wager. But Garreth refused to accept the money or go back on his word, even though Edith's behavior had only worsened since they'd announced their engagement. She seemed to think she was entitled to the best of everything now, and she wanted Garreth to make sure she got it.

"I still think I should have been chosen as Rowena," Edith complained. "After all, she was a fair Saxon maiden. Lacey has brown hair, for goodness sake."

"You won't be able to see her hair beneath that ridiculous pointed hat," Francie said. "Besides, we all agreed we'd draw names for the characters and you drew Queen Eleanor."

"The old bag," Edith snorted.

"You have a very attractive costume," Francie said testily, brushing a hand over her brow. Her cheeks were flushed as she added, "Besides, it's too late to change anything this close to Mardi Gras."

Edith ran her hand across her forehead and sighed dramatically. "I suppose," she said, casting a cunning glance in Garreth's direction.

The three women went back to the task at hand, painting the all-important crests on the remaining pennants, and their discussion temporarily moved away from Edith's ill mood and obvious displeasure.

Lacey couldn't have cared less about being Rowena, except that Garreth had been chosen as Ivanhoe. That would mean that he would wear her colors on his lance as they played out the tournament scene. Sebastian, as the black knight, would try to win her favor.

The parallel to the real-life game they played

was almost eerie. Even though they all knew the score and were aware of the drawbacks in their individual plans, their situations had nevertheless begun to bother Lacey more and more.

Despite Stone's threats and Sebastian's family obligations and Garreth's noble attempt to salvage his father's life's work, she no longer felt right about what they were doing.

Though society wholly accepted their actions as responsible and customary, her heart told her they were, each of them, making a terrible mistake.

"Mumps! How can she have mumps now?"

Francie's angry voice echoed through the main hall as she read the message she'd just been given.

The Bishops' servant backed toward the door, his eagerness to escape the infuriated woman plainly written on his face.

"Lacey!" she called, forgetting the man in her rush to find her friend. The servant slipped away unnoticed as Francie darted toward the stairs.

Removing her spectacles, Lacey looked up from her writing as Francie bounded into the upstairs sitting room.

"What in the name of heaven are you screaming about?"

"She has the mumps! That rotten girl has ruined everything."

"Who has the mumps?" Lacey asked, concern driving away the last traces of her concentration on her latest article.

"Edith Bishop! She's gone and gotten the mumps and won't be able to play Eleanor on the float tonight. Who can we possibly get at the last minute? I swear I think she did it on purpose because she wanted to be Rowena."

"Nonsense, no one can make themselves have mumps. Besides, we should be worried about Edith. Is she going to be all right?"

"Oh, you can bet she'll recover fully. Hardy peasant stock, and all that," she mumbled, sounding much like the noble character she was scheduled to play in a few short hours.

"Francie!" Lacey cried, horrified at her friend's callousness. She realized her own attitude toward Edith hadn't been much better lately and she suddenly felt ashamed. The girl was unpleasant, but if her parents were as bad as everyone said she could hardly be held responsible for that. In any case, Lacey knew it was her connection to Garreth that had her disliking Edith so strongly.

Francie looked properly chastised and she slumped into a chair, a look of real distress on her face as she fanned her heated cheeks.

"Don't worry," Lacey said. "We'll find someone." Setting aside her paper and pen, she tucked them into her satchel. "Come along; we'd better get started."

After several frantic minutes of discussion, the two women penned a note to Sandy Fitzpatrick, who immediately sent a response back saying Andi would be happy to take Edith's place on the float. The resolution calmed Francie somewhat, but by then the hour to dress was fast approaching.

"We'd better get into our costumes," she said.

Lacey agreed, and they turned to go up the stairs when the door chimes rang again.

"Now what?"

Francie went to the door. She pulled it open and was nearly run down as Garreth burst into the hall.

"Have you seen Sebastian?"

Lacey rushed forward. "No, I haven't seen him in two days, not since we finished the float."

"What's happened now?" Francie fretted.

Raking his hands through his hair, Garreth paced in front of the petticoat table, his reflection jumping to and fro in the gilt mirror. "Sebastian and I were in the stables behind the Averys' town house. We were decorating the horses like they were part of the joust since they help pull the float."

The women nodded.

"He looked out the door of the carriage house and got this crazed look in his eyes. The next thing I know he's on his horse, shouting about finally putting an end to something once and for all. He was in quite a state, and I had no idea what he was talking about. But I followed him out and saw him chasing a carriage. I tell you, the look he wore was as black as the villian, de Bois-Guilbert, he was supposed to be portraying."

"Good heavens," Francie cried. "Where could he have gone?"

"I don't know. By the time I went back inside to get my horse, they had disappeared. I waited, thinking he'd come back, but that was over three hours ago."

A desperate look crossed his face, and his hazel eyes darkened with concern. Again he furrowed his fingers through his hair, separating the part and disheveling the thick strands.

"Have you checked his house?" Lacey asked.

"His house, the club, everywhere. I tell you he's disappeared."

"We've got to tell his parents," Francie said, pacing before the window and back again.

"No, they're gone for the rest of the day. Some of the older folks had opted to do their own float and the Averys were in charge of getting it to the starting line. I have no idea where to find them."

"It's just as well," Lacey said, her mind finally beginning to function once more. "I think I know where Sebastian may have gone."

"You do?" Garreth and Francie chimed together.

"Yes, and I don't think he's in danger, so calm down," she warned, glancing behind them.

"Not in danger? Then where the devil is he?"

The shock on Garreth's face would have been comical at any other time. But Lacey saw no humor in the situation.

She turned to Francie. "Remember I told you about the carriage that showed up at Emerald Oaks the day Sebastian proposed?"

"That's right! You said he seemed upset by it."

"Yes, well I saw it again as Sebastian and I left

the German Relief Hall following the New Year's celebration. The driver hadn't been quick enough that time and I caught a glimpse of long black hair beneath the caped cloak.

"Sebastian denied knowing the occupant, but I didn't believe him this time. However, I didn't want to upset him further so I dropped the subject, knowing he wouldn't confide in me anyway. But I saw him look back when he thought I wasn't paying attention. And the look on his face was full of sorrow."

"I still say we should notify the Averys," Francie shrieked.

"No, keep your voice down," Lacey said, drawing them both by the hand into the front parlor. She closed the wide double doors behind them and glanced around nervously. "I don't want your parents to hear us," she said, her tone barely a whisper now.

"Why? Do you know what's happened?"

They both faced Lacey and she slowly nodded her head. "I don't know for sure, but I can guess."

"Well, don't keep it to yourself," Francie said. "Tell us."

Lacey chewed her bottom lip, wondering if she should say anything more. What if this was truly what Sebastian wanted? Did any of them have the right to try to stop him? She'd had doubts about their engagement ever since the beginning, but lately she'd felt more and more confused. Maybe Sebastian was the only one thinking clearly. Maybe she and Garreth were the ones in danger. In danger of making irreparable mistakes with their very lives.

"Lacey?"

She looked up and met Garreth's worried eyes. Again she hesitated.

"He's my best friend, Lacey. If you know something, you have to tell me."

Swallowing hard, she nodded. "I think—that is, I'm pretty sure he's eloped."

Chapter Fifteen

"Eloped!" Francie squealed.

"Shhh!" Garreth and Lacey hissed in unison.

Francie waved away their warning. "How can you two be so calm? He can't elope. He's engaged to you," she cried, clasping Lacey's arm.

"But he's in love with someone else. I think, deep down, I've known it ever since the day he proposed. But we made a deal. He said he would never mention the fact that I schemed to marry him, and in return I pretended I didn't know his heart still belonged to his Cajun."

"I don't understand. If he's not in love with you, why is he marrying you?"

"Oh, Francie. What a strange question coming from you. You were the one who helped me plan this whole marriage scheme, and you knew I not only didn't love Sebastian but I had never met him."

"That's different. You had no choice."

"Neither did he," Garreth said, finally realizing the extent of the sacrifice Sebastian had tried to make on his behalf. He finally understood the strange, haunted look Sebastian had worn that day in his office. His friend had been willing to marry Lacey in order to spare Garreth's pride and keep him from ruining his life by marrying Edith.

Lord, what a tangled web they'd created with their schemes and machinations. It continued to enlarge and reach out, pulling in more and more prey. First Sebastian, then Edith, now an unknown woman none of them had ever met.

Somehow the cycle had to be stopped. It could go on no longer. He and Lacey would have to right the wrongs they'd started when they made their bargain in the beginning. But for now, he had to help Sebastian.

"I've got to stop him," he whispered.

Both women turned to him, their faces lined with shock. "What?"

"I've got to stop him. His parents will never accept that girl as his wife. They've threatened to cut him off without a penny, and I believe they'll do it. Sebastian is spoiled and impulsive. He's liable to do something rash and then not be able to live with the consequences."

"No, wait," Lacey said, grasping his arm. Despite her own troubles, she couldn't stop the stirring she felt when she considered how much

Sebastian must love this woman to risk the results of his parents' wrath.

"What if he has thought about all that? What if he doesn't care about his parents' objections anymore?"

"Then he'll have to tell me that himself," Garreth said, recalling the last words Sebastian had spoken to him that day in his office. *Remember, twice now I've tried to help you.* And now it was Garreth's turn. No matter how much he hated the idea of Lacey marrying Sebastian, he couldn't stand by and watch his best friend ruin his life. "I'm going after him. You two just stay here and pretend everything is normal."

"I'm going with you," Francie stated flatly.

"That's the most featherheaded idea you've ever come up with, Francine Thomas." Garreth scowled.

"Featherheaded or not, I'm going. If Sebastian Avery elopes with an unknown Cajun it'll be front-page news."

Garreth swore. "Don't you think I know that? Sebastian can't afford a scandal like this. Not when the Averys have just begun to forgive him for loving that girl in the first place. He's pulled some stunts in his life, but I'm afraid this will be the last straw."

"I'm going with you," Lacey said calmly.

Staring at Lacey as if she'd gone mad before his very eyes, Garreth shook his head violently. "No, absolutely not. I swear, you've gotten as featherheaded as Francie."

"It's the only way."

"It's crazy! You cannot go along."

Lacey glanced at Francie and nodded. "You can't stop us," she told Garreth. "We're going after Sebastian, with or without you. I am his fiancee. If he has chosen to marry another woman over me, I have a right to know. I won't have you dragging him back here in some misguided attempt to force him to marry me. And Francie has a vested interest in this story."

"What are you talking about? Why would this concern Francie?"

"Because," Francie said, "if you two don't succeed in stopping him, I intend to be the first one to report the story."

"Report? What are you talking about?"

Ignoring Garreth's puzzled look, she rushed to the door and shouted for Jeannie, her younger sister.

The girl rushed to the parlor so fast Lacey suspected she'd been eavesdropping.

Francie pulled her sister into the parlor and slammed the heavy doors shut. "How would you and your friends like to be on the *Ivanhoe* float tonight?"

"What? Are you serious?" the younger girl asked excitedly.

"Yes. We need your help."

"Sure, we'd love it. Mama wasn't even going to allow me to go this year."

At sixteen, Jeannette Thomas still had another year until she'd be accepted as an adult. But she'd filled out in the last year and she was nearly of a size with her older sister.

"The costumes are laid out on my bed. All you have to do is be at the starting point at eight o'clock. We all designed elaborate masks, no one will know the difference as long as you're careful. I'll tell the Fitzpatricks what we're doing; they'll help you. Can you get three more friends to go with you?"

"Of course, all my friends want to go!"

"Good," Francie said, sharing a smile with Lacey. "Just sit on the float and wave; it should be fine."

"What about the party?" Lacey cried, suddenly remembering the gala they were expected to attend after the parade.

"I tell you this is a ridiculous scheme and you'll never pull it off," Garreth said, pacing in front of the fireplace.

"I hadn't thought about the party," Francie admitted.

"It'll still work," Lacey said. "Jeannie, all you have to do is stick by the Fitzpatricks. Everyone will think Francie, Garreth, Sebastian, and myself are there as long as you don't remove your masks. Talk little," she warned, "and disappear before midnight, when everyone removes their masks."

"We can do it," the girl boasted. "Don't worry." She grinned from ear to ear, obviously thrilled to be included in the subterfuge. Then she added, "Does this have to do with you being Phillip Truman?"

"Truman?" Garreth shouted.

Lacey and Francie exchanged startled looks.

"How do you know about that?" Francie asked.

"I've known about it for a long time. I read your diary."

"Brat," Francie scolded. Then she frowned. "Does Mother know?"

"Know what?" Garreth demanded, still unable to piece together what he'd heard.

"No," Jeannie said. "I told you, I can keep a secret."

"Good girl." Francie hugged her sister. "Now go get ready. And remember, don't tell Mother and Father anything, no matter what. Cover for Lacey and me until we get back."

"Sure."

The girl hurried from the room, a wide grin splitting her pretty face.

"Now, tell me what the hell is going on."

"Later," Lacey cut in. "Right now we've got to get going. They could be long gone by now."

"This is absurd," Garreth said. "You two should just stay here and let me handle this."

"No," the women chorused.

"Sebastian is your best friend," Lacey reminded him. She didn't add that she'd come to care for Sebastian herself the past months. "But I'm his fiancee."

Garreth frowned, his brows pulling together. He scrubbed his hand over the afternoon stubble on his chin. She could be right. With their friendship on the rocks, Sebastian might not listen to Garreth. But Lacey's presence could remind Sebastian of his promise and perhaps make his friend see reason.

"Maybe, just maybe, I can see why Lacey would want to go along. I can't agree, but I can understand it. But why do you want to put yourself in that kind of predicament, Francie? This whole thing could blow up in our faces and cause a scandal Mobile will never forget."

Lacey took his arm, ignoring the thrill of desire that shot through her at the first hint of his warmth. She had to think of Sebastian now, and his problems. Not her feelings for Garreth.

"Francie will collect the things we need while I explain to you what's been going on around here."

Francie offered Lacey a nervous smile and sped from the parlor, leaving the two alone.

"Do you read Truman in the *Register?*" Lacey began.

"The reporter?" Garreth frowned at the delay as Lacey calmly led him to the door. "Certainly. He's very good."

"Yes," Lacey agreed. *"She* is."

They hit pay dirt at their first stop.

"You're sure the couple in this carriage are the same ones who bought tickets on the train?"

"I done tol' you, they left the rig here in my livery. The man said they'd be back for it in three days. Then he bought two tickets for New Orleans on the morning train."

"Did you see them get on the train?" Garreth asked.

The man rolled his eyes. "I got better things to do than watch the train load and unload. I reckon if you buy a ticket you usually take the ride you've paid for."

"He's right," Lacey said, clutching Garreth's sleeve. "It makes perfect sense that they'd leave Mobile if they planned to elope. They must be on that train."

He rubbed his hand over his face and sighed. "I suppose you're right." He turned back to the stationmaster. "When is the next train for New Orleans?"

"Tomorrow morning, same as today."

"That's too late," Francie cried. "We'll have to ride."

"Are you crazy?" Garreth shouted. "I can't take two women to New Orleans alone and on horseback."

"Oh, stop fretting like a mother hen. No one will ever know. The way I figure it we have three days to find Sebastian and get him back here without anyone being suspicious," she said.

"Three days! You are crazy."

Even Lacey had to admit that seemed too risky. She turned to Francie, hoping the woman had a strategy figured out.

"Yes, three days. No one will notice our absence tonight as long as Jeannie does what we told her to do. Tomorrow, Mother will sleep late after being out until all hours of the morning. When she wakes, Jeannie will tell her we've already gone for the day. Tomorrow night is the annual Mystic Founders ball. She and Father will be out late again. Mardi Gras is always frantic around here. They won't think anything of not seeing us as long as Jeannie keeps feeding them information. That gives us until the Druids Ball Tuesday night when you two are to be crowned king and queen. That's three days."

"She's right, Garreth. We've got to do it. We can't wait until tomorrow for the next train. If we leave now on horseback we still have a chance to find them before they elope."

"I must be the one who's lost his mind," Garreth told them. "You two are starting to make sense."

The women shared a smile, but Garreth could only shake his head in disbelief.

"I still can't believe it. You two, reporters for the *Mobile Press Register*."

Garreth gripped the reins of his horse as they sped along, staring ahead at the deserted road. While not the most well traveled, it was the shortest route to New Orleans.

Which might be a wild-goose chase, he thought angrily. He should never have listened to Lacey and Francie. He should have come alone.

"Francie is the reporter; I just write the society articles."

" 'Trifles,' " he said, glancing at her with what looked like pride in his eyes. "My mother loves the column. Especially the last few months."

She flushed, turning her attention back to the road.

Francie shoved back the hood of her cloak and

groaned. "God, it's hot in this wool habit. I wish I'd worn the chambray."

The wind whipped through the trees on either side of the road and Lacey felt the chill to her bones. Freezing, she wished she had a wool riding habit instead of the plaid surah.

She glanced sideways in the fading light of dusk and saw Francie shiver.

"Are you all right?" she asked.

Garreth looked over at the women, a worried frown drawing the corners of his mouth down.

"I've felt rotten ever since we left the city limits," Francie admitted, pulling her hood back up and huddling in the folds of the garment.

Lacey and Garreth exchanged concerned looks.

"There's a small inn about three more miles ahead. We can stop there and rest a bit."

"I'll be fine," Francie assured them, shivering once more.

They rode at a swift pace until dark completely engulfed the area. A full moon struggled to rise through the overhanging clouds, barely lighting the potholed road. Another hour passed.

If they were caught the scandal would be devastating. Garreth had almost decided to turn back when the inn came into sight.

A dark blur in a clearing—he recognized the place immediately and temporary relief shot through him.

"There's Sadie's place," he said. The widow's business had suffered when the railroad all but made this route to New Orleans obsolete.

They stopped in front of the clapboard house and dismounted, tying their reins to the horse-head post in front of the porch. Francie staggered as they climbed the four steps to the door, and Lacey steadied her, her own legs feeling weak from the rough ride.

Inside the old inn, a fire blazed warmly, and several lamps had been lit to dispell the early darkness of the winter night.

Sadie, a rotund woman in her late sixties with ruddy cheeks and full lips, met them at the foyer and quickly ushered them into the parlor.

"Coffee?" she asked.

"Please," they chorused, rushing to warm their fingers before the flames.

"Haven't seen much of you lately," the proprietress said, taking Garreth's coat and gloves. She collected the women's outerwear and hung the garments on a hall tree beside the door.

"How have you been, Sadie?"

"Fair to middling." She waddled toward the pot hanging on a metal arm beside the fire and poured them each a cup of the thick black brew. "The three of you looking for a place for the night?" she asked, a suspicious frown marring her otherwise cheerful face.

Knowing Sadie ran a reputable place, Garreth moved quickly to assure her nothing sordid was afoot. "No, nothing like that. We're looking for someone. We think a friend of ours might be in some trouble."

Sadie nodded, propping her hand on her hip.

"Well, I hope you find 'em. If I can do anythin' let me know."

Suddenly Francie swayed and set her cup on the mantel. She backed into a chair and sank down on the thick cushion.

"Are you all right, dear?"

At Sadie's question Lacey and Garreth turned their attention to Francie.

Rushing to Francie's side, Lacey stopped. "Francie? What's the matter?"

The other woman looked up and Lacey gasped. "Oh, Francie!"

Garreth bent for a closer look and immediately took Lacey by the arm, dragging her back from the chair.

"You look like a pelican hoarding snapper," he said, gaping at Francie's swollen neck. Her flushed face and sweat-dotted brow told the rest of the sorry story.

"Curse Edith Bishop," Francie swore, her hands going to her tender neck. She winced and pressed her fingers to her aching forehead. "That girl is worse than a plague."

"Back up, Lacey."

"I've had the mumps," she said, kneeling once more at Francie's side.

"You can't go on like that," Garreth said. "We'll have to go back."

"No," the women said in unison.

"You've got to go on," Francie said. "You can still catch him. You've got to stop him from doing something really stupid, for Lacey's sake as well as his own. I'll stay the night here and send word to Sandy in the morning to come for me."

"Lacey, you stay with Francie. I'll go on alone."

"No. I'm fine, really. You two go ahead."

He looked at Lacey and she nodded. "I'm going with you," she said.

She didn't know what made her risk scandal to go on with Garreth alone. Maybe she wanted to see for herself that two people with tremendous odds against them could come together and make it work. Maybe it was desperation to stop Sebastian for her own sake, although she didn't think so. If she saw that he truly loved the Cajun, Lacey would not interfere with their happiness.

Maybe, she thought, glancing at Garreth, she just wanted an excuse to be with him for a brief period of time before they had to go their separate ways. She wasn't sure. And it didn't matter. She was determined to go along, and he'd have to tie her to the post out front to stop her.

Reading her resolve, he nodded. "All right. We'd better get started if we hope to catch up to him before it's too late. Francie, are you sure you'll be all right?"

"I'll be fine, it's Edith you should be worried about. I'm going to kill her when I get my hands on her."

"Sadie'll take good care of her," the motherly proprietress said. "You two go on and catch up to that friend you're so worried about."

They said hasty good-byes to Francie and were off once more. Neither spoke for a long time, riding silently side by side in the light of the full moon. Now high in the sky, it lit the way and saved the road from being treacherous.

A heavy silence descended. They rode on without speaking until Lacey could barely sit upright in her saddle. Her muscles ached, her legs trembled with fatigue, and she had a cramp in her neck. Her mare had grown increasingly restless and Lacey found it more and more difficult to keep her seat.

"Garreth, I need to rest for a minute," she finally said, twisting her neck to rid it of the painful crick. "And I think something is wrong with this horse. She's been acting strange since we left Sadie's."

"There's a small cabin up ahead. It was deserted the last time I past this way. If it's still empty we'll stop and rest a little while. My mount seems a bit spooky himself."

She nodded, focusing on the dim outline of the road. Ahead, the trees grew thick from neglect. They shadowed the narrow road, and blackness cloaked the area. She shivered and tucked her cloak tighter around her.

It was terrible the things people would do for money, she thought. Garreth, Sebastian, herself. They'd all been willing to trade their souls for it. She should never have devised such a cold-blooded scheme in the first place.

But almost immediately she pictured her mother and Georgie and knew she couldn't give up. Stone would tear her family apart if she didn't come up with the money they owed him before the deadline. She had no other plan, no other way to save her family. Yet here she was hoping Sebastian, at least, had found happiness. She hadn't stopped to consider what she'd do if he had.

The road narrowed and Garreth's mount drew close to hers. The mare whinnied nervously and sidestepped. Lacey could smell horseflesh and leather. She felt the mare's coat twitch beneath her.

In the waning light Lacey could see the shadow of stubble darkening Garreth's rigid jaw. Then the trees overhead came together in an arch and the moon's light disappeared altogether. Thrust into pitch blackness, he reached across and took her reins.

"Let me lead the way," he said, grasping the leather straps and aligning his mount with hers.

For a moment Lacey settled back, content to let him go ahead. Her fatigue caught up with her all at once and her eyes drifted closed. She felt her muscles relax for the first time in hours. The soreness eased somewhat and she almost thought she could doze given the opportunity.

She glanced over Garreth's shoulder and saw the pinpoint of light which signaled the end of the leafy arbor.

Suddenly her horse whinnied, sidestepped, and screamed in protest. Surprised, Lacey fumbled for the reins, but Garreth had them. He whirled in the saddle, shock etched on his face as his stallion nipped the mare's tender flank.

"What the hell," he cursed. His stallion rounded swiftly, nearly unseating him. The horse pawed viciously at the pocked road, dancing in the age-old steps of a mating ritual.

Garreth's next words singed Lacey's ears and brought a red-hot flush to her cheeks.

"That damned mare is in season," he snapped, fumbling with the reins of Lacey's horse.

Lacey struggled to grip the pommel as the mare reared, baring her teeth.

The reins snapped from Garreth's hands and, sensing freedom, the mare reared once more, unseating Lacey. With a startled cry, she slid from the saddle onto the hard-packed road.

"Lacey! Are you all right?" Garreth's shouts could barely be heard over the cry of the mare as she raced away into the night.

Breathless, Lacey tried to answer him, but only a small squeak escaped her lips. In a rush of fright, Garreth sprang from the saddle and, holding his stallion's reins, bent next to Lacey's supine form.

His hands quickly raced over her, searching for injury. In the panic of the moment the leather straps he held slipped to the ground. It was the only incentive the randy horse needed. With a wild roar he followed the trail of dust left by Lacey's mare.

Garreth jumped to his feet, torn between going after the stallion, their only source of transportation, and staying with Lacey. He jogged a few steps after the horse, then threw down his hat with a scathing curse and knelt beside Lacey once more.

She was pushing herself up, and he gripped

her elbow and helped her to her feet.

"Are you all right?"

She dusted her bottom and he heard her wince. "Yes," she said, staring into the darkness where their mounts had disappeared. "What do we do now?"

Garreth retrieved his hat from the ground and beat it against his thigh. "We walk."

"Walk?"

"Yeah. You can walk, can't you?"

"Of course I can walk. But what about Sebastian?"

"Sebastian is on his own. We can't go all the way back to Mobile, get more money and horses, and still hope to catch up to him in time to get him back before the Druid Ball Monday night. His parents will just have to know what's going on."

"But what about the horses?" she said, rubbing her behind.

"To hell with them. Unless I miss my bet they're having a damned sight more fun right now than we are."

Chapter Sixteen

Almost immediately it began to rain. Garreth cursed, turning up the collar of his coat. Lacey covered her head with the hood of her cloak but soon the fabric was drenched.

Icy droplets ran over her nose and dripped into her eyes. The hand Garreth held was warm and somewhat dry, but the other was chilled to the bone and she kept tucking it into the folds of her cloak.

They finally reached the cabin, wet and exhausted. The door was ajar, hanging by a single leather hinge. The window had long since been broken, its shattered glass pieces already buried beneath the layer of dirt which seemed to cover everything. Sitting about ten yards off the road in what must have at one time been a clearing, the lower part of the cabin was almost obliterated beneath a thick crop of brush and weeds.

Garreth stomped down the heavier shrubs and undergrowth, clearing the way for Lacey. Her slippers had not been made for heavy walking and already her feet ached so badly she could barely go on. Her ankles felt swollen and tight from the constant jarring of soft flesh and bone against hard-backed earth, and a chill permeated her body from the freezing rain.

Pushing open the ineffectual door, Garreth led her into the deserted cabin.

"I'll see if there's anything to make a fire with," Garreth told her, going toward the brick fireplace that had seen better days. A slice of moonlight partially cut the blackness of the room, and she glanced around.

"Wouldn't you know it," Garreth spoke behind her. She turned to see him holding a dusty old lamp. "The oil, if there ever was any, has evaporated. But I did find these." He held up two long, wooden lucifers.

He disappeared into the shadows of one corner and came back holding a broken chair. "Not the best firewood, but it's dry."

He tossed the splintered wood into the fireplace and bent before it. Almost immediately she heard a scratch and smelled sulfur as Garreth lit the first match. The old chair went up like a pitch torch and the room filled with muted light and a hint of warmth. She took a moment to glance around at the filthy, sparsely furnished cabin.

Lacey stared at the rough shelves over the old cookstove, the sunken mattress on a cot in the corner, a single unbroken chair, and dirt everywhere.

Garreth shook his head, then turned back to the hearth. "You'd better get out of those wet clothes."

"Wh-what?" Lacey shivered, the word forced out through lips blue with cold.

"You're going to make yourself sick if you don't."

He didn't face her; she was thankful for that at least. Did he realize how his words made her feel? Could he know how just the simple, sensible statement had set her heart racing and stirred her blood?

"I won't look," he added, using a chair leg to poke the fire to life.

Lacey's eyes went wide with shock at his words, but she realized he thought she didn't trust him. How ridiculous! She trusted him with her life.

The knowledge surprised her a little, but at the same time brought her a measure of comfort. Yes, she would trust Garreth with her life.

She turned toward the cot in the corner and saw it was covered with a single, moth-eaten blanket. Without glancing back, she shucked off her wet clothes down to her slightly damp chemise and wrapped the blanket around her. The only other thing on the cot was a thin, homespun sheet and she gathered that up as well.

Garreth was bent over the fire, his damp shirt stretched tight across his wide back. As he reached to poke at the flames with a chair leg, the fabric of his trousers flexed with the expansion of the muscles in his thighs. Lacey swallowed hard.

The fire blazed beneath his ministrations and she attributed the heat rising in her cheeks to the flames' leaping higher.

"There, that's better," Garreth said, turning on his heels.

He saw Lacey standing behind him, the blanket wrapped around her shoulders, the sheet clutched in her trembling hands. Her hair was loose. Why hadn't he noticed that before? Her cheeks were pink with the glow of the fire. Her eyes, beautiful and blue, stared at him with wide-open innocence. He swallowed hard and forced himself to speak without betraying the raging emotions that had engulfed him at the sight of her.

"Feel better?"

She didn't answer for a moment, her eyes watching him closely. Then she seemed to shake herself out of the daze she was in and she nodded. "Yes. I found these. They're not in very good condition, but they're somewhat clean and they'll keep us warmer than our wet clothes."

Garreth rose and stepped forward. His hands reached for the sheet and Lacey's gaze followed his fingers as they closed over hers. A rush of heat spiraled up her arms and centered in her breasts, and suddenly the cabin was warm as toast.

"Thank you," he whispered, taking the sheet and stepping behind her. Nervously she cleared her throat and went to lay her wet things on the hearth before the fire to dry. She stood close to the flames, although she couldn't remember ever being warmer than she was at that moment.

Even with her back turned, she could hear every move he made, and her mind conjured pictures to match the sounds. The rasp of damp cloth against hair-roughened skin, the buttons of his trousers giving way beneath steady fingers.

She shivered and drew away from the fire, feeling aflame herself.

"That's better," she heard him say, and turned toward his voice.

He stood beside the bed, the sheet wrapped around his body and tucked under his arms. Despite the desire coursing through her, Lacey couldn't help smiling.

"What's so funny?" he asked, seeing the grin.

"Nothing. It's just that I've never seen you so...so disheveled. Except when you rescued me from the lake."

"I was thinking likewise. Every time we're together I seem to find myself drenched."

She smiled.

He smiled.

The moment stretched out, cozy and comforting, until finally Garreth broke the thread of longing holding them in its grasp.

"I'd better check that fire."

He passed her, and she smelled the scent of rain-wet hair and damp wool. She followed him with her eyes and saw the cover part as he stooped before the hearth. The folds fell open to show hardened calves and narrow, well-shaped feet.

She'd never imagined a man's legs could stir such primal feelings in her. She tried to stifle the desire coursing through her, whirling her insides into a frenzy of pleasure. She was technically still engaged to Sebastian, after all.

But she'd never been able to rouse the feelings for Sebastian that seemed to blossom at the mere sight of Garreth. He was her heart's desire, the one man she'd longed for her whole life. The soul mate, the perfect match. She knew that now as surely as she'd ever known anything. Had they been wrong to deny their feelings? Most certainly. Nothing as strong as the wanting she felt could be suppressed for long.

He pivoted on the balls of his feet and she met his gaze. In his eyes she saw mirrored the hunger she felt. An arc of awareness shot between them. Her breath caught in her throat.

Almost immediately, Garreth rose and strode past her to the shelves over the stove. She felt the loss of his gaze like a cold wind whipping through the warm cabin. She wanted to go to him. And then what?

She cleared her throat and stepped closer to the fire.

"There doesn't appear to be anything here to eat. A bag of flour it seems the rats have been in, a tin of rancid lard." He turned toward her once more. "I guess we'd better just get some sleep and start for Sadie's as soon as possible in the morning."

Lacey nodded, willing her nerves to still. She tightened the blanket around her shoulders and pasted on an unconcerned expression.

"I'm not really hungry anyway," she said. Then her eyes went to the cot in the corner and the feelings she'd tamped down burst to life.

"There's only one bed," she blurted nervously, stumbling back so fast the blanket came dangerously close to the flames of the fire.

Garreth leapt forward and they collided as Lacey shot away from the heat. He steadied her with a frown, looking down into her face as though he couldn't imagine what had her so jumpy.

"You take the cot," he said. "I'll sit up in the chair over there."

"You can't sleep in that chair."

He quirked an eyebrow at her statement. "I'll be fine," he said.

Knowing how her words must have sounded, Lacey hurried to the cot and sat down, crying out in surprise as she sank into the hollows in the old straw.

"Not the luxury you're used to, I imagine."

She looked up and saw the quirky grin tipping one side of Garreth's mouth.

"I've slept on better," she admitted.

Settling onto the mattress, she wondered if she should turn her face to the wall. Could that get her mind off the sight of Garreth in nothing but the sheet? Could it erase the image of his bare feet and legs from her brain?

She watched as he added several more sticks

to the fire, then went to the chair. Carefully tucking the cover around his body, he sank into the wicker seat. And immediately crashed to the floor in a tangle of legs, arms, wood splinters, and rough cotton.

"Oh, my God," Lacey cried, stumbling from the cot, her feet tangling in the blanket as she rushed toward him.

Garreth struggled up from the floor as she reached him, clutching his arm and tugging him up. Her grasp caused him to lose his footing and he tumbled back, pulling her off balance and causing her to fall to her knees.

"Let go," he said shortly.

She jumped, startled by his anger, and scrambled back, dragging the cover down in her effort to get away.

She realized he'd been holding his cover with the hand she'd grasped and her tugging had loosened his hold. The cover slipped down to reveal the wide expanse of chest and hard-muscled stomach. She saw the golden brown path of hair that covered both copper nipples and trailed down to the indent of his navel.

Her heart jolted, slamming against her breastbone, but she couldn't draw her gaze away from the sight. Breathing was painful as she saw his gaze slip over her face and neck and then widen.

Following his glance, she saw that her cover had been likewise dislodged, revealing the crests of her breasts beneath the sheer, clinging fabric of her damp chemise.

As they both stared down, her nipples puckered and tightened beneath the cotton. She heard his indrawn breath and felt the heat of a scarlet blush cover her cheeks.

"I—I—" She tried to draw the blanket up, but found she was sitting on the edge and couldn't budge it. After several frantic moments it finally came free and she snatched it up to her neck.

"I'm sorry," she mumbled, trying to get to her feet.

He rushed to help her up and they both stood. His cover pooled on the floor as it slipped to his hips. But he didn't remove his hands from Lacey's shoulders. Their eyes met and held. He drew her slightly closer. She didn't resist. Couldn't resist.

His lips came down on hers and she leaned up to press her body full against his bare skin. The heat blazed through her and she forgot the tenuous position of her blanket as her arms snaked around his neck.

The kiss deepened; neither wanted to end the moment they'd waited so long to share.

"Lacey," he murmured, feathering kisses along her neck and jaw. "Oh, Lacey. How I've wanted to hold you like this. To feel you in my arms. God, I can't let you go. Not ever," he vowed fiercely.

"I don't want you to, Garreth," she admitted, realizing the shame of her words, but not able to stop them. She loved him, craved his closeness. She needed to be with him, and she forced aside the reasons why they should resist their feelings.

"Are you sure? Do you know what you're saying?"

"Yes, I'm sure. I think I've known this would happen since the moment we first met, I just didn't want to admit it. But I can't deny it any longer. I love you."

"Oh, Lacey. I love you, too. God, how I've ached for you."

"Show me, Garreth. Show me now, tonight, while we have this chance."

He met her fervent gaze, his arms drawing her against the warm, dry flesh of his chest.

Chapter Seventeen

No words were necessary as Garreth led her to the cot and pressed her down against the lumpy mattress. His body covered hers as his lips found her mouth once more.

Lacey slid her arms around his neck, drawing him closer, reveling in the feel of his muscled arms around her, his heavy weight atop her.

Almost desperately, he prolonged the kiss until Lacey could no longer breathe. But she didn't care. She'd have gone on kissing him until she passed out from lack of oxygen but she'd never have pushed him away. It felt too good, too right, to finally be with him this way.

He reached between them and parted the blanket, revealing her body through the thin chemise. She gasped as the air hit her skin. But she had no time to feel chilled.

Garreth lowered his mouth to the hardened point of her nipple and ran his tongue over the rosy circle outlined for his perusal.

Lacey arched, the feeling like nothing she'd ever imagined. She cried out softly against his shoulder and pressed her lips to the muscle rising there. He made a noise deep in his throat and she gently sank her teeth into his flesh.

She heard his choked groan and felt a power and wonder she'd never dreamed possible. His reaction spurred her on. She let her hands slide over the hard curves of his back to the edge of the sheet. She pushed it down, letting her fingers explore every inch of his sinewy buttocks.

The cover gave way and she pushed it to the side, revealing his beautiful body to her gaze. As his head bent over her breast, she glanced beyond his shoulder and saw the mounds beneath her hands. The sight aroused her beyond reason and she gently raked her fingernails up over his buttocks and his back, all the way to his shoulders.

He cried out, arched, and buried his face between her breasts. His arms tightened around her as he gathered her close.

"Oh, God, oh, God," he whispered, one knee settling between her thighs to softly part them. She felt the rough skin caress her exposed womanhood, and white-hot flashes of pleasure rippled though her. She clenched her thighs against the pleasure-pain, capturing his leg between hers.

Shifting, he rubbed his thigh against her

until she could hear her own panting in the stillness of the night. A molten heat encompassed her, pushing her on to something climactic and unexplored.

"Garreth? Garreth?" Her voice sounded strangely rough and far off. Something was happening. She could feel the building tension gripping her limbs, like the springs of a watch being overwound.

Garreth's head dipped once more and his mouth lavished her breast. His thigh continued to stroke her mound until she imagined she could feel each tingling sensation from that part of her individually. Her senses heightened as never before, and suddenly the watch spring broke and she shot apart in a spasming shudder as lights flashed behind her eyes and a roaring in her ears drowned out the cries she uttered.

His lips swallowed her moans as he kissed her harder and deeper than ever before. She quivered in his arms, frightened and thrilled by the sensations controlling her body.

Wanting more, but unsure just what, she opened to him and felt his hips slide between her thighs. His hard, hot shaft probed her for a second. The heated tip sent her spiraling back into the vortex of pleasure and she arched, forcing Garreth into her with one hard thrust.

She cried out, and he stilled. For a moment neither moved. Then she couldn't resist the call of desire, and she wriggled beneath him. It was all the encouragement he needed and he slowly withdrew, only to resheathe himself deeper each time.

Again Lacey felt the building pressure in her middle. This time she knew what lay at the end of the feeling and she gripped his buttocks as she pulled him closer.

"Lord," she heard him whisper. "You're too eager. I can't hold back."

"Don't. Never," she said, her words disjointed and harsh. "Don't hold back."

"No," he said, driving into her deeper and harder. "No."

His hand slid down her leg to her knee and he drew it up to press against his side. Lacey immediately saw the advantage of the position and lifted her other leg, catching them behind his back as he drove into her.

They clung, arched, and struggled to get closer, all the while touching, feeling, caressing. Gasps blended, breaths mingled. Sighs flowed into sighs.

Too soon, Lacey felt the shudders ripple through her once more and she cried out, not wanting the feeling to end. But this time, she felt Garreth's body quiver inside her as they rode the final wave of passion together.

For a long time they lay still. Then Garreth shifted, rolling onto his back and draping Lacey across his chest. She shivered and he reached for the end of the blanket and drew it over them. His hand stroked her hair back from her face tenderly, as her fingers played in the soft swirls of hair covering his chest.

For the first time, Garreth didn't know what to say. He knew how he felt, had known for some time. But he also hadn't forgotten the impossibility of their situation. A situation made more perplexing now.

Still, he couldn't summon a morsel of regret for what they'd done. In fact, he couldn't remember ever feeling so right about anything. He could only hope Lacey felt the same. He found he didn't have the courage to ask her thoughts, fearing he'd hear remorse in her voice.

After a long silence, he heard the soft sounds of her steady breathing and knew she slept. A dream. A fantasy come true. Lacey slept in his arms, just the way he'd imagined a hundred times. The way he'd thought she never would. The way he'd pictured her sleeping with Sebastian. A pang of sorrow deflated his happiness. He'd made love with his best friend's fiancee.

Raking a hand through his tangled hair, he pressed his lips to Lacey's forehead. She was his. Had been his heart's only desire since the day she walked into his office. He'd been a fool to think he could marry another. Or allow her to. He'd make Sebastian understand. Somehow he'd undo the ties which held him to Edith Bishop.

As he listened to the soft sounds Lacey made in slumber, he wondered how the hell he would do what he vowed.

Lacey drifted up from a deep sleep, aware of the warmth pressing against her nude body. Somewhere along the way her chemise had been removed and as her eyes fluttered open she knew what the warmth represented.

Daylight streamed into the cabin. The fire had long burned out, leaving a bitter nip in the air around them.

"Garreth."

"Were you expecting someone else?"

She grinned and tucked her chin into his chest. "No."

"Good, because I intend to be the only one you ever awake to find in your bed."

"Oh, Garreth," she moaned, trying to pull away. He held her close and she was forced to meet his gaze. "What have we done?"

"We've made love, Lacey. And it was beautiful and good and right."

She cocked her chin up and stared at the hard glint of determination in his eyes. "Yes, it was." A flush covered her cheeks and she grinned. "Is it always like that?"

He chuckled, the rumble from his chest sending sparks of desire through her and rekindling the banked flames of their passion.

"Don't ask me," he said roughly. "I seem to have forgotten everything beyond this moment. You have literally left me mindless."

His words fanned the flames and she settled more closely against his side. "Have I?"

He clutched her close and nodded.

"Good," she said, unable to hide the satisfaction in her tone.

His hand slid down to her bottom and he gave it a soft pat. "You siren. I think you know precisely what you've done to me."

"And what is that?" she whispered, unable to resist pressing her lips against the muscled expanse of chest beneath her cheek.

"You've made me love you even more, if that's possible," he admitted, hooking her beneath the arms and drawing her fully atop him.

"Oh, Garreth, I love you, too. I love you so much," she said, pulling back once more. "But we can't—"

"Don't." The sharpness of his voice stopped her. His eyes softened the rebuke. "Don't you dare tell me you're sorry for what we did, Lacey. I couldn't bear that."

"No, not sorry. Never that." She felt the hardness of his body, the softness of his embrace. "I love you."

Beneath her she could feel his body's response to her declaration. Feelings she had never known she possessed rushed to the surface now like old friends. All the emotions he'd made her feel only hours ago came crashing back.

She was a woman, *his* woman. She knew it; his body acknowledged it. They belonged together. Nothing, no one, could change that fact.

"I love you," she said, more forcefully this time. His eyes lit with fire and a beatific smile illuminated his features.

"I love you, too. And I want you again, Lacey. I can't help myself. I've never known the kind of passion I've felt for you over the last months. I tried to fight it, for both our sakes, but I should have known from the first it was no use."

"What are we going to do?"

Again she felt the growing evidence of his desire and he grinned. "The obvious, it seems. I can't get enough of you."

Again they made love, this time slowly. They explored, caressed, clung. Garreth staved off his fulfillment until Lacey could bear it no more. As she cried out, digging her nails into the satin-covered steel of his back, he exploded within her.

Too soon, reality came to shadow their happiness once more. Garreth knew they had to discuss the harsh truths he'd tried to put off. They had decisions to make which could wait no longer. Difficult decisions that would affect more than themselves.

"Lacey, you know I won't be happy until I've made you my own, legally."

A burst of exuberance mushroomed in Lacey. She reveled in the feel of excitement his words stirred in her. She wanted to belong to Garreth, and he to her. She wanted them to be together, like this, for the rest of their lives.

"But," he said, bringing a wave of apprehension to douse her joy, "you must know what this means for both of us."

He pushed her gently away and drew himself up to lean against the rough, log-scalloped wall of the cabin.

Lacey shifted to a sitting position, drawing the blanket with her to cover her nakedness and cut the morning chill. "What do you mean?"

"The wager, Lacey. You came to me for two reasons. You needed money, and you knew my company was on the verge of bankruptcy. If anything, my situation has only gotten worse."

"The *Mirabella*?"

He nodded. "I had a lot riding on her. Without the payment I was to receive for her cargo, Armstrong Shipping was dead. The wager would have kept it afloat temporarily, until I could..."

His words trailed off and he raked a hand roughly over his face. Lacey sank back on her heels.

"Until you could marry Edith."

His hand dropped to the mattress, his eyes grief-stricken. "Yes."

"I see." Feeling as though the other woman had somehow invaded the privacy of the moment, Lacey made to rise.

Garreth sprang forward and grasped her arms. "Lacey, look at me."

She did as he said, knowing it was useless to try to resist him now.

"What I'm trying to say is, I have ruined things for you. For both of us. For surely I won't allow you to marry Sebastian now any more than I could go through with my plans to marry Edith."

"But you told Sebastian you were honor-bound to go through with your wedding to Edith."

"This," he said, motioning to the bed. "This changes everything. My duty is to you now, no matter what the consequences."

"I have something to tell you," Lacey whispered, her lips close to Garreth's ear as she snuggled beside him. The sunlight of the clear morning peeked in through the gaps around the door frame, making a square of light on the dirt floor. The chilled air whipped around the edges, but they were warm in each other's embrace.

"What is it?" he mumbled, his attention on the exposed flesh of her neck now that she'd cuddled so close against him.

"I was meant to marry you all along."

The cloud of passion dissipated and he leaned back to look into her face. "What are you talking about?"

"You asked me how I found out about the wager, and about your finances."

He nodded.

"My father planned to marry me off to you before his death. Apparently he'd had some business dealings with your father and thought you'd be a fine catch. However, when he uncovered the truth of your finances and learned through a friend about the money in the Bank of Alabama, he changed his mind."

"He was right to," Garreth said, all his earlier regrets coming back to haunt him in the full light of day. What could be ignored in the darkness of night with Lacey's passion to buoy him could not be discounted now.

"No," she said, brushing the hair from his forehead and pressing tiny kisses along his brow. "He was right from the first. You're the only one for me."

"Lacey, I won't deny my love for you. And I won't let you go, no matter how much I know I should. But you've got to realize the difficulties we'll face when we return to Mobile."

"I don't care. As long as you're with me, I can face anything. I don't care about the money, Garreth," she said, lifting her face to meet his gaze. "You must know it wasn't for my benefit that I approached you in the first place."

"I know. But you must realize I can't save Emerald Oaks. Hell, I'll be lucky to keep the house in town. I'll have to sell Armstrong Shipping and find work. Your mother and brother will have to live with us in the town house; we won't be able to afford a place outside Mobile. It won't be the life they're used to, the life you are used to."

She looked away as reality crashed through the fragile bubble of happiness they'd made together. He was right. He couldn't save Emerald Oaks, and he couldn't stop Stone.

"That's impossible, Garreth. I can't move my mother from Emerald Oaks. Not now, maybe not ever. And Georgie...you don't understand how it is with my brother. He'd never adjust to living anywhere else."

"It'll be hard on your mother and Georgie," he admitted. "But you've known all along your plan might not go the way you hoped. We'll help Georgie adjust. And maybe when your mother sees how happy we are it'll help her get over the loss of your father."

"No." She cut off his words abruptly. "No, you don't understand. That's not possible. There has to be another way. A way we can be together and I can still pay off the mortgage on Emerald Oaks."

She thought of Stone's threat to charm her

mother into marrying him. If she went to Katrina and told her she would have to move to town, leave Emerald Oaks, and take Georgie into the very heart of the masses of society they'd always sheltered him from, she knew her mother would not understand. She'd be horrified, and with good reason. Katrina would be at Stone's mercy. Why, she'd probably jump at his offer of marriage if it meant her only chance to remain at Emerald Oaks. And even if Lacey tried to warn her about Stone's treachery Katrina probably wouldn't understand in her present state of mind.

Garreth's face tightened and he gently set Lacey aside. He rose from the bed, gathered the abandoned blanket, and wrapped it around his waist. He went to the fire and stoked the embers to life, tossing in the chair leg to be used as the last firewood.

"I know about your brother, Georgie." He turned to face her.

"How?"

He dusted his hands on the blanket and came back to the bed. "I did some checking after you came to my office that day. I was curious why I'd never seen you around Mobile before."

"We did very little socializing. Mother preferred to stay at Emerald Oaks with Georgie. Father was never far from them. He insisted I have my debut, but then he left me alone, knowing I was happier at Emerald Oaks with them than I would have been if I'd married and had to move away."

"Until you had no choice."

She nodded and he sat on the mattress beside her. He took her hand.

"And now all your carefully laid plans have been ruined. Despite all you've done, you're going to lose Emerald Oaks. Because of this, because of us."

Lacey shook her head. "No, I was wrong to go after Sebastian in the first place. We should leave him alone. He must love this girl. That's all that matters."

"Maybe it should be," he said, staring down at her small hand clutched in his. "But it isn't, is it? Not for any of us."

"What are you saying?" Her voice shook with the doubt and trepidation his words caused in her. Was he now regretting what had happened between them? Did he wish it had never occured so he could go on with his plan to marry Edith Bishop?

"Sebastian's parents will never accept his choice. Bishop will probably try to ruin me for what I've done to his daughter. And your family will be forced to move to town. And I feel so damned helpless, there's nothing I can do about any of it."

Anger sharpened his tone and he saw Lacey's eyes go wide with fear. Immediately he softened, leaning toward her.

"Don't you dare say you're sorry," she whispered, mocking his earlier demand.

Garreth could see the bright sheen of tears in her eyes, the dread she couldn't hide. He pulled her into his embrace and forced a dry chuckle. "Don't worry about that," he told her.

She looked up and he reached a finger to catch the tear on the edge of her lashes.

"I love you, Lacey Webster," he said. "I'll always love you. I'm only sorry I don't have more to offer you."

She smiled and touched his cheek. Releasing the blanket, she let it drop to the bed. His eyes roamed her creamy shoulders and rose-tipped breasts. His hands reached out to touch her and she went into his arms.

She didn't want to think about Stone now, not with the memory of Garreth's lovemaking still warm within her. She would have to find another way to stop Stone, to help her mother and Georgie so they wouldn't have to leave Emerald Oaks. But not now, not this minute. Right then, all she wanted was to revel in the new sensations Garreth stirred in her.

"This is enough for now," she said. "There'll be time to worry about the rest later."

Chapter Eighteen

"We'd better get started. It's going to be a long walk back to Sadie's."

They found their clothes and dressed, only slightly uncomfortable in the stiff garments. Garreth turned his back as Lacey dressed, but she knew it was only an act of consideration for her modesty. He'd seen every inch of her body the night before.

Adjusting her skirts into place, she stepped up behind him. A shyness overcame her as he turned, his eyes raking her figure as though memorizing her.

"I'm ready," she said.

"I'm sorry there isn't anything to eat. It'll be a long walk to Sadie's without breakfast."

"It doesn't matter."

"We'll have to discuss our plans on the way. If

anyone should learn we stayed the night in the cabin—alone—there'll be talk."

She nodded, silently agreeing to whatever he proposed. Garreth took her hand and drew her fingers to his mouth. Pressing a kiss against the softness there, he closed his eyes.

"Don't worry. We'll think of something."

She nodded, drawing her hand away. She should have told him about Stone. If he understood...

No, she thought. Thaddeus Stone was a problem she alone would have to deal with. She'd known from the beginning it would be up to her to stop the man; that was why she hadn't even confided in Francie. No one, not even Garreth, could help her this time.

"Come on, then. Let's go."

Still gripping her hand, he shoved aside the crooked door and led Lacey into the sunlight of the bright, crisp morning. The cold reminded them that winter had not yet given up its hold over the area.

Garreth moved forward and she saw his spine suddenly stiffen.

"I'll be damned," he said.

Lacey looked past his shoulder and a wide smile lit her face.

"Oh, thank God!" she cried, rushing forward.

Garreth strode across the road to the abandoned pasture on the other side, where his stallion carelessly grazed in the deep, yellow grass.

"What about the mare?"

"She'll follow his scent. You should have her

back before the day's out."

He stepped close to the horse. "So you came back, did you?" he scolded. "And wearing a fat grin, I see." Inching closer, he patted the horse's side. The reins dangled free, trailing in the brush. His saddle and saddlebags were intact.

The stallion glanced up, still eating. "Well, lucky for you I'm feeling a bit more favorable to your romantic pursuits this morning, seeing as how I enjoyed a few of my own last night. Otherwise I'd probably be making glue out of you when we get back to Mobile."

He turned to Lacey. "Well, we might have breakfast after all," he said, opening the pouch.

"We can go on now?" Lacey asked.

"Damned right, we can do whatever we want," he crowed.

"Should we?"

Her hesitant tone succeeded in gaining Garreth's full attention and he turned to face her.

"What do you mean?"

"Should we try to stop Sebastian? Shouldn't we allow him to find his own happiness?"

For a long moment Garreth didn't respond. Then he slowly nodded. "Perhaps. But we have two days left. I have to make sure this elopement is truly what Sebastian wants. I have to know he's considered the consequences of his actions, much the way we have, and that he's not rushing headlong into a foolish scheme he'll later regret."

"I understand."

Garreth felt he owed Sebastian that much. They were friends, and Sebastian had tried to help him by agreeing to marry Lacey. If Sebastian were making a mistake he'd only regret later, they had to at least try to talk to him.

"Here."

Removing a strip of cheesecloth from the saddlebag, Garreth unrolled it to reveal soft cheese and bread. He handed the biggest piece to Lacey and she broke the bread and slipped the hunk of cheese inside.

They finished their meal and Garreth helped Lacey onto his horse. He pulled himself up behind her and settled her derriere in the juncture of his thighs.

Lacey couldn't stop the feelings that engulfed her as Garreth's warmth surrounded her, penetrating the layers of damp clothing between them. She reveled in the feel of his arms around her as he gathered the reins and led the mount toward the road.

The bustle of activity they encountered in New Orleans was a mixed blessing. While slowing their progress and ending any hope they had of following Sebastian's trail, it also served to conceal them and keep them from being conspicuous arriving in clothes hopelessly rumpled from the rain and ride. At least Garreth had guessed right about the mare, so they hadn't had to arrive atop one horse.

Merrymakers lined the streets and filled the alleys. Costumes of every description paraded by them as they made their way to a nearby hotel. Sebastian had chosen his destination well. Mardi

Gras in New Orleans assured him anonymity.

"Now what?" Lacey asked, eyeing the man in a jester's suit coming toward them. As he approached, he pulled the string on a paper cone and multicolored streamers shot out in every direction.

Lacey smiled at the man but Garreth only scowled.

"There isn't much we can do. Sebastian picked a good place to get lost. Unless we get lucky and he's staying somewhere nearby, I'm afraid we've wasted a trip."

Looking back over her shoulder, Lacey smiled. "I wouldn't call it wasted," she whispered softly, trying to lighten his mood. The last day had been trying, and she knew Garreth was tired. His mood had been solemn and brooding, but his concern had all been for her.

"No, indeed." He reached across the saddle and squeezed her hand. "I'd definitely call it time well spent."

She smiled up at him, but she couldn't help the twinge of disquiet she felt. His voice sounded strained, his cheer forced. Something had been bothering him since they left the cabin, and his pensiveness increased with each passing moment.

They made their way through the throng of masqueraders until they drew up in front of a grand hotel. The elaborate sign over the glass and brass doors read HOTEL RUE ST. CLAIR. Beside the fancy doors were scrolled cornices in a gilt-leaf pattern. Lacey stared up at the fine place and felt ill at ease in her rumpled dress and mussed hair, arriving without even a single traveling case.

Garreth dismounted and helped her down, but his attention seemed focused elsewhere.

"I'll see about rooms," he said, wrapping the horses' reins around the log post and leading Lacey through the lavish doors.

Rooms, she thought. Not room. He didn't intend to share another night with her. He obviously intended to try to salvage what was left of her reputation, but she'd have preferred spending what time they had left with him. Stone was still a problem, and until she found a way to stop him she couldn't begin to plan a future.

Was Garreth now wishing they hadn't shared their passion? Did he have regrets he wasn't telling her about? Or had the one regret he'd admitted to, that he had no means to support her, continued to weigh on his mind, causing his doleful mood?

She wished she could assure him it didn't matter to her. And the truth was, to her it didn't. But it would matter greatly to the well-being of her mother and brother. She'd tried to hide her doubts about the future, but they remained beneath the surface, gnawing at her happiness. How would she rid her family of Stone's dark cloud of disaster without the money she needed to pay off the loan on Emerald Oaks?

Four months ago she couldn't imagine moving from Emerald Oaks. A month ago she still thought marriage to Sebastian was the only way to secure their future. Nothing had changed. She had told Garreth they had this time together, and that it would be enough. But that was a lie. For now she couldn't imagine her life without him. And their prospects weren't rosy, the way she'd pretended while in his arms.

The lobby of the hotel was decorated in polished gilt and crimson velvet. High-backed chairs with matching tea tables sat in clusters, elegant ladies and gentlemen seated around them. They looked up as Lacey and Garreth entered and Lacey's confidence slipped another notch. Noses twitched and turned up and eyes quickly glanced away.

"May I help you?" she heard the man behind the desk ask. She turned toward him and saw the look of disdain he cast them both. Garreth must have seen the expression on the clerk's face, and his tone turned harsh.

"The lady and I will require rooms for the night," he announced.

The clerk didn't even pretend to look at the register open before him. He sniffed and tugged the corners of his brocade vest down.

"I'm afraid we have no vacancies."

"Look, you little weasel—"

"Garreth, let's just go. We can get a room somewhere else. It's not important."

Shaking off Lacey's hand, Garreth reached across the desk and seized the man by his shirtfront. "The lady," he ground out, "would like a room and a bath. Now. I suggest you find a vacancy."

The man looked scared witless, but he tipped

his chin up another notch. "I told you, we are full up. It is Mardi Gras, you know."

Lacey clutched Garreth's elbow once more and tugged. "Garreth, he's right. Please let him go." She glanced around and saw all the eyes in the lobby trained on them. She tugged harder. "Please," she said.

Garreth let the man go. The clerk stumbled back and swallowed, tugging harder on the vest. The prominent Adam's apple in his throat jumped and quivered. "Garreth, let's go," Lacey pleaded.

"Wait," Garreth said, leaning toward the man. The clerk stepped back nervously. "We're looking for a man and woman. They would have checked in sometime last night." He went on to describe Sebastian, and the clerk turned the register toward him.

"No one here like that. I told you, we're booked up. Have been for months. *No one* can get a room here during Mardi Gras unless they reserved a room in advance."

Garreth look down the row of names in the register, then, feeling remorse for his rough treatment of the man, pulled a coin from his pocket and tossed it on the counter. "Thanks," he mumbled.

He turned and Lacey followed him out of the hotel. They walked the horses down the street to the next hotel, and the next. After four stops it was apparent they weren't going to get a room for the night. Every available space was taken with revelers. And no one had rented a room to

anyone matching Sebastian's description or using his name. They wandered on, past the stylish
hotels and inns to the not-so-stylish rooming
houses. As they trudged on Garreth's mood
blackened.

Lacey wished there was something she could
do to assure him she wasn't regretting their decision, or blaming him for his failure to secure
them accomodations. But she suspected bringing the subject up would only convince him she'd
been worried about it herself.

Feeling helpless, she followed him on until
they finally found a room in a small, well-kept
boardinghouse on the riverfront. The proprietress told them she had one room available and
Garreth glanced at Lacey for her approval. She
nodded, a bit apprehensive about having to share
a room after realizing Garreth didn't want to
share a room with her. But there was nothing to
be done about it now.

They went up to the door the woman indicated
and she assured them she'd have a bath sent up
right away for Lacey. Garreth disappeared, only
to return a few minutes later with his saddlebags.
He took out his wallet, removed some bills, and
gave them to Lacey.

"I'll be back later," he said, not bothering to
offer her an explanation. "Order dinner."

He left the room and she wondered if he would
return at all. Her self-confidence was taking a
beating beneath his surliness.

"Stop acting foolish," she chided herself. "He's

probably just going to find a place to stable the horses."

But Lacey couldn't quite get over her trepidation at Garreth's hasty departure. His mood spoke volumes, silent words Lacey couldn't bear to acknowledge.

She stripped down to her small clothes and sat on the bed to wait for the owner of the boarding-house to bring up the promised bath. That would surely make her feel better, she thought. After all, she didn't feel desirable in the travel-worn surah. How could she expect Garreth to be interested in her in such an outfit?

The woman brought up the hip tub, followed by several pitchers of steaming water. Lacey rinsed her hair and scrubbed her body until the water grew cold and gooseflesh pebbled her skin. She stepped from the bath and dried herself on the thick cotton towel provided, wishing she had a pretty nightgown to don before Garreth returned. They might not be married, but she felt like a nervous bride nevertheless.

A knock on the door had her scanning the room for something to wear. "Just a minute," she called, her heart pounding furiously in her chest.

Finally grabbing her wrinkled skirt and jacket, the only clothing she had, she quickly tugged them on. She fumbled with the ivory buttons on the jacket, restarting when she found she'd mismatched the holes.

"It's just me, honey," the old woman called. "I've brought your dinner."

Forgetting the jacket in her disappointment, Lacey opened the door.

Mrs. Leon held a tray filled to the edges with food. "I've brought you some pastries and meat. After Fat Tuesday they'll be scarce until Lent is over. I hope you enjoy them."

Lacey accepted the tray. "Thank you, but my, um—my husband hasn't returned yet."

"Oh, that's for you. Your man said as how he wouldn't be back to eat with you. Thought he must've told you, but he did leave in a rush. Didn't even bother to stable his horse out back. Did ask me to bring you this, though." She handed Lacey a plain white cotton nightgown, two sizes too large, but clean.

"Thank you, I appreciate this. You have stables here?" she couldn't help asking, though her heart told her she didn't want to hear the answer.

"Sure. And good ones too, no smelly place here."

"Did my—did Mr. Armstrong say anything else?"

Lacey hated having to ask a stranger for information about Garreth, and some of the commiseration she'd felt for his mood was replaced by a touch of irritation.

The woman eyed her curiously, as Lacey had suspected she would. "Not a word," she said, obviously inquisitive and interested in what she perceived as a rift between the couple.

Lacey nodded and pretended to eye the contents of the tray. "Well, thank you. This looks delicious."

The woman, knowing she'd been dismissed, backed out of the room. Lacey set the tray and nightgown aside and went to the window. Outside, the merriment of Mardi Gras was still going strong. She knew from past experience that the revelry wouldn't end until midnight on Fat Tuesday, when Ash Wednesday would bring a halt to the celebrating and start the abstinence of Lent.

They would have to be back in Mobile by midnight, Tuesday night, for the unmasking. She and Garreth would be crowned king and queen of Mardi Gras. She and Sebastian had planned to announce their engagement at the end of the festivities. So much had changed in so short a time, she couldn't seem to think straight. But one thought resounded clearly through her mind, settling with a painful certainty in her heart.

Garreth had left her at the boardinghouse alone. Without a word of where he was going or when he'd be back. Or even, she realized, if he would be back.

Chapter Nineteen

Snuggling deeper into the blankets, Lacey squeezed her eyes tight and tried to ignore the stream of sunlight coming in through the opening in the curtains. But the rosy glow soon turned to the yellow flash of dawn and she forced her gravelly eyes open.

After quickly scanning the room in an attempt to orient herself, her gaze focused on the sleeping figure draped across the oversize armchair by the window. Immediately she came wide awake.

Garreth! When had he come in? Why hadn't she heard him? And why was he sleeping in the chair?

The answer to the last question seemed painfully obvious and she crept from the bed on silent feet. She stripped off the borrowed nightgown and hurriedly dressed in the hopelessly wrinkled riding habit, carefully watching Garreth in case he should waken. He didn't. Apparently he'd been out late last night.

Lacey's ire blossomed and as she combed out her hair and donned her ruined slippers her anger got the better of her and she began to purposely make noise in an effort to stir him from his sleep.

Her ploy soon worked. Garreth stretched and came awake with a confused frown. As his eyes met hers, the frown deepened, fueling the fire of her displeasure.

"Is something troubling you, or are you always this cranky in the mornings?"

Lacey barely resisted the urge to throw the comb at him. "Oh, were you out late?" she said acidly. "I hadn't noticed. Tell me, what exactly were you doing until the early hours of this morning?"

He shot her a dazed glance and rubbed his hands over the stubble of his beard. The raspy sound sent her senses into a frenzy of awareness and she turned away quickly so he wouldn't see the longing on her face. She ached to wake in his arms again, to reach over and touch the rough surface of his jaw first thing in the morning. To feel the scratch of his beard on her cheeks as he plied her with kisses.

A knot formed in her stomach and she pressed her hands to her middle to still the pang of distress.

"I thought you said you didn't notice how late I was out?"

Lacey flushed and slammed the comb down on the solid oak of the dressing table. "I didn't," she lied.

He arched an eyebrow in her direction and then looked away. "We'll have breakfast and then start for home," he said.

"Home? After coming all this way? What about Sebastian?"

"Sebastian is the reason I was out so late. I was trying to locate him."

"Why didn't you tell me? I would have gone with you."

"Because some of the places I went to you have no business seeing. I checked every hotel in the city, but I visited every gaming house and saloon, too. If he's here, he's made himself scarce. We've got to catch the morning train if we hope to get back in time for tonight's unveiling."

The wood of the chair groaned as he pushed out of it. He went to the washstand and poured the icy water into the bowl.

Lacey heard his gasp as the cold liquid hit his face and she realized for the first time the chill that pervaded the room. Why hadn't she noticed it before? Because Garreth's presence alone could warm her?

She saw him glance at her again. His cheeks were red from the cold and she couldn't stop the surge of pleasure his dishevelment brought her. As he stared at her she didn't bother to hide her longing. She needed him, his understanding. She wished there were some way she could confide in him about Stone, but Stone was her problem and she alone would have to solve it.

Still, she needed Garreth's reassurance that he wasn't regretting what had happened between them. And maybe he could reassure her as well, she thought, fighting her own demons of dilemma.

Garreth's attitude was undermining her courage, making her more and more uncertain. His frame of mind only gave her own fears room to grow.

The small niggling of uncertainty she'd felt after they made love had taken root in his hesitancy and was choking off all the beautiful hopes she'd allowed herself to consider possible.

And she was damned mad about that, now that she thought about it. What they had shared should have been beautiful and special, and should have had the power to overcome all the problems standing between them. Again, Stone had robbed her of the tenderest of moments. His threats had stolen her chance to bask in the warmth of Garreth's love and absorb the magic of what they'd shared.

Glancing across the room, she saw him stomping his feet into his boots. Obviously that was not to be, and she couldn't even tell him why.

"What's the matter? What are you looking at?"

She hadn't realized she was staring at him, and she turned back to the cheap mirror. "Nothing," she said, watching his reflection in the wavering glass as his eyebrow rose another notch.

He continued to ready himself to leave and she set aside the comb she'd found in his saddlebags last night and went to the window.

Outside pockets of revelers still drifted by, some early risers, others left over from the night before. She pushed aside the lacy curtain of inexpensive cotton weave and watched the costumed people wander by.

Garreth watched Lacey's stiff back for a long moment, then returned to dressing. What could he say to her? He could see she was confused by his attitude, but he couldn't find the words that would reassure her. How could he? He had no more to offer her now than he had the first day they met. In fact, he had less.

What had possessed him to take her in that cabin as if she belonged to him? She didn't belong to him. She would belong to Sebastian if he could find that fool before he ruined his own life. And Garreth was tied to Edith Bishop as surely as if they'd already spoken their wedding vows. Garreth would bet his last dollar Bishop wouldn't let him out of that arrangement without a scandal the likes of which Mobile had never seen.

And with the man's money to back him up, Bishop could ruin what little hope Garreth still held for the future.

He loved Lacey; he wanted the best for her. Loving him was the worst thing she could do. And she'd all but said marrying him would destroy her life.

But what choice would she have now? He'd taken the choice away from her when he'd taken her in the cabin. They would have to marry soon, no matter the consequences to any of them.

And as happy as that thought made him, he knew she would suffer for it. Her family would suffer for it. And soon enough she'd realize his selfishness in making her his own had cost her everything she held dear. And she'd grow to resent him, maybe even hate him for it.

And God help him, even knowing all that, he couldn't stop the joy he felt in his heart to know she'd soon be his forever.

A man in the garb of a nobleman from the last century, a woman decked out like a Moorish princess. Another jester, or perhaps the same one they'd seen when they first arrived. A shiek's harem girl. A man and woman in dark cloaks dressed as—

Lacey leaned closer to the window, rubbing away the condensation caused by the cold combined with the early morning dew. A dark cloak. A man in a top hat. Neither in costume, she noticed suddenly.

"Garreth," she hissed, still not believing her eyes. He didn't answer and she tapped the glass anxiously.

"Garreth," she called, louder this time.

He hurried to her side. "What is it?"

"Over there." She pointed as the couple quickly crossed the street, the man's hand gripping the woman's elbow as they stepped up onto the walkway flanking the river's edge.

"Is that...?"

"Sebastian," he shouted, grasping Lacey's hand. "Let's go."

They quickly collected their small amount of belongings and Garreth tossed enough money on the bed to cover their stay. Down the back stairs they flew, the saddlebag draped over Garreth's shoulder and Lacey's hand still gripped in his.

Bitter cold air hit them as they pushed through the door and stumbled into the alley behind the boardinghouse.

"This way," he said, already circling the brick building and darting into the street, heading in the direction Sebastian had gone.

Lacey was thankful for Garreth's hand, which spurred her on and lent her a measure of support. She quickly became winded trying to keep up with his pace, but she didn't slow down.

They gained the walkway, both searching the path ahead for any sign of the other couple. Trees, as well as other strollers, blocked their view. They rushed on.

Garreth rounded a bend and Lacey decided she would have to stop for a moment. She pulled her hand free of his grasp and opened her mouth to tell him she couldn't go on any farther. But Garreth's cry of triumph spurred her on.

They spotted the couple leaving the path and darting through the grass of an open field. Hand in hand, Lacey and Garreth followed.

Nothing obstructed their view now and they slowed their pace a moment to catch their wind. Dampness soon seeped through the thin satin of Lacey's slippers, and her feet grew chilled.

Across another street and down an alley they pursued their quarry.

Through the French Quarter, around stands smelling of ripe vegetables and raw meat. They pushed past the vendors setting up their wares, ignoring their beckoning calls.

Garreth rounded another corner and collided with a quadroon carrying a basket of flowers on her head. The basket tilted, spilling the buds onto the bricked alley. Hastily, Garreth and Lacey gathered the flowers and assisted the woman in putting them back in her basket. A furious pout turned down the corners of the woman's mouth until Garreth dug deep in his pocket and drew out a coin.

"Sorry for the trouble," he called, already pulling Lacey away up the alley. The woman went back to hawking her blossoms and Lacey and Garreth raced toward the adjoining street.

"Damn," Garreth cursed, searching the empty street.

Lacey rested against the stone of the building nearest them and struggled to catch her breath.

"I think we lost them."

Glancing around, Lacey saw a flash of black fabric disappearing around another corner. Still winded, she tapped Garreth's arm and pointed.

"Come on."

Letting Garreth lead her on, Lacey followed. Up Burgundy Street to Bourbon Street and across to St. Charles. Every time they thought they'd lost the couple, one or the other of them would spot them again and the chase would resume.

Time after time Lacey wondered why they were racing through the streets of New Orleans after a couple who obviously didn't want to be found. But she knew Garreth's concern for Sebastian drove him on, and she'd all but begged to come along. She couldn't cause him to lose the trail after fate had graced them with such a timely sighting.

On St. Charles they were overrun by a group of costumed revelers very much into their cups from the night before and looking for another party. Lacey watched as Garreth was swallowed up by the crowd, shouting her name as their hands were ripped apart and each was tossed in a different direction.

"Garreth," she called, buffetted to and fro by the carousers. One young man in the costume of a Scottish clansman took her in his arms and began to dance her along the street. Lacey tried to push him away, but the youth was caught up in the merriment and wouldn't be deterred.

"Hey, pretty lady. Want to know what's beneath me kilt?" he drawled, his accent almost as bad as his proposition.

Lacey gasped and stomped his toe as hard as she could with the ineffectual slippers. He threw back his head and laughed, gathering her against his chest and lifting her feet off the ground. She screamed, batting him with her fists as she shouted frantically for Garreth.

The pseudo-Scot twirled her in circles until she

felt as drunk as he obviously was.

"Put me down, you idiot," she yelled, pounding the top of his head and knocking his flat hat askew.

Suddenly she felt a strong arm encircle her middle from behind, and a massive fist shot past her cheek to connect with the Scot's jaw. The man's grip faltered and Garreth turned with Lacey in his grasp to rush through the crowd, her feet swinging inches from the ground.

When they cleared the group and reached the safety of the deserted corner, Garreth finally set her on her feet.

"Couldn't you resist dancing just this once?" he said, unable to refrain from teasing her.

"Very funny," she shot back icily, straightening her mussed clothes where the men had tugged her back and forth like a pulley bone.

"This way."

With no more warning than that, he took off across the street and down another alley. Lacey followed, now fearful of being abducted again if she should lag behind.

The couple led them up Canal Street to an alley in back of several fine town houses. The gardens were enclosed with brick walls, and a black wrought-iron gate led to each individual residence.

The two pushed open the second gate they came to and hurried through the brick enclosure to the garden.

Fearing they might disappear yet again, Garreth and Lacey rushed forward through the gate and plowed into the backs of the couple.

Startled from their embrace, the couple turned to face Lacey and Garreth.

"Garreth!"

"Sebastian!"

"Who is that?" the woman in the cloak asked, her thick accent making it sound like *dat*, instead of *that*.

"Who are we?" Garreth said, his words coming between pants for air. "Who are you?"

Sebastian stared as though seeing a ghost, his dark eyes darting between Garreth and Lacey. His arm went around the girl and her hood fell back, revealing blue-black hair and olive skin.

Her wide brown eyes closely inspected the intruders, a spark of fear and anxiety flashing in their depths. She shrank against Sebastian's side and he drew her protectively closer.

Lacey, longing to bend double in an effort to catch her breath, settled for clutching the stitch in her side and silently watching the byplay.

"Garreth, Lacey, what are you doing here? How did you find us?"

"It wasn't easy," Garreth said, anger now tinging his voice. Impatiently, he stepped forward. "We've been through hell looking for you. What the devil did you think you were doing disappearing that way?"

Sebastian didn't answer and after a moment Garreth muttered a curse.

"I suppose I can guess who this is," he said. "Do you realize what you're doing?"

"This," Sebastian said, seeming to snap out of

the surprised daze which had held him silent, "is Pascale. And yes, I know perfectly well what I have done."

"Have done?" Garreth's tone darkened.

Sebastian straightened and gathered the beautiful girl to him. "Yes, it's done." He cast an apologetic look toward Lacey, his expression pleading for her understanding. She couldn't fault his deeds, and so she offered him a small smile in return.

"Garreth, Lacey, I would like you to meet Pascale Avery. My wife."

Chapter Twenty

Garreth's curse took them all by surprise and they turned to stare at him. He seemed to collect himself and apologized.

"What are you two doing here?" Sebastian asked again.

Pascale seemed more confused than anyone, and her brown, doelike eyes continued to dart nervously around the small group.

"We came to stop you from making the biggest mistake of your life," Garreth said. He saw the way Pascale's face tightened with hurt, Sebastian's with anger. His tone softened. "Obviously we're too late."

"Damned right you are," Sebastian ground out. "Not that you could have changed my mind if you had arrived earlier."

He turned to Lacey and his dark eyes softened.

"I'm sorry, Lacey. I didn't intentionally mislead you. I really tried to forget Pascale, to go along with my parents' wishes. But I would have made both our lives miserable if I'd married you, I know that now. I love Pascale."

Lacey took his hand and smiled at them both. "It's all right," she assured him. "I understand. You did the right thing."

Garreth groaned and she turned to look up at him.

"We're supposed to convince him not to ruin his future," he said. "And here you are encouraging him."

"He's married her, Garreth. They're in love."

Her anger finally got the better of her. Couldn't he see, even now, that love was the most important thing? Not money, or position, or trying to please someone else. Love was all that mattered. Or at least it should be. It would have been for her, if not for Thaddeus Stone and his dire threats. If not for that she'd have gladly been a pauper, as long as she could be with Garreth.

"It can be annulled."

Three gasps met Garreth's bald statement and he had the grace to look sheepish.

"Maybe we should discuss this privately," he added.

Sebastian glanced around at the deserted garden. His eyebrow raised in question.

"You and I," Garreth clarified.

"That won't be necessary. Anything you could say I've already considered. Look, I know what you're trying to do and I appreciate your concern. Especially after the rotten way I've behaved lately. Hell, for most of our lives. But I've finally decided to grow up, Garreth. I'm making my own decisions now. And I feel great."

"How will you feel when your parents cut you off without a cent?"

Sebastian didn't look worried or alarmed. In fact, he seemed blissfully happy. "I don't think they'll do that," he said, holding up his hand when Garreth opened his mouth to protest. "But if they do, we'll live with it. Right, Pascale?"

"Then why were you running through the streets of New Orleans like the devil himself was on your tails?"

The couple exchanged looks of chagrin; then Sebastian spoke. "Pascale is staying with relatives here. I sneaked her out last night and we found a justice to marry us. We were trying to get her back before her aunt wakes up so we can tell her the news before she notices Pascale is missing and sends up an alarm."

"Then it's final. You're truly married."

The import of Garreth's question didn't go unnoticed. Sebastian nodded proudly. "We are truly married. There is no question of an annulment."

"I still don't understand," Garreth said. "You seemed furious when you went after that carriage. How did you come to this?"

Sebastian motioned them toward a white, wrought-iron lawn set and the four sat in chairs around the small table.

"Our relationship progressed while I was up-river at the plantation checking on things for Father. When Pascale's father notified my parents of what he termed our infatuation, they were furious. I was ordered to Springhill and Pascale was sent here."

He gripped her hand tightly in his and smiled at her. "But her cousin has been helping her and he brought her to Mobile to try to talk to me. I thought it was useless to see her again, knowing Mother and Father would never agree to a match between us. And I didn't think I had the courage to stand up to them. But Pascale wouldn't give up."

Lacey watched the love play between the two and her gaze went longingly to Garreth. How could he remain unaffected with such strong emotions flashing like electrical currents around them?

"I had to speak with Sebastian one more time," Pascale said, finally adding her bit to the story of the star-crossed lovers. "When I saw him with you," she said, looking at Lacey, "I thought my life would end."

Lacey felt ashamed that she'd played a part in the girl's pain, but she tried to tell herself she couldn't have known at the time.

"I knew Pascale was following me. I'd finally had enough that day with the horses. I chased her, determined to end things once and for all. Then she told me the most wonderful news."

Again they shared a knowing smile and Sebastian pressed a kiss to her forehead.

"I'm going to be a father, Garreth."

Lacey felt the breath rush out of her lungs so

fast her head spun dizzily. She shot a startled glance at Garreth and saw the color drain from his face.

"Oh, my God."

The realization of what they'd almost done shook Lacey to her very core. What if she and Sebastian had gone through with their wedding before he spoke to Pascale? What if he'd never known about the baby? What would have happened to Pascale?

"Don't look so horrified." Sebastian laughed. "I'm thrilled. And so is Pascale."

"A baby." Lacey's world tilted, righted itself, then settled into place. Suddenly a bright smile lit her face. "A baby!"

Three faces lit with happy grins. One remained solemn.

"I knew then that if I was ever going to grow up, it had to be soon. Pascale was counting on me. Our child needed me." His voice grew husky, his eyes soft. "No one has ever needed me before, not like this. I knew I couldn't let them down."

"I hate to be the one to break up the celebration, but what about money?" Garreth said, disrupting the festive mood which had enthralled the others.

Sebastian shrugged. "I think Mother will reconsider her decision when she learns she is finally going to be a grandmother. Hopefully she will accept Pascale as my wife and come to love her as much as I do. If not"—he shrugged—"then I will find work."

"Work?" Garreth laughed dryly. "What do you know about work?"

Lacey's brow furrowed and she resisted the urge to punch Garreth in the arm. How could he continue to be such a cynic in the face of so much love?

"Pascale's cousin has offered me a job in his stockyards. I was always good at mathematics in school and he needs someone to help with the accounts."

A spark of admiration lit in Garreth's eyes, but he quickly doused it. But not before Lacey finally guessed what he'd been doing. By making Sebastian defend his decision, he was showing his friend every possible difficulty and forcing him to face the truth. Never one for large doses of reality, Sebastian would have to swallow a lifetime's worth in one big gulp. Garreth was making sure he was ready for it.

Lacey settled back, content to watch the two spar now that she thought she understood his plan.

"I see," Garreth said slowly, folding his hands in his lap. "And what if your mother does change her mind and accepts Pascale? You'll go back to Mobile and your old ways, I assume."

Pascale met Lacey's eyes and the women exchanged secretive smiles. Now both knew what was going on with the old friends.

"No. I plan to take Pascale back upriver to the plantation. She wants to be near her father, and my father has wanted me to take over the plantation for some time. Mobile society will just have to get along without me from now on."

"Well, damned if you haven't convinced me," Garreth said, pushing to his feet. "But don't expect me to be the one to tell Anna. I plan on leaving town before that auspicious event."

Sebastian laughed and clasped his friend's hand. "I plan on telling Mother just as soon as possible. In fact, we'll travel back with you two if you can wait while we break the news to Pascale's aunt and pack her bag."

Garreth nodded, and Sebastian led Pascale up the path through the garden to the double French doors at the rear of the house. They disappeared inside and Garreth turned on his heel and began to pace the small clearing.

"Now what's the matter?" Lacey asked, wondering how it was possible the beautiful story hadn't moved him at all. She felt all warm and fuzzy inside and she longed to throw herself into his arms and tell him everything would likewise work out for them.

"I'm afraid he's fooling himself. Anna will never accept a Cajun daughter-in-law, especially one who is already expanding. I can just imagine the things she'll have to say about that."

"But they're so happy, Garreth. Can't you just forget the bad for a moment and look at the good? They're in love. And just maybe," she said, speaking of more than Sebastian and Pascale now, "maybe, love *can* conquer all."

He turned to face her then and she saw the pain in his eyes. His hands came up as though to touch her, then fell to his sides. A harshness swept his features.

"If only it were that simple," he said, returning to his pacing.

They left New Orleans before the day's activities could hamper their progress. As they put the city behind them they could hear the sounds of the festivities getting under way once more.

Today was Tuesday. The gala would continue throughout the day, growing bawdier and more raucous until the stroke of midnight, when all masks would be removed and the first day of Lent would begin.

Lacey and Garreth had 16 hours left to reach Mobile in time for the crowning of the king and queen of Mardi Gras.

Sebastian and Pascale accompanied them back to Mobile on the morning train after breaking the news of their marriage to Pascale's aunt.

Lacey had no time to talk privately with Garreth, but she could see his despondency growing the closer they got to Mobile. He had withdrawn from her completely and she vacillated between irritation at his silence and hurt at his seeming desertion.

They had made love. Yet he didn't seem to remember the wonderment they'd shared. Not the way she did, with her heart full to bursting and her arms aching to hold him once more, in case it should be the last time.

Instead he seemed troubled by her presence. Bothered by the memories.

By the time they all reached Mobile her temper was short and her mood as black as Garreth's. They went to Garreth's office, which was closed for Mardi Gras. It was the closest place they could rest and decide how best to proceed, and it was private.

"I'll send word to Francie that we're back and see how she's doing. I'll arrange for a carriage and someone to bring you something fresh to change into," he told Lacey matter-of-factly. "You two are on your own."

"We thought we'd rest a bit and then go and see my parents," Sebastian said. "Pascale could use some sleep before we face Mother with our news."

"You're welcome to use my rooms upstairs," Garreth offered. "I won't be needing them."

He started to leave, leaving a flustered trio behind. Sebastian called out to him and he turned in the doorway.

"Aren't you forgetting something?" he asked, a wicked grin tipping his lips.

Garreth looked displeased with the delay and scowled. "What is it?"

"This." Sebastian reached into his coat and withdrew an envelope. Garreth took it, scanning the name written on the front.

"The proof you need to claim the money from the wager. I've written the solicitor that I'm legally married and therefore concede the bet. I've also instructed him to add the additional amount we discussed earlier. You're wealthy once more, old man."

Garreth stood, poised but unmoving. Could he take Sebastian's money? With it he could either save Armstrong Shipping, or Emerald Oaks. Not both. He'd still have to choose.

Without regret, he crushed the fine linen stationery. He'd meant it when he told Lacey they'd have to make it on their own. He'd been willing to compromise. Hell, he'd been willing to give up his business. But she hadn't been willing to give up her home.

His honor refused to let him turn his back on her after they'd made love. Even when she made it clear what he could offer would never be enough. But he still had pride, dammit. He'd get her on his own or he wouldn't do it at all.

His eyes came up to meet Sebastian's and they were dark with anger.

"Forget it," he said, balling the envelope up with one fist and tossing it back at his friend. "I don't want your money. Besides, if you'd waited another day you'd have won that cursed bet."

Lacey's attention, which had held fast on the envelope until then, flew to Garreth. What was he doing? Why was he refusing the money? Had he gone mad?

"What do you mean?" Sebastian asked, his gaze going from the ball of paper on the floor to Garreth's stony face.

"I mean Lacey and I will be married. The sooner the better," he said.

Lacey gasped. Sebastian's eyes widened. Pascale looked confused as she sat in the chair beside Gramb's desk.

"What?" Lacey murmured, not believing her ears.

"Well," Sebastian said, ignoring Lacey's shock, seemingly in an effort to lessen her embarrassment, "you'll need the money even more then."

"No, we won't. We'll make it on our own, or we won't make it. It was a stupid wager and we both needed the seats of our trousers worn out for throwing away that much money. Besides, you and Pascale will need it as much as we will."

"But, Garreth—" Lacey began.

Sebastian held up his hands. "What do you suggest? You won the bet, fair and square."

"We'll go to the solicitor together and collect the money. Then each of us will take back the amount we wagered and hopefully never be so foolish again." That was the only answer. His share alone wouldn't help their situation much, but it was the only fair thing to do. He'd just have to make Lacey understand.

"Let's go," Sebastian said, no longer childish enough to ignore reason when it was presented to him. He knew he and Pascale might very well find themselves in a position to use a sizable amount of cash.

"Later," Garreth said. "I have something else to take care of first."

"What could be more important than saving your company? Wasn't that what you wanted all along?"

Garreth's gaze slid to Lacey. Her eyes filled with tears as the tenderness and longing she felt were momentarily mirrored there. He did care for her; she could read the love on his face. Then why was he behaving so strangely? she wondered. Why was he treating her with the coolest disdain?

"Maybe at first that was all that mattered. But not anymore," Garreth said cryptically. He turned and left the room without a word of explanation.

Chapter Twenty-one

All the way to the Bishop house Garreth fumed. His lust, his passion for Lacey had ruined her hopes of an advantageous marriage. Even without Sebastian she could have found no less than a dozen men with more to offer her than he.

But that was not to be now. He'd made sure of that when he made love to her in the cabin. And the worst part was, he couldn't find an ounce of regret within himself. All the while he cursed himself for bringing her down on a level with him, he reveled in the knowledge that soon he would make her his wife. One way or another.

If Bishop didn't call him out when he told the man the news.

He rode up to the house still uncertain what he'd say. How could he tell the man he'd decided, rather at the eleventh hour, not to marry his daughter?

As he drew up to the town house, his stomach dropped another notch. It seemed a party was going on, something he should have considered, as this was the last day of Mardi Gras.

Glancing down at his travel-worn suit, he wished he'd taken time to change and bathe before facing Bishop.

But he'd had a single thought in mind and that had been to dissolve the arrangement with Edith Bishop as soon as possible and get back to Lacey. He had to convince her to marry him before she had time to consider the alternatives and come up with another crazy scheme.

The door was answered by a servant in full purple livery. Garreth eyed the elaborately outfitted man, hoping the costume was part of the festivities, but, knowing the Bishops, not quite certain.

"Garreth Armstrong to see Mr. Bishop," he said, feeling more than a little foolish.

The man bowed, then led Garreth to a paneled study and left him there. Garreth paced the small dark room like a caged tiger until he heard the knob rattle and turned to face Bishop.

"I was wondering where you'd gotten off to," Bishop said. "Did you forget about the soiree?"

"Yes, I'm afraid I did. You see, sir, something has come up."

"Has it now? Well, let me pour you a shot of whiskey and you can tell me all about it. I assume that's why you're here now, looking like something a rat wouldn't drag back to his hole."

Garreth ran his hand over the stubble on his cheek. He'd forgotten how disreputable he must look. Besides his clothes, he hadn't shaved in over two days.

He tried to think of a delicate way to break the news to Bishop, but nothing came to mind. Obviously this was not going to be a congenial conversation, no matter how he chose his words.

"I can't marry your daughter," he finally blurted, seeing no purpose in postponing the inevitable battle.

Bishop paused in the middle of pouring whiskey into two identical crystal tumblers. Slowly he turned to face the younger man.

"What did you say?"

Garreth saw the shock and rage cross the man's face and he swallowed hard. The money from the wager would never be enough to save Armstrong Shipping if Bishop set out to ruin him. And Garreth damned well knew the man had the power to do it.

"I'm sorry. An engagement between Edith and myself is no longer possible."

"You're already engaged. Or have you forgotten?"

"No sir, I haven't. And I wouldn't do this at such a late date if there were any other way."

"I see." Bishop continued pouring the drinks and handed one to Garreth. After a moment he narrowed his eyes and stared at Garreth.

"You've gotten some girl in trouble? Is that it?"

Fury nearly overtook Garreth, and he felt his

hand tighten on the fragile glass of the tumbler. He met Bishop's hard gaze, but refused to answer.

"Well, at least you're man enough to make an attempt at chivalry. Drink up."

Garreth eyed the amber liquid in the glass and then swallowed it in a hasty gulp.

"I assume you're going to let Edith break the engagement. She'll say she's changed her mind. Found someone more suitable."

Bishop's words were not a question. Garreth nodded, knowing the least he could do would be to let Edith Bishop save face.

"It'll take at least a week. I expect your plans, whatever they are, can be postponed that long?"

Garreth didn't want to wait a week to marry Lacey. He wanted her for his wife as soon as possible. But his honor demanded he go along with Bishop. He nodded.

"Good. I also assume your plans will not interfere with the Indies shipment."

Garreth froze, his glass halfway to his lips. "Sir?"

Bishop took his glass and refilled it. He handed it back to Garreth.

"The jade deal. Your troubles won't affect our business, will they?"

"Do you mean," Garreth said, a high-pitched tone of disbelief in his voice, "that you still want me for the jade deal?"

"Of course I want you. I chose you for that job because you were the best man for it. You still are. I might be accused of being a lummox but

I've never been mistaken for a fool."

"No, sir," Garreth stammered, still unable to believe his good fortune. The money from the wager would keep him going until summer. If everything went according to schedule the jade deal would secure their future. There might even be enough left to pay off the mortgage on Emerald Oaks.

How could this be happening, just when he'd thought things were as bad as they could get?

"You might be the biggest toad in the puddle, boy. But you weren't my only pick. With my money Edith won't have any trouble replacing you. I have to tell you, now that it won't make no nevermind, you never were her style."

"Sir?"

"My girl, she's a fun-loving little thing. Likes parties and gossip. You don't mind my saying so, you're somewhat dull."

Garreth felt a lightness in his chest he didn't immediately recognize. But it blossomed until he felt full of it, and the unaccustomed happiness spilled out onto his face in the shape of a huge grin.

"Yes sir, I can see where I might be too serious for someone like Edith. I'm glad to know she won't be too disappointed that our engagement is off."

"My little girl is never disappointed, Mr. Armstrong. I see to that."

"Thank you, Mr. Bishop. I'll go now."

Bishop showed Garreth to the door. They had

an understanding, and Garreth would hold to it
no matter how difficult it would be to keep from
shouting his joy from the rooftops of Mobile. He
was free to marry Lacey, and he wasn't poor!

"What do you mean she's already gone? I told
her I'd send word to Francie and arrange for a
carriage."

Sebastian sipped his drink and motioned for
Garreth to lower his voice. Pascale was sleeping
in Garreth's room upstairs, worn out from the
hasty trip to Mobile.

"You weren't exactly in danger of charming her
out of her stockings, you know. She decided not
to wait until you'd returned from your mysterious errand. I hailed her a cab and she left right
after you did."

"Damnation, everything is finally falling into
place and she has to run out on me."

"Who ran out on whom, old man?" Sebastian
asked, clapping Garreth hard on the shoulder.

"I know it must have seemed that way. But I
had to straighten out the mess I'd made with
Bishop. I couldn't marry Lacey until I'd ended
my engagement to the old guy's daughter."

"Edith, huh? Yes, well, I can see where you
might have had trouble convincing the two girls
to share you, handsome though you are."

"Don't joke, Sebastian. Lacey means more to
me than anything in the world. I never would
have thought I could feel this way about a
woman, but I love her. I love her so much I
wanted better for her than I could offer. And it

was tearing me up inside, because I knew I'd keep her with me despite all that."

"That's when you know it's real," Sebastian said, more serious than Garreth had ever seen him. "When nothing else matters except being together."

"Yes, but now everything is finally going good and she's gone."

"What happened with Bishop?"

Garreth told Sebastian how Bishop had taken the news of the broken engagement. Then he went on to add that the jade deal was still on.

"Sounds like a damn fine investment," Sebastian said. "What do you say about taking on another partner?"

"A partner? Who?"

"Me. I never was too keen on that idea of working in the stockyards. Oh, I would do it, if it came to that. But if you invest my share of the wager in the Indies venture, we can both be sitting on top of the pile again by summer's end."

"I thought you hated the shipping business?"

Sebastian laughed. "That was when I was young and stupid."

"Last week?"

This time they both laughed.

"Yeah," Sebastian admitted. "Besides, I didn't hate the business; I was jealous of you because you had something you cared enough about to work for it tirelessly. I never had anything that important in my life. Not until now. What do you say?"

"I say sure. Partner." He held out his hand and

Sebastian shook it; then the two clapped each other on the back and stepped apart.

Garreth's smile died instantly. "What am I going to do about Lacey? She left not knowing how I feel about her. It'll all be worthless if she refuses to marry me now."

"You could always go back to Edith."

"Dammit, Sebastian!"

"I'm joking, for God's sake. Settle down, will you? It isn't as though you'll never see her again. You two will be crowned king and queen of Mardi Gras in less than four hours, if you get yourself ready and get down to the Relief Hall for the ceremony."

"The ball! Good Lord, I'd almost forgotten." He scrubbed his hand over his jaw and began to unbutton his shirt. "I have to get ready."

"Whoa, get ready at your mother's, will you? My bride needs her beauty sleep."

Garreth remembered Pascale was asleep in his room and he refastened the button he'd undone. "Right," he said, grabbing his saddlebags from the top of Gramb's desk and shooting out the office door.

Chapter Twenty-two

The lamps positioned around the massive dance floor had been covered with Japanese lanterns, so a profusion of color reflected off the white walls of the Relief Hall. Candelabras graced every surface in an effort to lend a festive glow to the otherwise plain room.

Lacey fussed with the yards of white satin and lace that made up her elaborate costume. A huge, sun-shaped mask covered her face, feathers and ribbons fanning out in every direction. Francie, still puffy from her bout with the mumps, had insisted on coming for the crowning.

Lacey was glad for the mask, which hid her red-rimmed eyes and the shadows which lay like half-moons under her lower lashes. She scanned the room for any sign of Garreth, cursing her own weakness that she couldn't seem to get him out of her mind.

Her gaze fell on Edith Bishop, in the corner of the ballroom, her attention focused on Marshall Sutherland. She seemed to be flirting. Lacey frowned, pain gripping her heart like a fist. She didn't want to be reminded of Garreth's engagement. Not now, with the memory of their lovemaking still fresh in her mind. It would appear Edith didn't want to remember the entanglement either.

"Francie, what do you suppose that is all about?"

Francie looked over at the couple and shrugged. "I haven't the vaguest idea," she said, her nose already twitching with the scent of a story. "But I'll find out."

She sped away into the crowd, leaving Lacey alone in the center of the room. Gathering her courage—and the fabric of her dress so she could walk—Lacey hurried to the dais where she was to stand. She prayed her trembling legs would hold her and that she wouldn't step on her train before she could get there.

The younger members of the Mystic Society who had been chosen as the court were already on the dais. One of the girls darted forward to capture the frothy bundle of satin and lace, her face all but buried behind the mass.

"What a beautiful dress, miss," the little girl whispered.

For a moment Lacey let herself enjoy the pleasure of the ball. She hadn't attended many pageants, preferring to stay close to Emerald Oaks and her family. This was a first for her. And if it had not been for her apprehension over Garreth's desertion, she knew she would be enthralled with all the pomp and ceremony.

And the gown Francie's mother had commissioned was truly stunning, albeit cumbersome. The sleeves were billowy and full, gathered at the elbow and falling in soft ruffles to her fingertips. The train was decorated with butterflies made up of pearls and rhinestones. The cummerbund waistline was encircled with three strands of perfectly matched seed pearls.

Tears rushed to Lacey's eyes. Her mother and father would have been so proud!

For the first time since her wild trip to New Orleans she let herself consider her family's future. She admitted it looked bleak. The alliance with Sebastian was off, and she could feel no regret at that fact since she'd seen him with Pascale. But their happiness could not alleviate her apprehension.

Immediately following their love-making Garreth had told her he loved her, wanted to marry her. But then he was acting like a maniac earlier, at the office with Sebastian and Pascale. He'd declared that they would be married. But he'd refused Sebastian's offer of money. Money that could have helped them both!

And she still had the problem of Stone to worry about. How was she going to save Emerald Oaks and her mother and Georgie?

At what should have been the most beautiful

moment in her life so far, Lacey realized she had reached her lowest point of despair.

And then she saw Garreth and the tears disappeared. He seemed to be scanning the room, looking for someone. Immediately Lacey's eyes went to the corner where Edith and Marshall Sutherland had been. They were gone. She turned back and gasped. Garreth stood at the bottom of the dais, his eyes fixed on her, wide with wonder.

He leapt the step and rushed to her side.

"You look absolutely ravishing," he whispered, his mouth close to her ear.

Heat surged through her body. Her breath caught in her throat.

"Th-thank you," she finally managed to say.

He took her hand and together they walked to the two high-backed chairs which would serve as their thrones. No expense had been spared to make the night's event the most lavish ever held.

The mayor arrived, his entourage encircling him, and he fought his way past smiling women and hand-clasping men to the dais.

Raising his hands, he struggled to silence the eager crowd. "Ladies and gentlemen," he shouted, barely heard above the din of excited voices. "Please, if I may have your attention."

Lacey tried not to notice the way Garreth continued to hold her hand. She fought to keep her heart from beating out of her chest. A flush of crimson covered her cheeks as the warmth of his touch seeped through her extremities. As he looked at her, she imagined all the doubts and worries which had driven them apart were gone from his features. Only a softness remained, combined with a love glow she knew she might be fabricating in her mind's eye.

Fool, she called herself. He'd left in haste earlier, seemingly eager to be rid of her. Too rushed to even consider his share of money from the wager, or discuss what it would mean to them. Or, indeed, if there was a *them*. She couldn't be sure after his earlier behavior.

How could four hours have made that big a difference in his attitude?

She withdrew her hand, frowning when he turned to her with a wide grin.

"I present to you," the mayor was saying in his best official voice, "the king and queen of Mardi Gras, for the blessed year eighteen hundred and ninety two, Miss Lacey Webster, daughter of Victor and Katrina Webster, and Mr. Garreth Armstrong, only son of Gladys and Wilson Armstrong, of Armstrong Shipping."

The mayor went on to introduce the court, but Lacey barely heard his words as Garreth took her hand and seated her in the chair on the right, himself on the left. She placed her hand on the carved armrest and he placed his hand over hers. She shot him a confused frown, but he only smiled.

The past king and queen stepped onto the dais to pass on their crowns and Lacey was forced to smile and murmur words of thanks, praying it would all soon be over so she could go back to Emerald Oaks and lick her wounds in the temporary security the place offered.

But it was not to be. The mayor announced the first waltz of the evening and Lacey remembered with a shock of dismay that she and Garreth were required to dance the first dance and open the ball.

He seemed too eager as he took her hand and helped her onto the dance floor. His arm went around her, his hand carefully positioned on her waist. She tried to look down, but he softly called her name and she found she couldn't resist looking into his eyes.

"You really do look stunning," he said.

"Thank you," she said stiffly. "You look very handsome yourself."

In fact, he looked scandalously desirable in tights of pale cotton and a jewel-studded jerkin with a silk undershirt and a train equally as long as hers. The butterfly motif was continued on his costume.

The music began and he stepped to the side, leading Lacey around the floor. The crowd encircled them, exclamations of admiration reaching toward the ceiling and filling the room.

They spun together, seemingly in their own world, as the candles wavered and flickered and lent a surrealistic quality to the dance. Maybe it was the bad lighting that made Lacey think she saw desire in Garreth's green-gold eyes. Whatever it was, she caught her breath on a gasp and missed a step.

"Easy, love," he whispered, tightening his hold

and correcting her mistake without missing a beat.

"What the devil do you think you're doing, Garreth Armstrong?" she demanded, suddenly tired of his cat-and-mouse game. First he treated her with the greatest tenderness and passion she'd ever known in her life, making her dream impossible dreams. Then he ignored her as if she were a bad memory he was trying to forget. Now, just when she least expected it, he was tender and loving again. She couldn't bear the uncertainty any longer.

"I'm dancing with my queen, Lacey."

"I'm not *your* queen," she said.

He laughed and waltzed on, seemingly unaffected by her anger.

"Yes, you are, darling. You're my queen for tonight, and for always."

He stared down into her blue eyes, eyes that would never seem less than extraordinary to him if he looked into them a thousand times. He smiled and touched her cheek gently.

"I love you, Lacey. And I hope you'll be more than just my queen. I hope you'll be my wife."

Lacey stopped dancing and for once Garreth didn't cover her misstep. Her eyes misted and she swallowed the lump of emotion lodged in her throat.

"Don't tease, Garreth."

"Tease? Darling, I've never been more serious in my entire life. I love you, Lacey. I need to hear you say you'll share your life with me. Please don't make me wait any longer. I'm desperate."

344

"I don't understand. After we made love you were so cold."

"I was so confused. I wanted to give you everything you needed, but I knew I couldn't. I wanted the best for you, Lacey. Even if the best wasn't me. But I knew at the same time that I'd never be able to let you go. The night I spent in your arms was the most perfect time of my life. And I would have claimed you for my own despite your protests and my obligations to Edith. I had to have you, and I hated myself for the weakness that threatened to hurt you."

"But you were the only one I wanted. Oh, Garreth, I love you. I wanted desperately to accept your proposal right then, in the cabin. But I—I couldn't. I knew I would have to do whatever was necessary to save Emerald Oaks. I know it seemed selfish, but there's more involved in my not wanting to move mother and Georgie to town."

He frowned, his step slowing as he studied her anxious face. "What are you talking about? What else is there?"

She knew she had to tell him. She should have told him the truth right then and there, in the cabin. Despite the trouble it would cause, she could not let him go on thinking she had denied him out of selfishness.

"We were being threatened, Garreth. Thaddeus Stone—"

"Thaddeus Stone? What has that blackguard got to do with anything?"

"Thaddeus Stone is the one who holds the loan on Emerald Oaks. He is using it to get revenge for my mother's rejection of him years ago when they were courting. He means to marry Mother by using her love of Emerald Oaks and her need to stay on there as coercion. And then he plans to send Georgie to an asylum. Oh, Garreth, I don't know what I'm going to do."

"You're not going to do anything. You've worried about this alone long enough. I wish you had told me. I don't know how we would have solved it, but at least you wouldn't have had to deal with it by yourself."

"I should have told you. But I thought Stone was a problem I had to take care of on my own."

"You're not on your own anymore, Lacey. We have each other now." He smiled and tightened his hold on her. "And we've got enough money now to stop Thaddeus Stone."

"But your company—"

"First things first. And the most important item on the docket is helping your family. And putting a stop to Thaddeus Stone, once and for all."

"Garreth," she breathed, her face alive with happiness. "Do you mean it?"

He nodded and took her in his arms. Lacey would have sworn her feet never touched the floor for the rest of the dance. She couldn't remember being so blissfully happy.

Then she remembered Edith, and the joy crashed down around her like a house of cards.

"Oh, Garreth, what about your engagement?"

"What engagement?" he teased.

She frowned and shot a look across the room to the crowd waiting to start the ball. She spotted Edith, again in the company of Marshall.

"Oh, Edith Bishop. Well," he said, twirling her so she could no longer see the woman, "I'm afraid I'm going to be jilted tonight. In fact, I'm afraid nothing short of a quick marriage to a very beautiful society columnist will mend my broken heart."

"She's let you go? Just like that?"

Garreth chuckled and snapped his fingers. "Just like that," he said. "Claims I'm too serious by far."

"Yes," Lacey laughed, her feet floating over the parquet floor once again. "Yes, indeed, you are definitely too serious for Edith Bishop."

"But just right for Lacey Webster, I hope," he said.

"Absolutely perfect," she told him, beaming.

The others crowded onto the dance floor, and Garreth moved closer to Lacey. They danced for what seemed like hours. He refused to let her go, even when Sebastian stepped up to claim a dance.

"Where is your lovely bride?" Garreth asked.

"In the corner with her esteemed mother-in-law," Sebastian bragged slyly.

"I'll be," Garreth said, looking to see Anna Avery and Pascale with their heads together.

"One thing about Mother," Sebastian said. "When she knows she's been defeated she can turn every situation to her advantage. You'd think my marrying Pascale was all her idea from the first. Father is thrilled I'm taking over the plantation, thinks I may have some good in me after all."

"I'm afraid I agree," Garreth taunted his friend. "As much as it grieves me to admit it."

The three laughed and Sebastian took his leave, convinced Garreth had no intention of relinquishing his hold on Lacey.

"I'm so happy for them. I hope everything works out well."

"So do I," Garreth said. "Especially since he's now my business partner."

"Your partner! Garreth, what has been going on in the last four hours?"

"A great deal."

The waltz ended and the tempo picked up. Garreth led Lacey to the edge of the room where tables of fruity punch had been set up. They each accepted a glass from Francie's little sister, who'd been pressed into servitude as a means of getting into the ball.

"How was the parade?" Lacey whispered.

"Fabulous!" Jeannie cried, her eyes dancing with delight. "We came in third place! Or rather, you all did."

They all laughed and Francie swept over to join them. "I've got the goods," she said, motioning toward Edith and Marshall. "But I'm not sure how you're going to feel about this, Garreth." Her earnest expression reminded Lacey that her friend had no clue what was going on around her. For the first time ever.

"It seems Marshall has had a setback," Francie

told them. "Of the financial variety. He's been cozying up to our Edith for some time in case she changed her mind about Garreth. Which it seems—"

"Don't tell me," Lacey said, glancing mischievously at Garreth. "Edith has decided Garreth is not the man for her after all."

Francie stepped back and blinked rapidly. "How did you know that?"

Instead of answering, Lacey leaned in closer. "I've got another scoop for you," she told the startled reporter. "Garreth's broken heart will lead him to marry on the rebound, almost immediately."

The couple exchanged loving looks and Francie giggled with glee. "I knew you two were meant for each other. Oh, I've got to get out of here and start my story. This is going to make the front page." She turned to leave, then whirled around, a wicked smile lighting her face. "I might even sign my own name to this one," she announced.

On her way out the door Francie collided with a harried and winded Gramb. Garreth saw his secretary's flushed face and set aside his cup.

The man easily found Garreth in the crowd, the ridiculously large crown making him a full foot taller than anyone else in the room. Lacey took his hand as she saw his face and read the distress Gramb's appearance had caused.

"What is it?" Garreth demanded, not waiting for the man to come to a full stop or catch his breath.

"You'd better come right away," Gramb said, his voice trembling. "You're never going to believe what has happened."

Lacey and Garreth exchanged startled looks and clasped hands as they rushed out the door behind the frantic secretary.

Chapter Twenty-three

Francie's article about the broken engagement and subsequent attachments didn't make the front page of the *Register* the following morning. But her story of the miraculous return of the *Mirabella* did.

As Garreth and Lacey rushed from the Relief Hall they were met by the captain of the ill-fated ship.

He explained how they'd been buffeted off course during the hurricane and about the damages the vessel had sustained.

"We limped into port where we docked for two months while she was repaired. We sent letters, but since we'd made our delivery and pickup, we knew we'd beat the mail back to Mobile."

"Are you telling me the cargo is undamaged?"

Garreth asked, grasping the man's pea jacket by the collar.

"Yes sir," the captain beamed. "Safe as a babe in its mama's arms, she is. And every hand on board is present and accounted for. Not a single casualty."

Garreth whooped and grabbed the man in a bear hug. They danced a silly jig on the walkway as the other guests of the ball filtered out to see what the commotion was about. All the hands were sent to collect their families, who'd spent the last months grieving for their lost loved ones, and the streets filled with happy revelers.

Sailors danced with socialites. Officials celebrated with shipping clerks in the biggest street party Mobile had ever seen. The flurry of activity went on until dawn despite the arrival of Lent, each person feeling they had special cause to frolic.

Francie frantically scribbled notes as she wound her way through the crowd.

"Knew you were the best man on the bay when it came to shipping," Bishop boasted, passing Garreth and Lacey with a wide grin. Marshall danced by with Edith in tow a moment later, neither noticing the other couple as they stared deep into each other's eyes, rather like lovesick puppies.

"You are my good-luck charm, Lacey Webster," Garreth told her, gripping her about the waist and ducking into an alley where they could share a private moment.

"Am I? You wouldn't have thought either of us

lucky a few months ago," she told him, thinking of the way things had changed in both their lives.

"Ah, but look how wonderful everything turned out. Our lives have gone from disastrous to marvelous. And it all started when you walked boldly into my office with your crazy scheme. Now it seems we can't lose."

Garreth kissed Lacey then, slow and sweet, and she knew she was indeed the luckiest woman in the world. She'd known when she'd gone to see him that day that it would change her life, but she'd had no idea in what way.

Sebastian and Pascale passed the opening of the alley and Garreth called out to them.

"Ho, partner. How're the newlyweds doing?"

"Couldn't be better," Sebastian shouted back. He stopped, grinned at Pascale, and strode over to Garreth.

"Feeling lucky, are you?" Sebastian laughed.

Garreth gazed at Lacey and smiled. "You better believe it."

"How about another wager?"

"What kind of wager?" Garreth asked, narrowing his eyes suspiciously.

Just then Thaddeus Stone appeared and Lacey saw Garreth's expression harden in rage. He nudged Sebastian and motioned him along as he took a step toward the man.

"What are you going to do, Garreth?" Lacey asked, grasping his arm frantically. "We've got the money to pay him now and save Armstrong Shipping. He can't hurt us anymore."

Ignoring Sebastian's look of confusion, Garreth gently removed her hand from his arm and placed a tender kiss on her cheek. "He isn't ever going to hurt anyone like that again," he said.

He and Sebastian stepped into the crowd and Lacey held her breath as she saw them approach the man who'd made her life a living hell the past months.

"Stone," Garreth called.

Stone turned to face the two men, a triumphant look on his face. "Fellows, how about this party," he said, raising his glass in a mock toast.

Garreth stepped toward him, close enough to smell the liquor he'd consumed. His eyes narrowed and his fists clenched at his sides as he thought of how this man had made Lacey suffer.

He smiled at the man and draped his arm around his shoulders.

"Stone, I hear you've graduated from cheating at cards to blackmailing innocent women and children," Garreth said, his tone deceptively calm. His arm tightened around the man's neck and he saw Stone go pale. His eyes widened and he tried to step away. Garreth tightened his hold even more.

"I don't know what you're talking about," the man sputtered.

"Oh, I think you do. I just wanted to let you know I'll be around tomorrow to pay off the loan on Emerald Oaks. If you want my advice, you'll take the money I give you and use it to get the hell out of Mobile. I may not have the money my father once did, but the Armstrong name still counts for something in this town."

"Now just a minute..." Stone mumbled.

Sebastian had caught on to the essence of the conversation and he stepped forward. Grabbing the front of the man's shirt, he shook him once, hard. "I suggest you do as Mr. Armstrong says, Stone. The Avery name carries a lot of weight as well, and we do have the resources to see you suffer for what you've done. You're through in this town. Get out, before we change our minds about letting you off so easily."

Stone stumbled back and both Garreth and Sebastian released him at the same moment. He straightened his vest and tugged the collar of his shirt.

"I don't know what you're talking about," he babbled. "But I planned to leave anyway. Lacey Webster told me she'd get the money to pay me." He sneered at the two men before him. "Judging by your actions here tonight, I can guess how she got it, too."

Garreth and Sebastian exchanged furious looks and Sebastian nodded.

"Be my guest," he said, waving toward Stone.

Garreth grinned and whirled with his fist raised, catching Stone off guard with a roundhouse punch that sent him into the crowd. The rowdy group only laughed and hoisted the man up, tossing him back toward his two assailants.

"I never could stand that man," Sebastian said, catching Stone under his arms and lifting him to his feet.

"Be my guest," Garreth said, repeating Sebastian's invitation.

Sebastian grinned and, holding the man by his shirtfront, landed a stunning blow to his jaw. He collapsed, unconscious, and Sebastian let him drift to the ground in a crumpled heap.

The two friends left him there and returned to Lacey and Pascale.

"Are you all right?" Lacey asked.

Garreth hugged her to him and softly caressed her cheek.

"I'm fine now."

He kissed her quickly on the lips and turned to Sebastian. "You were saying something about another wager."

"The first one to produce a son wins the proceeds from the jade deal."

Identical gasps came from behind both men and Pascale claimed Sebastian's arm as Lacey took Garreth's.

"Oh, no you don't," the women said in unison.

"Besides," Garreth added. "You have a head start."

"You've still got a chance. Nothing saying this one will be a boy."

He patted Pascale's tummy and she slapped his hand away. "Stop dat," she said, swatting him. "And come on before you get into more foolishness."

Sebastian laughed and good-naturedly followed his new bride as she dragged him away from his best friend and worst temptation.

Garreth, still laughing, turned to find Lacey frowning at him, her hands on her hips.

"Haven't you learned anything, Garreth

Armstrong? You can't wager for love."

"Ah, but we took a chance, didn't we? And just look how it turned out."

He pulled her into his arms and she went willingly. His lips found hers and they kissed while the party raged on around them. In their own world there was no longer any room for chance. They'd gambled——and won the greatest prize of all.

"TRIFLES LIGHT AS AIR" FOR THE LADIES OF MOBILE

This will be this reporter's last column, as I will be traveling to the East Indies with my husband, Garreth Armstrong, of Armstrong Shipping. I have enjoyed writing this column for the ladies of Mobile, and hope it will continue in my absence as a source of social knowledge and information. Before I go I would like to congratulate Francine Thomas on her position with the New Yorker, and wish her the best of luck as their newest reporter. Also, as my last story, I'd like to relay the wonderful details of the wedding of the season that took place last night and joined Miss Edith Bishop with Mr. Marshall Sutherland. It was a gala event....

Author's Note

Dear Reader,

I hope you enjoyed reading *Blind Fortune* as much as I enjoyed writing—and researching—it. Many of the things in Lacey's and Garreth's lives were factual and I wanted to share a few of them with you.

For instance, Mardi Gras was born in Mobile, Alabama, contrary to popular belief, and all the details of the celebration were gleaned from actual accounts of that year's festivities (except Lacey and Garreth as king and queen).

Also, the *Mobile Press Register*, still the only newspaper in Mobile, was run for many years by Col. Rapier. Although there's no evidence he hired women reporters, the "Trifles" column was indeed a regular feature.

All of the homes featured in *Blind Fortune* were

taken from actual historical homes still standing—and open to the public—in Mobile. I invite you to visit them, and say hello to all the lovely ladies who made my stay there so pleasurable and informative.

I welcome letters at:
P.O. Box 63021
Pensacola, FL 32526

Their First Noel

DON'T MISS THESE FOUR HISTORICAL ROMANCE STORIES THAT CELEBRATE THE JOY OF CHRISTMAS AND THE MIRACLE OF BIRTH.

LEIGH GREENWOOD
"Father Christmas"

Arizona Territory, 1880. Delivering a young widow's baby during the holiday season transforms the heart of a lonely drifter.

BOBBY HUTCHINSON
"Lantern In The Window"

Alberta, 1886. After losing his wife and infant son, a bereaved farmer vows not to love again—until a fiery beauty helps him bury the ghosts of Christmases past.

CONNIE MASON
"A Christmas Miracle"

New York, 1867. A Yuletide birth brings a wealthy businessman and a penniless immigrant the happiness they have always desired.

THERESA SCOTT
"The Treasure"

Washington Territory, 1825. A childless Indian couple receives the greatest gift of all: the son they never thought they'd have.

_3865-X **(Four Christmas stories in one volume)** $5.99 US/$7.99 CAN

Dorchester Publishing Co., Inc.
65 Commerce Road
Stamford, CT 06902

Please add $1.75 for shipping and handling for the first book and $.50 for each book thereafter. NY, NYC, PA and CT residents, please add appropriate sales tax. No cash, stamps, or C.O.D.s. All orders shipped within 6 weeks via postal service book rate. Canadian orders require $2.00 extra postage and must be paid in U.S. dollars through a U.S. banking facility.

Name_____
Address_____
City _____ State_____ Zip_____
I have enclosed $_____in payment for the checked book(s).
Payment <u>must</u> accompany all orders.☐ Please send a free catalog.

TIME'S HEALING HEART

MARTI JONES

No man has ever swept Madeline St. Thomas off her feet, and after she buries herself in her career, she loses hope of finding one. But when a freak accident propels her to the Old South, Maddie is rescued by a stranger with the face of an angel and the body of an Adonis—a stranger whose burning touch and smoldering kisses awaken forgotten longings in her heart.

Devon Crowe has had enough of women. His dead wife betrayed him, his fiancee despises him, and Maddie drives him to distraction with her claims of coming from another era. But the more Devon tries to convince himself that Maddie is aptly named, the more he believes her preposterous story. And when she makes him a proposal no lady would make, he doesn't know whether he should wrap her in a straitjacket—or lose himself in desires that promise to last forever.

__51954-2 $4.99 US/$5.99 CAN

A LOVE THROUGH TIME

TIMESWEPT

MARTI JONES

Although tree surgeon Libby Pfifer can explain root rot and Japanese beetles, she can't understand how a fall from the oldest oak in Fort Pickens, Florida, lands her in another century. Yet there she is, face-to-face with the great medicine man Geronimo, and an army captain whose devastating good looks tempt her even while his brusque manner makes her want to wring his neck.

__51991-7 $4.99 US/$5.99 CAN

DREAM WEAVER

MARTI JONES

Bestselling Author Of *Time's Healing Heart*

Brandy Ashton peddles homemade remedies to treat every disease from ague to gout. Yet no tonic can save her reputation as far as Sheriff Adam McCullough is concerned. Despite his threats to lock her up if she doesn't move on, Brandy is torn between offering him a fatal dose of poison—or an even more lethal helping of love.

When Brandy arrives in Charming, Oklahoma, McCullough is convinced she is a smooth-talking drifter out to cheat his good neighbors. And he isn't about to let her sell snake oil in his town. But one stolen kiss makes him forget the larceny he thinks is on Brandy's mind—and yearn to sample the innocence he knows is in her heart.

_3641-X $4.50 US/$5.50 CAN

Dorchester Publishing Co., Inc.
65 Commerce Road
Stamford, CT 06902

Please add $1.75 for shipping and handling for the first book and $.50 for each book thereafter. NY, NYC, PA and CT residents, please add appropriate sales tax. No cash, stamps, or C.O.D.s. All orders shipped within 6 weeks via postal service book rate. Canadian orders require $2.00 extra postage and must be paid in U.S. dollars through a U.S. banking facility.

Name _____

Address _____

City _____ State _____ Zip _____

I have enclosed $_____ in payment for the checked book(s).

Payment **must** accompany all orders. ☐ Please send a free catalog.

Christmas Carol
FLORA SPEER

Bestselling Author of *A Love Beyond Time*

Bah! Humbug! That is what Carol Simmons says to the holidays, mistletoe, and the ghost in her room. But the mysterious specter has come to save the heartless spinster from a loveless life. Soon Carol is traveling through the ages to three different London Yuletides—and into the arms of a trio of dashing suitors. From Christmas past to Christmas future, the passionate caresses of the one man meant for her teach Carol that the season is about a lot more than Christmas presents.

_51986-0 $4.99 US/$5.99 CAN

WINTER LOVE

NORAH HESS

"Norah Hess overwhelms you with characters who seem to be breathing right next to you!"
—Romantic Times

Winter Love. As fresh and enchanting as a new snowfall, Laura has always adored Fletcher Thomas. Yet she fears she will never win the trapper's heart—until one passion-filled night in his father's barn. Lost in his heated caresses, the innocent beauty succumbs to a desire as strong and unpredictable as a Michigan blizzard. But Laura barely clears her head of Fletch's musky scent and the sweet smell of hay before circumstances separate them and threaten to end their winter love.

_3864-1 $5.99 US/$7.99 CAN